Back Before Dawn

Back Before Dawn

Kerry Peresta

LEVEL
BEST BOOKS

This book is dedicated to single moms, some of the bravest women I know. I have shared your struggles and I've felt your pain. You have my undying respect. May life treat you well.

"I count him braver who overcomes his desires than he who conquers his enemies; for the hardest victory is over self."

~ARISTOTLE

Praise for Back Before Dawn

"*Back Before Dawn* is a fabulous read with relatable, fascinating characters and a plot that zigzags between the struggles of a single mother with an online dating addiction and a diabolical murder that lands on her doorstep. This book will have you turning pages until its very satisfying conclusion! Peresta's Best Book Yet!"—Susan Crawford, *NYT* bestselling author, *The Pocket Wife* and *The Other Widow*

"*Back Before Dawn* is a rollercoaster of a read that will have you holding your breath until the surprising end. A taut, propulsive thriller, Kerry Peresta's newest novel features a single mom still reeling from her second divorce and struggling to make a new life for herself and her children. The local newspaper she works for isn't doing well, her ex-husband is chronically late with child support, and her new boss has it in for her. Who can blame Izzy for diving into online dating for some relief? But this hard-working woman can't pull herself away from the dating obsession that takes her out of the house almost every night, even as it threatens to bring her world crashing around her and makes her the primary suspect in a too-close-to-home murder."—Mally Becker, author of *The Turncoat's Widow* and *The Counterfeit Wife*

"Fast-paced, precisely plotted, and with an engaging cast of characters, *Back Before Dawn* taps into very real nightmares about the promise and peril of online dating. With a sure hand, author Kerry Peresta sends her heroine, single mom Isabelle (Izzy) Lewis, into battle against interconnected personal and professional demons that threaten her life, her livelihood, and those she loves. Izzy is an appealingly flawed character, whose addiction to online

i

dating renders her vulnerable to a predatory boss, an abusive ex-husband, and a rejected suitor-turned-stalker. Izzy is not without resources. Her friends, her coworkers, even the barista at Starbucks are all determined to help her, but when she becomes the prime suspect in a murder investigation, she must rely on her own intelligence, grit, and courage. *Back Before Dawn* is a multilayered mystery with plenty of satisfying twists and turns."—Lori Robbins, Silver Falchion and Indie Award winner, author of On Pointe Mystery Series

"Having been happily married for just short of fifty years, I can honestly say I have never had any experience whatsoever with online dating. However, Isabelle Lewis, the recently single, first-person narrator of Kerry Peresta's new novel, *Back Before Dawn*, has had plenty, so much so that her online dating activities have developed into a full-blown addiction with nightmarish consequences. Isabelle ("Izzy") is an attractive advertising sales rep for a medium-market newspaper. She has three kids, a vindictive ex-husband, and a new boss determined to get her fired. Pages and chapters fly by as the novel unfolds, ultimately resulting in murder, Izzy's arrest, and a resolution that I guarantee not even the most seasoned reader will see coming. I loved this book, and only my wish to savor it kept me from finishing it in one sitting. *Back Before Dawn* is a winner, and unlike anything else you are likely to read this year. I cannot recommend highly enough."—Gregory Stout, author of *Lost Little Girl* and *The Gone Man*

"Meet Izzy, a single mom of three with a serious addiction…an addiction to online dating that introduces her to a stalker and threatens her job and her children. Can she pull herself out before it's too late? A tension-filled page-turner right to the end."—Judy L Murray, Silver Falchion and IPPY Award-winning author and Agatha Nominee for The Chesapeake Bay Mystery Series

Prologue

Ethan had expected blowback from his crazy ex-wife, but not like this.

He considers muting the shrieking voice, but lowers the cell volume instead. He lays the phone on the end table, puts it on speaker, and half-listens, distracted by the football game playing on his flat screen. When the Georgia 'Dawgs are on, she should know better than to try to get him to talk to her. The 'Dawgs had made it to the playoffs last year, and it looks like they'll do it again this year.

He loves Saturdays.

Ethan glares at the voice coming through his phone.

Resigned, he mutes the TV.

"What is this? Can't we talk this out? What the heck are you thinking?" she screeches.

"I told you it was coming, remember?" Ethan rubs the back of his neck.

"Since when do you carry out a *threat*," she hisses. "I can't believe you actually did it."

Ethan closes his eyes. Izzy's temper doesn't flare often, but when it does, it's epic. "I pulled the trigger on this for the good of us all."

"Are you serious?" Her voice rises an octave. "What, you see them maybe once every six weeks? Two months? Tell me how many of Peter's football games you've attended. Or Mimi's dance recitals, Ethan. Go ahead. Figure it out. I'll wait."

A beat of silence passes. "See? You can't even remember the last time. Full custody? My attorney will rip this thing to shreds."

He waits. Listens to her breathe. They'd been divorced thirteen years, but he could still tell her mood by the way she breathes.

Her breathing slows.

Ethan's shoulders relax. "Did you read the full Petition?"

"Not the whole thing. Is it full of surprises?"

He groans. "It's full of proof, Izzy. Times. Dates. Things the kids have said. The number of nights you are absent until two or three in the morning."

She gasps. "You've been surveilling me?"

He frowns. Kicks back the rest of his beer. "What did you expect? These are my kids we're talking about. You leave them alone almost every night. This can't continue, Izzy. It's dangerous."

"I...I'm getting a handle on it, Ethan. I've told you that."

He grunts. "As if."

"I am. I'm serious about it."

Ethan groans. "This isn't fixable, Izzy. It's done. *I'm* done. You can't back out; we're going to court."

"How about a change of custodial agreement? An adjustment?"

"Not interested."

"Ethan, you're not even in the same school district."

"So what? Kids are flexible. They'll be fine."

"Peter's a senior this year. Chad's going to be a sophomore. They've gone to school there all their lives. They won't be FINE."

There she goes again with that temper. He jots it down to bring up with his attorney. The more damaging criteria they can produce, the better. He grins.

"I'm watching football, Izzy."

Her laughter is brittle. "You love that damn football more than you love our kids. It won't work, Ethan. You'll be miserable, and so will they."

"You're making this too easy, Iz." He jots down another note. *Accuses father of making kids miserable.*

"Damn you, Ethan! I don't have the money for an attorney, and guess whose fault that is? You're three months behind on child support."

"Another reason full custody works out better." He chuckles. "You'll pay *me.*"

"And you won't provide what the kids need. You never did. Remember?"

"I'm done talking, Izzy." Ethan ends the call.

"Stupid broad," he mutters. Settling deep into his recliner, he adjusts his back pillow, puts his hands behind his head. Focuses on the game. Refs call a foul. He curses. A soft click sounds. Ethan's head jerks around. He mutes his TV, cocks his head and listens.

His cat strolls into the room.

"Buddy, you scared the crap out of me." He idly drops his hand to the top of the cat's head. The cat startles, drops into a crouch, then races away.

Ethan opens another beer, frowns at the cat. "You're stupid, too." He wolfs down half the beer. Wipes his mouth. "Now. Everyone leave me alone and let me watch my game."

He unmutes the TV and adjusts the volume to a higher level. Reclines his chair back as far back as it will go.

He doesn't hear the whisper of soft footfalls proceeding through the house. Or notice gloves pulled into place. Or see the reflection of the flat screen on the small, delicate, immaculately sharpened blade.

"Go! Go!" Ethan screams from his chair. Refs call another foul. "Dammit! You guys need a real coach." As he sits, his arm topples the bottle of beer. "Crap," he mutters and rises from the chair for a replacement and a clean-up towel.

Ethan doesn't notice the masked and hair-netted form sliding out of sight behind a closet door. Nor does he notice the same door opening or the sounds of disposable booties stealing across the carpet when Ethan returns to his seat. "There," Ethan tells his team when they make a first down. "Good job, boys." Halftime begins.

Ethan closes his eyes. He is now on his fifth beer, and halftime is the perfect opportunity for a nap.

The person proceeds toward Ethan.

Pauses five seconds. Ten seconds. Fifteen.

Ethan starts to snore.

Steps inch toward the back of the recliner.

The halftime show blares. Skimpy-costumed dancers gyrate across a stage. Sports announcers relate in ecstatic detail the way stats are lining up for this year's playoffs.

Garbed in jeans and black sweatshirt, the perpetrator inside Ethan's home weighs the next moves. The target is an arm's reach from the blade. Ethan shifts in the reclined chair and straightens his head on the headrest. A smile appears on the person's face. An arm raises. Light glints off a small blade.

The tool plunges into the carotid, rendering an impressive fountain of blood spray from the neck. Up, out, and down, down, down. A virtual bloodbath. The perpetrator steps back, pausing to appreciate the power, the vigor... of this particular artery. Ethan stirs. His eyes fly open. He tries to speak, but his words are garbled. "It's okay," the perpetrator whispers, patting the top of his head. Blood leaves the body in thirty seconds when the carotid is severed properly. You won't feel a thing."

The blade is wedged once more into the initial cut with determined pressure. The perpetrator bounces away from the fresh spurt of blood. The mission is complete.

Ethan's vibrant flesh pales. His eyes grow wide and pleading. Soon, the rapid, intermittent jets of blood lessen. The heart slowly yields until Ethan gasps his final, shuddering breath. The perpetrator reaches out to shut the eyelids. Blood pools on Ethan's chest and oozes into the carpet. The cat pads into the room and begins to lap up the blood.

The halftime dancers reach a feverish climax. A crescendo of spectator approval roars through the TV speakers.

The small weapon is slipped inside a baggie by gloved hands and stuffed into a pocket.

The footsteps are soft and silent as they depart.

Chapter One

A month earlier

September 1

With my fingers, I dip into my eye shadow and drag a slash of burnt umber across my eyelids. I curse when part of the burnt umber lands on my nose, and adjust the visor mirror. The morning rush hour traffic is making it impossible to get my makeup right.

I screech into *The Emerald Spring Sentinel's* parking lot a few minutes late, swipe on tinted lip-gloss, and speed-walk into the building, hoping my hair is not sticking out in all directions.

The ancient elevator in the lobby—a dubious attempt at historic preservation in the heart of downtown Emerald Spring, Georgia—creaks slowly from the third floor to the first. To add insult to injury, the blasted doors take a full four seconds to open. I enter the elevator, push the second-floor button, cross my arms, and resign myself to the fact that the ride to the second floor will take even longer. When the doors creak open, I exit in a rush.

"Morning, Iz," My advertising coordinator calls across the advertising sales workspace, a huge, open, carpeted area divided by a wide strip of linoleum. He points at the clock and shakes his head. I roll my eyes. Since when did my assistant start prodding me with guilt first thing in the morning? Single parents should get a pass. Besides, it's just a few minutes.

1

I toss my purse on my desk and thread my way through the cubicle-infested maze to the corner conference room, and jerk open the door. God help me if I'm late to a sales meeting again.

The ad director strides into the room with a laptop under his arm exactly two seconds after I place my butt in my chair.

Phil, advertising director of the *Sentinel*, wears an expensive suit, fashion-forward tie, and white, starched shirt. Office casual isn't tolerated at *The Emerald Spring Sentinel*, a respected daily newspaper in a sea of lesser newspapers going out of business. Phil hangs onto his staff's formal attire like a drowning man clinging to a life preserver. My eyelids have a permanent droop this morning, and I'm glad I'm on the back row. Phil douses the lights and I'm thinking maybe I can grab a nap. My stomach is a little choppy, compliments of three glasses of wine with last night's meet-up disaster.

Phil fiddles with his laptop until a PowerPoint presentation springs to life. From the look of Phil's somber expression, coupled with the graphs, statistics, and dour-looking predictions onscreen, I deduce this morning's meeting will not be a happy one.

The conference room holds forty vinyl and metal chairs, eight around a wood-veneered, rectangular conference table. Four rows of eight chairs each face the conference table. The retail advertising sales team fills most of the seats.

I stifle a yawn.

Someone starts passing out folders.

Phil pulls out a laser pointer.

A green laser dot slides across shorter and taller graph verticals on the large screen. "This is where we are, people. The folder you received contains the results of an extensive demographic study of our primary circulation area. Hang onto it."

I try to keep my eyes open.

Motivational posters scream at me from the walls. 'Every no gets you closer to a YES. Successful people never stop. They make mistakes, but they keep moving. The only failure is quitting, so don't quit.' In light of two failed marriages, I have adopted them as personal mantras. Like last night. The guy was a huge no. However, every no gets me closer to the big yes.

A colleague elbows me. "Phil is looking straight at you."

I straighten. Phil stares at me a beat longer than necessary, frowns, and continues whizzing the damn green dot across several super-sized pie charts, as if his bad mood has been spat out in bright colors and shoved in our faces.

Phil concludes the meeting with a litany of barely-disguised threats if we are unable to meet our monthly quotas and attractive monetary incentives if we do. I perk up at the 'monetary incentives' part.

I glance across the room to a wall of award plaques. Two slots bear my name, Isabelle Lewis, as salesperson of the month. If I win one more month, I have a good chance of scoring the biggest monetary incentive of the year.

I'm not ashamed to admit it. I am all about monetary incentives.

Ten minutes later, all of us are in our cubes perusing the fresh newspapers placed on our desks each morning by the ad coordinators. My landline rings.

"Izzy, *Sentinel*." I blurt, perturbed that my morning newspaper and coffee time is interrupted.

"Hey, beautiful," a breathy voice whispers.

My body tenses. The man from last night? "Umm, hey there…" I try to remember his name, but he'd dropped off my radar the minute I'd walked into my house at an ungodly hour. How did he get my landline number at the office?

"Tyler."

"Tyler, yes, of course. Thanks again for last night, and wow, that was awkward when your car got towed, huh?"

"Yeah, I thought I paid that ticket, and oops." He chuckles. "I need to make it up to you. When are you free again?"

Is he serious? Did my grunts of disapproval and periodic yawns not penetrate his thick skull?

"Listen, Tyler…I'm super busy, and it's not the best time."

I waited through a pause.

"I explained to you what happened."

"You…um, had quite the meltdown. It felt like…well, it doesn't matter what it felt like. I'm not interested in moving forward. But thanks."

"I am so sick of arrogant women like you," he hisses into my ear.

I pull back the receiver and stare at it. Who talks to a woman this way after one lousy date? His car had been towed, and on top of that, I'd had a front-row seat to a worrying and bizarre temper tantrum. Clearly, he doesn't understand social cues.

My cubicle-mate, Winston, eases into his desk in our three-sectioned pod. "Ethan again? What is that guy's problem?" he whispers.

I hold up a finger and shake my head. "Well, since you are 'sick of arrogant women like me,' it's a good thing you won't be seeing me again." I return the handset to its cradle as he hurls further derision, his voice receding until there is blessed silence.

My sigh is long. When am I going to quit doing this to myself?

Winston bids me a chirpy good morning over the eight-inch pod divide and toasts me with his coffee. I adore my podmate on several levels. For starters, he convinced the *Sentinel* to hire me when I was a desperate, newly divorced, broke, single mother of three young children. My marriage had blown up, and I had no child support, no sales experience, and even less confidence. He'd twisted Phil's arm to hire me on gut instinct.

I will always love him for that.

Winston has clear blue eyes, a closely trimmed white goatee that matches his short, white hair, a penchant for bursting into song, and a light-hearted disdain for management.

He leans forward. "And how are we this fine day? So, it wasn't Ethan this time. That's good, at least."

I nod my agreement and turn my attention back to the fresh newspaper open on my desk. "It was a scumbag I met last night that won't take no for an answer, that's all. Otherwise, I'm peachy, Winston. What's happening in your world today?"

"Have you heard?" His eyebrows arch.

"Heard what?"

"Phil hired a new advertising manager. He starts next week."

I can't blink for several seconds.

"It'll be okay." Winston has an uncanny ability to read my mind.

"Yeah, whatever. Last time this happened, look what we got. Who is it?"

"I used to handle his account many moons ago." He strokes his chin. "Birdie Costanza used to be one of our biggest clients. Furniture business. He opened his own chain in Missouri somewhere. I'm not sure what happened, but it tanked. He needed a job, and we needed a retail sales manager." Winston flips up his palms. "C'est la vie."

"*Zero* advertising experience?"

He sips his coffee. "Should be fun, don't you think?"

I slide down in my chair, my chin on my chest. "What's he like?"

"People can and do change, Izzy."

With this cryptic observation in my head, I hope I can eke out a decent attitude with my clients. I grab my purse and head out to my car to start a busy day of client meetings.

Chapter Two

I have three kids. Sixteen-year-old Peter, the responsible rule-abider; fourteen-year-old Chad, the lawless rascal; and twelve-going-on twenty Mimi, adorable baby sister. My morning routine consists of getting them out the door to school on time, racing to work, getting home at a reasonable hour, and connecting with them at some point during the day. Around ten o'clock p.m., when the kids disappear into their second-story bedrooms, a breathless anticipation shivers through me, and I grab my laptop to log onto three dating sites. When I'm away from home, I check in on my phone apps, but it's a work-issued phone, and I feel guilty. Besides, it's much more fun on my laptop. The images are as big as life. It almost feels like the few lovely men vying for my attention are right in the room.

I know in my heart it's becoming an issue.

Don't judge me.

I work hard. I deserve a reward at the end of long, crazy days.

Tonight's response is fabulous. Four gold-plated potentials. I smile and swipe right four times. The attention I'm getting online is a lot cheaper and more effective than counseling has ever been, that's for sure.

My second divorce had blindsided me. I'd waited five years after my first divorce before marrying a second time, and we'd dated a year before I'd accepted his marriage proposal. My entire family had stamped him with their seals of approval, and I don't know what happened. I thought I'd done everything right, and three years in, we started having problems. Everyone told me they were fixable. Well, turns out they weren't. In fact, *disturbing* was the word my therapist had used to describe my husband's behavior.

6

I click on my personal dating profile.

Dusky blonde, shoulder-length hair. Big, blue eyes. Full, pouty lips compliments of my mom. Oval face. The full-length photo is a photoshopped professional shot in business attire. The others are casual and fun. "Locked, loaded, and ready for love" is the ending line on my blurb. I frown. It sounds like a hooker's tagline. I update it with something else and considered more edits. Writing a profile is an art. In some ways, similar to the sales copy I create for my clients, except that I'm marketing myself instead of a product or service. I back out of my profile and sit in my cozy, candle-lit den, thinking.

My mind backflips eight years to the small counseling office crammed with well-meaning friends. My second husband and I had a lot of support when we separated. Expectations had been high.

After six months of marriage counseling and his ten-day stint in rehab, the concluding session had been a real eye-opener. My husband sat in a chair in the middle of the room, his arms crossed and lips pursed. Everyone held a collective breath, awaiting the happy, tearful conclusion to a long period of counseling. Reconciliation was inevitable, we'd all thought. If not, why the hard work?

In a stunning twist, instead of hugs and promises of a future together, my husband responded with a blank look on his face and empty eyes. He'd stared at all the expectant smiles in confusion, spread his arms, and said, "I am not going back. Ever. I want a divorce."

Later, I found out he'd hooked up with a woman in rehab.

I swipe a single tear off my cheek and push away the memory.

Never again.

My kids' gentle snores behind their bedroom doors make me smile.

A message from one of my matches lights up the screen.

My response is quick.

Chapter Three

For some reason I cannot put my finger on, a new manager tends to regard me as a challenge. And this one—a product of close-knit business relationships instead of a killer resume—could affect my bottom line. I park, drag my purse strap across my chest, and stride toward the building. Today is Birdie Costanza's first day, and my outlook is bleak.

I consider taking the stairs and ditching the elevator. What if I get trapped on the ancient elevator with the new guy? How awkward would that be?

I spin around to take the stairs and accidentally collide with a man. He is tall, older, and wears a sport coat, tie, and an irritated expression.

"Oh gosh. Sorry." I try to smooth his sport coat with a flutter of my hands.

"In a hurry, sweetheart?" His smile is thin. He adjusts his tie and scans me up, then down. Which I hate. Why do men do that?

His hair is blond, laced with silver, and slicked straight back.

"I guess so," I say with a half-hearted laugh. "You okay? Really sorry."

The man nods and walks to the elevator.

"Have a good one," I tell him, my voice pure sugar, and trot up the stairs. Sweetheart? I mean, I know it's Georgia and all, but come on, buddy. Get with the program.

I burst out the second-floor door from the stairwell in advance of the elevator, toss my purse on my desk, grab my mug, and hurry toward the breakroom.

I smile at Darlene as I pass.

Darlene is my staunch ally and best friend. She is married to a colleague on the sales team and works in billing. Her desk is between the break room and the workspace so she hears...everything. After I grab coffee, I pause beside her desk and give her a quick recap of my latest meet-up disaster.

Darlene laughs. "You know there's about a ten percent chance one of these men will live up to their profiles, right?"

I shrug. "Whatever. Every no gets me closer to—"

"A yes," she finishes for me. "But that doesn't mean you have to kill yourself."

"Good things come to those who persevere," I tell her with a wink and walk toward the introductory meeting.

The conference room is packed.

My co-workers are all spiffed up in honor of the ritual introduction of a new manager. I look down at my own thrown-together ensemble I'd pulled out of the dirty clothes and notice a stain on my blouse as I slide into the back row.

We hear Phil's loud, 'impress the New Guy' voice before he steps through the door. When they walk in, my heart sinks. New Guy is the man I almost knocked to the floor.

Of course he is.

Phil stands in front of the conference table, clasps his hands behind his back, and gives us a somber call to attention with his silence.

We all straighten in our chairs.

"As you know," he begins, "We've been looking for a new advertising manager for some time." He sweeps his hand toward his prize. "Birdie Costanza was the advertising decision-maker for one of our biggest clients a few years ago. With his leadership experience, we feel he is going to excel in the role."

With a smile, he stares at us in anticipation.

A strained silence fills the room. My eyebrows pull together. Are we expected to applaud?

Phil waits a few more disappointed seconds before he turns his dog-and-pony show over to Birdie. "Go ahead and introduce yourself, Birdie."

Phil and Birdie exchange places. Birdie clasps his hands behind his back, just like Phil, but manages to look more like Hitler than a sales manager.

"Now, I know some of you are thinking, who *is* this guy? What does he know about advertising? How can he be an effective manager if he doesn't have an advertising background?" He grins and scans our faces. He pauses a few seconds on mine, trying to place me. I see the recognition hit his eyes. I look away.

"I'll be going out with you on calls and meeting the clients for a while. I want to be up close and personal with the front end and the back end of this business."

We glance at each other and suppress groans at the suggestion of ride-alongs.

Birdie is oblivious to the depressing bomb he dropped. "I'll be scheduling one-on-one meetings this week and next. I look forward to it."

Phil gives a few half-hearted, positive strokes, bludgeons us about missed sales goals, and dismisses the meeting. Winston and I walk together back to our desks.

"Just what we need, a day or two of ride-alongs," he whispers.

"I know, right? This is going to kill my schedule for the next two weeks."

"And mine."

Darlene watches the mass exit with interest.

I make a beeline for her desk.

"How vas it?" she asks, with the slightest leftover accent from her Austrian mother.

"Another new manager?" I say, disgusted. "I just got used to the last one."

She nods. "It will work itself out. My husband knew him. What did he say...oh yes! Very successful, but something happened. The company..." she snaps her fingers. "Gone. A mystery."

"I'm wondering how he is to work with."

"Time will tell." She turns to her computer. "Better get started on these invoices." Her blue eyes look washed-out and gray.

"You okay?"

"Things will be fine."

"*Will* be fine? What is not fine?

Tension scoots across her features, her eyes suddenly liquid.

"Can you go out for a drink after work? An hour or so?"

I tell her that I can. Of course I can. I'd do anything for her.

My desk is lonesome without Winston, and he is not back in the pod yet. I like to bounce depressing thoughts off him, as he is 'glass half full' and I'm more 'ohmigod what now.'

My assistant, Lonnie, plops into his chair with a stack of proofs from the production department. I give him a quick thumbs-up and leave for the day on sales calls.

When I plunk all my sales paraphernalia down in the passenger seat of my Honda Accord, I stare at my hands on the steering wheel. Motivation to make a sale leaks from me like a deflating balloon. I need to give Birdie a chance...but all I feel rolling around in the pit of my stomach is dread.

I need to re-inflate. A smile tickles the corners of my mouth.

I pull out of the parking lot, and fifteen minutes later I'm at my favorite spot overlooking the Savannah River. Two minutes after that, a few deft strokes on my cell reveal several matches, just waiting for a right or left swipe. My fantasies take flight, and all thoughts of Birdie and sales goals and ride-alongs and mysterious business revelations vanish into thin air. Two hours pass in a series of texts or Facetime calls, at which point, I feel re-inflated. With a happy sigh, I drive home to touch base with the kids as they arrive after school before I head back out into the wild.

The thuds of each car door closing, the tread of three pairs of feet on the stairs, and the clunk of backpacks on the kitchen table reverberate through the house.

Mimi, twelve, smiles at me through a mouthful of Oreo cookie when I come downstairs. "What are you doing home?"

"I have to go back, but I wanted to see your faces." Peter races out the door back to football practice. I spend a few minutes with Chad and Mimi and tell them I'll be late tonight. Then I make a call to Ethan. The kids' dad and I sustain a testy friendship on behalf of our kids and on behalf of the fact that

I'm too broke to pay a babysitter. He sometimes agrees to hang out with them if I'm busy. Especially if he's late on child support.

"Snacks first, then homework. No exceptions. I want to check it when I get home. I'm calling your dad to come over."

Chad rolls his eyes, digs around in his backpack. Mimi already has her homework out. At twelve, she's so dependable I tend to forget she's still a young girl. I plant a kiss on top of each head and leave.

Starbucks is deserted mid-afternoon. I pull up to the drive-in window and order my standard latte. My favorite barista extends it to me from the drive-by window and makes jokes about my dating life. I shouldn't be so transparent with baristas.

As the caffeine begins to take hold, I think about the weekly quotas Phil has instituted for cold calls. Since Phil's been prodding the retail sales staff to pull advertising dollars from the classified ad budgets, I set my sights on a nearby Ford dealership. Ten minutes later, I pull into their parking lot. A young salesman approaches, thinking I'm a customer, then frowns when he sees my bag and perky demeanor. His shoulders slump as he leads me to the general manager's office. I figure he's not having a good sales day.

The GM's office is paneled in dark wood and anchored by a desk larger than the size of my entire three-seater pod at the office. The man at the desk turns from his computer screen and waves off the salesperson.

We shake hands. "Isabelle Lewis. Call me Izzy. Thanks for seeing me on the fly like this."

"Tom Burke. You're welcome."

His eyes linger on my face. "I'm confused…we already have a sales rep from the *Sentinel*. Jon Hoyt."

"We instituted a new policy. One rep for classified, another for retail ad buys. I'll be your retail rep if you agree."

We hit it off, go over some ideas, and set a date to meet again to discuss a contract. I float from the dealership on a cloud, feeling afresh the thrill of the *Yes*.

The popular River's Edge District, which had arisen practically overnight on the heels of the city's decision to develop the riverfront, is alive with activity. A red and green trolley rumbles by, and groups of laughing people make their way to River's Edge restaurants. A street musician pounds a trio of trashcans, and passers-by toss in a few bucks. Multiple frothy wakes from boats churn the Savannah River in the background. I have to park five blocks away and hop on the trolley. Standing room only, so I grab a strap and hang on. At one of the stops, a man stares at me through the trolley window. His hair is dark, and his hands are jammed deep in his pockets. But he is staring right at me. It is unsettling. Wait. Do I know this guy? The trolley jerks me off my feet as it takes off. I frown. Was that the creep whose car got towed?

I walk to the bar and order a drink. Darlene waves from a table in the back. I'm fond of this restaurant. It is one of my favorite places for first meets with one of my online dudes. I drop into a chair across from her. "So, what's up?"

Darlene fiddles with her martini glass. "I'm sure it's nothing. I'm paranoid, probably."

"Right. Darlene, you are the most trusting woman I know. If you've noticed something, it *is* something. So, what's happened?"

My wine arrives, and I relish the first taste.

Darlene pushes her shoulders back and sits up straighter in her chair. "I think Richard is having an affair."

I spend a few seconds attempting to force the liquid down my throat instead of spurting it out my nose. "The only thing you could've said that would have shocked me more is that you're moving back to Germany. Austria. Wherever it is you're from." I grab a napkin and blot my nose.

Darlene looks past me out the window and into the busy street.

"Are you *sure* this is happening? Have you approached him about it? What have you noticed that makes you think he's involved?"

Her eyes are sad. This bothers me. Darlene is not a sad person. She doesn't come to conclusions without a reason. There must be something to it.

"I'm shell-shocked. I've suspected for a while, but last night and the night before, he was out late, and his shirts smelled of perfume." She frowns. "He's out often too late. I don't believe the excuses anymore."

I gulp my wine. It is a sin to gulp wine, but I am horrified.

Darlene's smile is glum. "I'm hoping to find an online group or something. I...I don't know how to approach it."

She reaches for the new martini that's arrived.

"Some women have forgiven and worked it out, and others left. And then, I think, maybe I am paranoid." Tears spring to her eyes. "I love him, Izzy."

My heart turns over in my chest. I feel helpless. Moronic.

"Darlene, you know I'm here for you. I would open up to him and see where the conversation goes. Maybe it's a friendship. Maybe he has something going on that is different from what you think. But whatever it is, you can count on me to help you through it. You're the one who's said that I shouldn't be anxious about something that hasn't happened yet." I think about what I said. "Something like that. Anyway, it's not productive to worry; it doesn't help anything."

She smiles, pats my hand, and finishes her latest martini.

I am a terrible comforter.

Exhaustion spirals through my body. Once again, I was stupid last night and stayed out too long. Not tonight. I pull out my phone. My eyebrows jerk together at the many missed calls.

"I know you have to get going, Izzy. I think I'll stay awhile and listen to the music. I just wanted someone else to know."

I get up, hug her, murmur reassurances, and race to the trolley stop, my cell pressed to my ear. Why isn't anyone answering? I try my reluctant babysitter, Ethan's, phone. It rings and rings and goes to voicemail. I leave a terse voicemail, text him for good measure and wait for the trolley.

Chapter Four

My workday passes in a fog of client appointments, the threat of ride-alongs with Birdie, and assorted complaints and assessments about the new manager. I think about the futility of using my ex as a dependable presence with the kids as I walk to my car. The sun is sinking, but at least it's still light outside, and I'll get home early. Early-ish.

Last night he'd taken the kids to get ice cream, which would've been fine if he'd answered my calls. My suspicions are that he'd taken them out to meet his girlfriend and told them not to tell me. They'd hedged big time when I asked them about it after I got home, so I'm pretty sure that's what happened.

The jerk. I'd lit into him like a damn tornado. He never did admit anything, or explain why he hadn't answered his phone. Instead, Ethan fumbled through excuses. I didn't know what to believe.

Single parent problems. They never stop.

I pull my Honda into the garage and walk into the kitchen. Rake my hands through my hair, shake off my workday, and slip into 'Mom' persona. Mimi is splayed on the couch, watching TV and scrolling through social media. I sit beside her and ruffle her hair. She minimizes her screen, which makes me think...she's *twelve*. Do I need to start stalking her social media? I've already put parental controls on every device.

"Hey, sweetie, your teacher called today. She's missing homework. That's not like you. Is there anything going on? That I need to know about?"

She glares at me. "What do you think, Mom?"

I spread my hands. "You're going to have to get specific, honey. Listen, I need to work around a time frame with this. I have to go out later, so—"

"Mom!" Mimi shifts into high gear. "You just went out last night. I...I need you here. I need to know you're *here*." Mimi jumps from the couch and runs to her room. The door slams shut behind her.

My stunned silence lasts a few seconds before I walk up the stairs and open her door. She is face-planted on her bed. I sit beside her and stroke her back. She pushes me away.

"Honey, it's just for a couple of hours. Chad will be here, and you'll be fine. Peter should be home by ten o'clock, even if I'm not."

She rolls over and stares at the ceiling. "Is this another one of your internet guys?" Her eyes bore into mine. Mimi's eyes are that rare, perfect hazel: sometimes green, sometimes chestnut brown. Right now, they are shooting green spikes of adolescent wrath.

"It's a friend I haven't seen in a while. He wants to get together to catch up." I'm surprised how easy lying has become. Rationalization says this tiny lie is necessary because finding *the yes* trumps honesty with one's children.

Doesn't it?

Besides, it's only a couple of hours.

Mimi's wrath is short-lived. She picks up her phone.

"I won't be gone long. For now, let's get your homework done and talk about what's going on with you, okay?"

An hour and a half passes. Two. Parents of Chad's girlfriend arrive and drop her off. Chad and the young lady go into the kitchen and start homework. Still, Mimi unloads. I wrestle with becoming offended by the depth of her complaints about me—but also by her lack of appreciation for a mother who pays the bills, works each day, tries to be at her kids' extra-curricular activities, and more. The list is endless. I can't expect a twelve-year-old to understand, so I push my self-pity away and listen hard. We forge an uneasy truce. I check in on Chad and his friend, then leave around nine p.m. Peter will be home in an hour.

I scoop up car keys, purse, and set the security alarm.

16

Fifteen minutes later I arrive at The Rooster, a funky, eclectic bar. I remind myself to keep my word to Mimi and get home before midnight.

Nervous anticipation zings through me like electricity. Meeting men has become my favorite elixir. My drug. My balm in Gilead. The one pleasure I allow myself. Well, other than the occasional wine.

I strike a pose in the doorway in case he's arrived first.

No one rushes up to offer their hand in complimentary awe, so I drop the pose and find a table in the corner. Pull out my phone and check for texts.

A small person approaches and hovers near my elbow.

"Are you, umm, Izzy?"

It takes a second for the words to register. I turn my head and look into a face that reminds me more of a Shar Pei than a human male. My exhilaration dips somewhere around my ankles.

The man standing—or rather, stooping—beside me has sparse, dyed-too-dark hair, weighs one hundred and thirty pounds soaking wet, and could be the poster child for someone in desperate need of cosmetic surgery. He holds a wilted flower bouquet, which he slides onto the table. I am at a loss. The profile bio said he is forty-one, six feet tall, and works out. This arthritic, ancient man is *not* the man I'd met online. I scan the room. Where is he? Wait. Is the leprechaun going to sit at my table?

He pulls up a chair. My lips part. I can't feel the top of my head…a vacuum has sucked me into a dark, dark joke.

I stare at him. The leprechaun grins. Even his teeth look old.

"Well, Izzy, I pulled a fast one on you." His grin widens. "I have a hard time meeting beautiful women like you when I put my own photo on my profile, but when I put the *new* one up, my message box got full overnight." He cackles. I look away because his teeth are beginning to bug me. In fact, everything about him is bugging me.

"Who is in the picture?" I ask, hoping, at the very least, that it might be him at a younger age.

"My younger brother." He winks, cackles again, and ends up coughing sputum into his hand. Yes. His. Hand. I recognize a smoker's hack. His profile indicated that he is a non-smoker. I fold my arms. I am fuming.

17

"That photo was taken about a decade ago," he adds.

I left my darling Mimi for *this*?

"May I ask, umm, *Dan*, why you would think that women would be okay with this?"

He looks mystified. "My brother may be the nicer-looking one, but I'm the one with the spunky personality. I figured if I could attract a woman for a first date after she got to know me, she'd forgive me for puttin' up the picture." He resists another cackle, for which I am grateful.

"Did it ever occur to you that most people are really, *really* not into liars and that it doesn't matter how great you think your personality is…a woman can't trust you after something like this. Besides, looks matter."

He shrugs his tiny, leprechaun shoulders. "No need to be insulting. I thought women were more interested in personality and intelligence."

Intelligence? And what guy uses the word *spunky*?

"For the record, this is fraud. And also, for the record, stupid on steroids." I hike my purse over my shoulder, rise from the chair. "And your personality can never, in a million years, be classified as *spunky*." His face is beet red. I'm out the door in three seconds. For once, I'm home before ten p.m.

Chapter Five

The Starbucks by my house on the way to work the next morning is packed. I need the jolt of a three-banger, so I wait in the long line of cars snaking around the building. My head is killing me, and the dark circles under my eyes needed a double portion of undereye concealer to do any good at all. After meeting the leprechaun, I'd zoomed home to the kids. When they turned in for the night, like an idiot, I'd gotten back online. Several matches kept me up until the wee hours. It's become a game. Like potato chips, I can't stop at just one. And the leprechaun experience had been so depressing I needed something. Anything.

So I'd attacked the damn dating game and conquered all, but it took the whole night. I'm paying for it now. I feel like a fist-crumpled, empty beer can at the bottom of the trash. Probably smell like one, too, since I didn't have time to shower this morning.

I curse. Smack the steering wheel in frustration. What is wrong with me? I have to stop this.

"Good morning!" The cheery barista beams when I arrive at the window.

I hold my forehead and mmmph a reply. "Izzy, are you okay? You look exhausted." She relays my order to a co-worker. From long experience, she knows when I need a three-shot latte.

I try to smile at her, but it feels more like a grimace. Even my cheeks hurt. I grope in my purse, locate sunglasses, and put them on.

"It's not easy raising three kids and working full-time." She slides a heat protector on the cup and hands it to me from her perch in the window. "Take some time for you. Have a great one."

I smile. Isn't that what I'm doing with my concerted effort to track down the appropriate man for my family? Taking time for me? Of course it is.

I soar to the second floor in the decrepit, ancient elevator, somewhat buoyed by three shots of espresso. I've been at my desk three seconds when Jon Hoyt from the classified department storms up to my desk. He's not happy, and he wants to talk.

Privately.

I rub my chin. What is this about? I don't even know the guy.

He strides toward the empty conference room. I guess I'm supposed to follow?

He closes the door after I enter. Pulls two chairs from under the conference table and places them facing each other, maybe three feet apart. He sits in one. I take the other.

"I want to know what the *hell* you are doing pitching my client, Tom Burke. He told me you sent him an idea for a campaign. That's *my* account. Last I heard, poaching's a sin around here."

I am confused. "But Jon, we've been told to call on those accounts. Didn't you know?

He didn't.

"Phil felt we could increase market share. I'm just doing what I was told." I said, my lower lip quivering a bit.

Jon holds my gaze. After a few seconds, he brushes off his slacks, rises.

"We'll see about this," he says and strides from the room.

My heartbeat returns to normal. I take the chairs, one by one, and place them back under the conference table. Then I walk to Phil's office.

Phil is at his desk staring out the second-story window in his corner office. In the neighboring office, I hear Birdie unpacking boxes, shoving books on the shelves, organizing drawers. I fidget at the door, waiting for Phil to acknowledge me. He waves me in.

"Jon's already been in here. He's pretty hot about it."

I frown. The ad department has favorites, and Jon is a big one. It isn't fair.

My lips pull into a pout. "Didn't you tell us a couple weeks ago we should go after automotive budgets for retail? That we were missing opportunities? I deserve a shot, even if it upsets Jon. I have an appointment with Tom next week, by the way."

Phil's eyebrows shoot up. "You do? He never sees anyone but Jon." He stares out the window, chews his lower lip. "Okay. I'll let you have a go at him. I'll tell Jon. If any problems arise? It all goes to Jon. You're off the account."

I blink. Had I just smashed the invisible barrier between classified and retail budgets?

"You'll be happy about this. It'll bring more of his ad dollars in-house, Phil."

"I hope so," Phil mutters, turning toward his computer. "We need something to drag us out of the red."

I float back to my desk, searching for my podmate. Where the heck is Winston? I must share my good news. We will fist-bump about it for weeks. I am the queen of precedents.

My cell vibrates. My neighbor. My forehead wrinkles. She never calls me at work. "Hey, Annie."

"Hi Izzy, sorry to bother you, but some weird guy is outside asking to see you. He says he knows you and wants to come in and wait until you get home, that it is important that he talk to you. I am like—seriously? Izzy, is this one of your online admirers? He is creeping me out. I need you to get rid of him."

He wants to insert himself into my neighbor's house and wait for me? Who would do that?

"I'll take care of it, Annie. Do you know his name?"

"Tyler."

The man with the car that got towed—the one that freaked out on me because I didn't want to go out again. I smack my forehead and groan.

"I remember that guy. Don't let him in."

"All well and good to say Izzy, but what if he won't leave? He's been sitting on my front steps for an hour, like a...like in protest or something."

"Annie, tell him that I'm out on calls and won't be home until late. I don't

21

think I told him I have any kids, but I sure don't want him hanging around to watch them come home from school."

"Okay, Izzy, I'll tell him, but could you call the cops and make a report or get them to drive by here or something? At least get this on the record?"

I agree. With shaking fingers, I scroll through my texts, but I think I already deleted his number and the thread.

I attack my keyboard looking for the site I'd met this jerk on. I barely remember his first name, much less his full name to put on a police report.

A deep voice booms by my shoulder. "Gotta love a woman that looks for online matches on her work computer. Don't you know they monitor your log-ins?" Jon Hoyt stands behind my chair with a lop-sided grin on his face.

"I, ahh…there's a situation." Jon's grin gets bigger. I throw up my hands in frustration. "So, Jon, whatever…it would take a while to explain. Did you need something?"

He crosses his arms. "Phil came down on your side, and I have no choice but to back off on this. Listen, Tom's a great guy and a good friend of mine. Maybe I overreacted. But he's not a fan of two reps on one account. Just sayin'. If it gets too confusing, he may just push his ad budget into broadcast or social media and ditch the newspaper. That's what I told Phil, too." He shrugs and reaches out his hand. "Friends?"

"Friends." His handshake is strong. Warm.

As he walks away, I notice for the first time his broad shoulders and the way his pants fit. I watch for a bit.

Then I remember I am in the midst of a crisis, and mutter soft curse words. A text pops up, and it's my official slimeball, Tyler.

I call him, cautioning myself to take it easy. No use causing him to go nuts on me again. What if he's a psychopath?

"Hey, Izzy," he says.

"Hello there."

"I came over today to see you in person because I knew you wouldn't talk to me on the phone. It's important. Just thirty minutes." His voice is devoid of emotion, and I try to remember all those TV shows where detectives talked people out of suicide or off ledges and things. *What did their voices sound like?* Use that voice, don't get upset, Izzy, *don't!*

"Okay, but can we discuss it later?" I hear a beep and look at my phone; Annie is trying to get through. "Hold that thought. I'll be right back." I switch over to the other call. Maybe he doesn't know where I work. Does he? I was drinking that night. I may have screwed up.

"Izzy!" Annie's voice is close to panic.

"Tyler's on the other line holding. What now?" I chew on one of my fingernails.

"He's leaving. As he passed your house, he parked, got out, yelled something at your front door, then walked back to my house and told me through the window to tell you to watch your back. Izzy, it felt like a threat to me."

I long for a mega-dose of Xanax.

"I'm going to try to talk some sense into the man. Then I'll call the cops if I can't settle him down some. Do me a favor, keep an eye out for the kids and make sure they get in and call me when they do, okay?"

"You got it, Izzy. Be careful."

I clicked back over to Tyler. "Hey, sorry, had to get that. So as I was saying –"

"Yeah, as you were *saying*, you were going to ditch me again, like the other night."

"Tyler, I appreciate that you want to talk. I'm flattered, but it's still a no," I manage through gritted teeth. He's breathing hard into the phone, and somehow I feel the moist warmth of it in my ear. I clutch my stomach and wonder how to extricate myself from this situation without getting shot or tortured or something.

Tyler continues, "You didn't even give me a chance. Your next-door neighbor didn't understand, and *you* don't understand. I'm not the man you think I am…."

You're not the perfect candidate for lifetime therapy? Or prison? I know exactly the kind of man you are. I married a couple of them.

"I know there is a woman out there for you that is perfect for you." I hate myself for sucking up, but I'm desperate. "Trust me. I would be a waste of your time."

I hold my breath. Please, God.

"You don't understand. I went to the website…I found something…."

"What website?"

"Your newspaper. You told me where you worked, remember?"

Crap.

"I know something about someone you work with."

What did this guy want? My head throbs, and I clamp my palm around my forehead.

"And that would concern me…how?"

Tyler clears his throat. "I need to see you. I…I don't want to be on a recorded landline."

Ah. It's a ploy to get me to give him my cell number. My temper sizzles. "Look. Let me make this very clear. I don't want to see you again. Stay away from my house, and stay away from my neighbor's house. Clear enough? What's your last name, by the way, Tyler?"

He ends the call.

My heart slams against my ribcage. I grip my desk and close my eyes in hopes I don't hyperventilate.

My next phone call is to Annie. The next one to the police.

Chapter Six

After a quick lunch at a nearby deli, I walk to the parking lot, my three-inch heels clicking on the sidewalk like a metronome. It is so hot the sidewalks float, a heat mirage that recurs in the hundred-plus degree heat that shrivels much of Georgia into late September.

My Honda has baked in the sun all morning, and I gingerly test the seat before I put my full weight on it. The air conditioner blasts hot air on my face. I lift my hair off the nape of my neck and wipe away the sweat. My phone vibrates. The word 'unknown' masks the number. After spending my lunch hour trying to push Tyler off my radar, all I can think is…now what?

"Izzy?" A deep, guttural voice. I try to place it.

"You got her."

I hear the clearing of a throat and a shuffle of papers.

"This is Birdie."

My mood plummets. I picture Birdie at his new desk in his new office.

"Izzy, I am schedulin' meetings with my team. You're up. Mind if a ride with you today?"

I run through a list of excuses in my head, but decide not to opt out because I already have three meetings set up for this afternoon, and the timing works.

"Okay. Want to meet me in the parking lot?"

"Ten minutes," he grunts. "Pick me up in front of the building."

The words that dance through my mind are not words one should entertain regarding upper management. *Pick him up in front of the building?* In spite of the fact there are no parking meters available and busy traffic is hurtling by? My attitude grows dark and negative and profane around the edges. Does this man have no sense of courtesy? He can't walk two minutes to the parking lot?

After eight minutes, I pull out of the parking lot into traffic and slide into the far lane in preparation to circle the *Sentinel* building and arrive at the front door. As I approach, no Birdie. I huff and puff and circle again. No Birdie. My phone chirps with a text. Birdie says he is running late and will meet me at my client's.

I text him an address. He tells me we'll take his car to the next appointments, and he'll drop me back at my car after we're done. I fantasize for a moment that I should text back how disrespectful of others' schedules he is. However, as the lone provider for my household, a critical text to my boss is a really bad idea.

The obligatory cheerful response drips from my fingertips in a return text.

St. Michael's Healthcare system is a vast, sprawling complex east of downtown. At its center sits a twenty-story hospital orbited by clinics and peripheral facilities. The complex includes lush, manicured grounds, meandering pathways, and plenty of parking.

When I park, my hands stick to the steering wheel. I pull them away and wipe away the nervous dampness with a towel I keep in the console. Will Birdie make a decent impression? What if he doesn't like my presentation? What are his expectations? Why do I feel so self-conscious?

It had taken me over a year to get Nellie, Communications Director of St. Michael's, to carve out a budget for our newspaper. She holds the purse strings to one of the more hefty budgets on my account list—over a million a year. My commissions would dive if she diverted those funds to other advertising venues. My mission with Nellie is simple—keep her happy, show her results, stay connected about the value of our product, and re-up her annual contract.

I don't have a good feeling about inserting Birdie into our meeting.

As I'm touching up lipstick, Birdie raps on the window and gives me his super-sized grin. I almost hit my head on the liner. Did he mean to sneak up on me?

I grab my laptop bag and step out of the car.

Birdie hasn't learned the two-foot personal space rule, and instead of moving a healthy pace away, he moves closer. I can smell his after-lunch cigar. Or Camels. Or something.

His tanned face creases into a thousand fissures, an after-result, I suppose, of an acne-scarred childhood. "Ready for round one?"

I resist screaming NO at the top of my lungs.

"Sure. This client is one of my bigger accounts, so this is a good one to start with. She doesn't have a lot of time, and I can't see her as much as I'd like, but—"

Birdie frowns. "Why not? You just have to get in the door. When a client says no, they mean 'maybe' or 'not yet'. John tells me you're one of his superstars. You should know that a 'no' doesn't mean 'no'." He strokes his chin. "So, what's this account worth?"

I blink, startled at the question. I'm uncomfortable sharing this information with him, for some reason. Maybe because he is, at first blush, despicable? "St. Michael's is one of my larger accounts. I assume you have an account list and recap of revenues?"

He assesses the words, registering faint disapproval. "When I ask a question, I need a direct answer, not a lecture."

I glance at my watch. "We're late."

To his credit, he lets this go and opens the door for me on our way to the elevator. We ride up without speaking. I sense his resentment, but I will deal with it later. This client needs all of my focus. I have several advertising opportunities for her that will fit her market niche and hope to increase her allotted print advertising dollars over the next couple of months. I decide, during the last few seconds of the elevator's ascent to the administrative offices on the top floor, to prep Birdie.

I clear my throat. "I'll take the lead on this…or do you have a different expectation?" I nod at the bundle of promotional materials in my arms. "These are opportunities I've customized for her, and my presentation is scheduled for today." He regards me coolly as we zip past the thirteenth floor.

"It'll be alright." His tone is dismissive.

We enter the communication department's suite of offices, where I check in with the receptionist. She smiles and presses a button that triggers a muted buzz somewhere deep within the labyrinthine offices and invites us to take a seat. A few minutes later, a forty-ish, bubbly, attractive woman in a dark green business suit bursts out of her office and walks down the hallway toward us. Her eyes light up when they land on me. She squints at Birdie, trying to place him.

Birdie turns on his dazzling smile, raking her length with his eyes. Nellie doesn't notice, but I do. She hugs me, then extends a hand to Birdie, which he takes in both of his and mumbles something that I cannot hear. She removes her hand from his and shoots me an uncertain glance. She bustles us into her office and seats us at a round conference table in the corner.

"So nice to see you, Izzy."

"The same. How's life been up here on the top floor of St. Michael's?"

"Crazy." She laughs. "Today is the deadline for our in-house newsletter and the quarterly magazine, and...well, I could go on, but I'm glad I could squeeze you in."

"Thank you. I know you're busy. I've got some good opportunities to show you, but first, I want to introduce you to Birdie Costanza, our new retail sales manager." I indicate him with a sweep of my hand, not that this was necessary, but because I felt he expected some kind of fanfare. He nods and reaches for her hand. Again.

"I've heard so much about you," Birdie says.

I give him a quizzical look. If he'd heard a lot about her, it hadn't been from me. "From, um, Izzy, here..." he says, as if I were a faithful but unnecessary pet.

My brows knit together.

"I'm doin' visits with the sales staff. Want to meet the important people, y'know, the ones that keep the lights on at the *Sentinel*." Birdie throws his head back and laughs. He is still clinging to Nellie's hand. She tugs it free, and smiles a tight-lipped smile.

I set up my laptop presentation. Nellie rubs her hand and gives me a look. I am about to switch topics when Birdie decides to continue chomping on the foot in his mouth.

"So," Birdie begins. My heart chugs a little faster. "What do you have to say about your relationship with our newspaper? Is it workin' for you? If not, we'll figure out why." Another blazing grin pierces his face. He leans forward, places both elbows on the table, tents his hands, and waits for her response. The smells of cigar and cheap cologne float across the table.

I'm sure my cheeks are blazing red. He must've skipped diplomatic small talk 101 that most salespeople internalize before being let loose in the field.

Nellie, ever the professional, responds, "Well, ahh, Birdie, is it?" He nods.

She tilts her head toward me. "Izzy is doing a great job. Her presentations and customer service skills are excellent. She makes doing business with the newspaper easy and shows me the results. She constantly updates me with studies that show the bottom line, which are forwarded to my Board of Directors to justify my budget with you. No complaints. How about you? How did you manage to become sales manager for *The Emerald Spring Sentinel*?" Her tone is somewhat punishing.

Birdie folds his arms across his chest, his thick lips pursed. I am beyond worried and closing in on mortified.

"Sweetie," he says, "I have been in management since before you were born." He smiles, but his eyes do not. "I came to the newspaper by way of earnin' it."

I rush to fill the silence.

"Nellie, ready to look over these ideas?" I open my laptop and go through my presentation. Afterward, I present mock-ups of the new sections and special magazines we've agreed to produce for the healthcare niche in Georgia. Nellie and I put our heads together afterward and talk details.

Birdie taps his fingers, wiggles his legs. We ignore him.

After twenty minutes and a firm commitment from Nellie to be involved, Birdie slaps his hands on the table and pushes himself up from his chair. "Good to meet you, Nellie. You be sure and give me a shout if Izzy isn't takin' care of things, y'hear?" In a final nod to his lack of manners, he winks.

Mortification is now official. After he shakes hands with Nellie (again), I hang behind and glance at Nellie, telegraphing my regrets. She smiles and rolls her eyes.

I trot to catch up with Birdie, who is striding toward the elevator with all the self-confidence and assurance of an absolute ass.

We walk side by side and pause at the parking lot. To say that I have mixed feelings is an understatement. I force out, "Well, how'd you think that went?"

He turns up the corners of his mouth without showing teeth. "Fine. Who's next?"

The rest of the day, I hover between nausea and outright shock. Since the remaining appointments weren't with women, it turned out okay...men didn't seem to mind Birdie's borderline-sexist, crude commentary. They'd snorted in laughter right along with him. I felt like an unwelcome fly on the wall and ticked off the minutes until the meetings were finished. Yeah, he 'good-ole-boyed' them to death, but where does that leave me? As if I approve? This is a nightmare.

As we drive back to pick up my car at St. Michael's later that afternoon, I try to figure out what makes him tick. As he's driving, one hand taps out a rhythm on the dash. He is a man who has a hard time keeping still. I wonder if his wife is driven as crazy by this activity as I am.

No doubt about it, there *is* something appealing about him in a sleazy way. But the guy is stuck in another era. The one where women are supposed to be pretty ornaments and listen to disgusting jokes and endure greedy male eyes on their bosoms.

If the situation were not so ridiculous, I would laugh it off. But he is my boss, so I'm not laughing about anything. I'm worried.

We glide to a stop next to my car. "Glad we got to do this today." An outright lie, but one sows seeds where one can. "Do you want to get together later in the week to discuss anything?"

Birdie winks at me with an expression that might have been cute, say, in 1962. His eyes bore into mine.

"You bet, sweetheart. We have lots to talk about. Lookin' forward to it. I'll be in touch." With that, he straightens his tie, pulls his shirt cuffs down, and drives away.

Lots to talk about? What does that mean? The lack of sexual innuendo in my conversation? That I need to wink more? Wear shorter skirts? Push-up bras?

I skid out of the parking lot, tires squealing. My Honda is a V6. It gets some serious traction. And when I'm mad, so do I.

Chapter Seven

I look out the front room window. Peter left his car out in the driveway instead of pulling it inside, and all the windows are down. Understandable. The onion and fast-food smell in that car would gag a camel. Maybe they decided to air it out. I walk into the kitchen to think about dinner.

Mimi sits at the kitchen table doing homework. When she sees me, she begins her non-stop adolescent monologue, which is fine because my boys don't talk much. Chad mumbles something about a nap and heads to his room. I watch him trudge upstairs as I listen to Mimi. Peter is standing in front of the fridge. He pulls out the key lime pie, cuts himself a huge slice, and holds it in front of his mouth.

"No football practice today?" I ask him.

"Uhh…yeah, Coach said we needed a day off, so I hung with Chad until Mimi was finished."

"Isn't a huge game just two days away?" I narrow my eyes.

Peter chomps a bite of the pie, grabs the milk, and closes the fridge with his foot.

"Ever heard of using a fork?"

"Hungry," Peter mumbles, shoves the rest of the pie into his mouth, then downs the glass of milk in one long swallow. "Like I said, Coach gave us the night. Said to rest."

I lean against the kitchen counter, perplexed. He is gone before I open my mouth to ask about homework.

I vaguely wonder what is going on with the boys. I wash my hands and pull chicken breasts out to bake for dinner.

I join Mimi at the table. As I watch her, my mind wanders to what life would be like, married to a thoughtful, kind man that would teach my sons man stuff. A man that would give me some breathing room, at least with the bills and the yard. Sure, we have to be in love, but experience has taught me if practical things aren't taken care of —keeping a job, paying the bills, being responsible —the love dies a slow, painful death. As Darlene had once stated, "Izzy, your *picker* is broken."

Since my kids' dad is not around much, teaching the man-stuff falls to me, and what do I know about man-stuff? Zero. My father's job had kept him on the road or in the air. When he was home, it was a whirlwind of vacations or fixing things around the house. There'd been no chill time, no margins in his life for family. As a result, the marriage choices *I* made resulted in acrimony because I had no idea what a healthy and whole, normal dad looked like.

My jaw clenches. The divorces had been tough, terrible situations, and the memories still haunt me.

Online dating helps. It's a lovely release, yes, but also a relationship instructor. That's what I tell myself—that I'm being educated in the ways of appropriate interaction with a prospective spouse. These experiences are helping to fix my broken man-picker. It makes perfect sense to me. I take the thawed chicken out of the package and begin hacking at the slimy, gristly stuff.

Yeah, Izzy, you're learning important relationship skills. Hack, hack. *Like how to avoid creepy men, for one.* Hack. Hack. Hack. *And how to zoom back to the house before the kids wake up and see that you're gone. Again.* Hack.

I set aside the butcher knife, my breath coming in short gasps. My hands grip the counter for balance.

Mimi is head-down, scribbling notes for her project, at the table. I am glad that she is unaware that her Mom is experiencing a panic attack. After I control my breathing, I put the chicken in a pretty baking dish. Dark green with fluted edges. I only cook because I have to—I don't like one single thing about it except presentation. If I can find a man who cooks and all I have to do is make the meal look magnificent on the table and clean up after, that will be perfect.

I grab a can of mushroom soup out of the cabinet, douse the chicken, and shove the dish into the oven. I set the timer and clap my hands together. Any attempt at cooking on my part is worthy of a small round of applause.

Drying my hands on a tea towel, I think about the Tyler situation, an unwelcome addition to my stress level. I have to stop handing out my address or where I work every time I meet someone! I promise myself to stop drinking too much during first meet-ups.

Afternoon sun streams through the kitchen window, bathing Mimi in a golden glow. She looks angelic. I tiptoe into the den and see that Peter is already snoring, one leg over the back of the couch, his arms splayed over his head. I picture him as a three-year-old and thread my fingers in his gold, close-cropped curls.

Great time for a dating app check. I back out of the den and check my phone while the chicken bakes.

The next morning I pop out of bed with a spring in my step. A good sign, and as a bonus, I'd proofed all my ads early and have nothing on my calendar with Birdie. The day is a blank slate, full of possibilities. I tug off the oversized T-shirt I wear as pajamas, and jump in the shower.

After making sure the kids are fed, equipped and mom-waved out the door, I run upstairs to finish getting ready for work. My cell buzzes with a call. I frown at the screen. Windsor Academy.

"Izzy? You up and about?" The voice is not one of the kids' teachers. At least none that I know.

"Yesss…"

"This is Horace McAllister, from Windsor Academy? How are you this morning?"

My jaw drops. The headmaster of Windsor. This cannot be good. "Fine," I manage. "Until now."

He laughs. "Why is that response the only one I ever get when I call parents?"

"Because the main reason for a phone call from you is that our kids have messed up. So have mine? Messed up?"

"Actually, Izzy, it's about the boys."

My airway starts to close.

I choke out, "I thought they were doing well. Their grades are okay, right? Their teachers aren't emailing me every two seconds. Peter is a starter on the football team this year...Chad's grades are better...." I know I'm blathering, but when I'm nervous, I blather. It just happens.

"Izzy, I know you have unique challenges. I've seen this before. Boys in single-parent homes sometimes act out. Nobody's fault. Just the way it is."

I murmur agreement, thinking how much worse it would be if their dad had stayed around. Ethan is worthless. Well, except for helping out once in a while if I'm gone for an extended period. Other than that, he mostly feeds me excuses for late child support and why he can't make it to the kids' school activities.

Horace clears his throat. "I got a call yesterday from the church across the street. This person saw your boys in their car in the church parking lot after school, smoking. At first, she thought it was no big deal, just cigarettes, and made a mental note to talk to me about enforcing private property stuff with the students, but she saw them throw the butts in the grass and ran out to check. Sure enough, it was pot. We have a zero-tolerance rule about that."

A confusing mix of emotions holds my tongue.

Horace continues, "I'm going to talk with them after school in my office. Would you like to be there?"

We arrange a time and end the call. The house is silent, except for the sound of the dryer in the laundry room and the muted tick-tock of an antique clock in the den. My aloneness drapes my shoulders like a shroud. My steps up the stairs to finish getting ready for work are measured and robotic.

I glance at the clock on my dresser. Twenty minutes to make it to work on time. I tuck the conversation with Horace into a corner of my mind. Then I finish my makeup and get dressed, trot downstairs, gather my work stuff, hop in my car, and go to work.

Just like every other day.

The office is quiet when I arrive. On the drive to work, I'd talked myself out of being overwhelmed. After all, pot isn't the worst thing in the world. Maybe it's an isolated incident? What disciplinary actions will the school implement? What should my own reaction be?

I scan the sales floor. Most cubes hold busy salespeople finalizing ads. The press deadline looms, and assistants fidget at various cubicle intersections, waiting for the green light to rush the ads to production. After deadline passes, the sales floor will empty. Winston immerses himself in today's newspaper. He looks up and smiles.

I slip into my chair and try not to show outward signs of distress about what's happening with my boys. Winston is hyper-intuitive, and I don't want to talk about kid issues all morning. I have to bring my A-game to work.

He looks at me over the reading glasses on the tip of his nose, picks up his coffee mug and toasts my arrival. "How are we doing this fine morning?"

"Good."

I scratch around on my desk, hoping he will not look too closely at my face. However, I *don't* have a funny story about a new guy or an interesting dating profile, and he will pick up on a mood.

"Busy day?" His eyes are questioning. He's already discerned my mood, and I'm not ready for a Winstonian life lesson.

"Gonna grab coffee. You want a refill?" He didn't. I grab my mug and streak across the linoleum to Darlene's desk for much-needed female empathy.

Her smile is like sunshine on a cloudy day.

Darlene reads my face even better than Winston, and since I am primed for a little compassion, I drop the mask.

Darlene's eyes round. "What happened?"

I give her the short version, shifting my weight from one foot to the other as I stand in front of her desk.

"You've not seen anything like this before with the boys?"

"No, but I'm gone a lot, and they're getting old enough to get to practices and stuff on their own and be more responsible. At least, I thought so. Peter's sixteen, and Chad's fourteen." My shoulders sag. I stare at the floor. "I don't think I'd know."

Darlene tilts her head, waiting.

"I know what you're thinking...that I have to focus more on them. It's just that...we need a man around, dammit, and how am I going to find one if I don't get out there and look?"

Darlene runs her fingers up and down a vase that holds the largest dahlias I'd ever seen. Her bouquets pop up everywhere around the office. I envy her green thumb.

"There's more to life than the perfect man, Izzy. Your kids need you, not just your paycheck. I know you think they're getting more independent, and no, I don't have kids, but I've seen some heartbreaking divorces and how the kids react. Sure, they take a hit but they're okay if at least one of the parents is stable. As long as they have someone to depend on, they're good."

I stand before her desk, mute. The implication weighs heavy that I am neither stable nor dependable. In my present state of mild hysteria, her correction feels like rejection. I push the hurt away.

"I hear you. I'll feel better about this after the meeting with the headmaster. By the way, how's your situation?" Deft topic-switching comes in handy as an avoidance tool when someone pierces the core of my guilt.

She averts her eyes.

"I vondered when you would get around to askink."

I frown. The thickened accent does not bode well.

"I got up the courage to confront him, and he admitted to meeting a 'friend' for coffee once in a while. I didn't press it, but...my gosh, Izzy, he's attracted to someone else." Darlene squeezes her forehead in an attempt to stop her tears. "It's a client."

I grunted. "Of course it's a client."

"He said she's coming on to him."

"At least it's out in the open, and you can deal with it. He's crazy about you. I can see it." Not exactly true, but it's what she needs to hear. I'm an optimist.

Her smile is half-hearted. "The weird thing is that I *know* we have a good relationship, but...how do I trust him now?"

I glance across the sales floor to the management offices and notice Birdie standing at his office door, surveying his domain. His lips tighten when his eyes rest on me.

"Darlene, I gotta go," I whisper. "Hang in, honey," I say and give her a quick hug.

My coffee has devolved into cold sludge. I slide into my cubicle and tuck my mug on its coaster. Birdie has slithered back into his hole. I am so relieved I let out a snort of laughter, and Winston perks up.

"What are we laughing about, Iz?"

"Nothing." I glance at the fresh newspaper on my desk. "Have you had a ride-along with Birdie yet?"

He grimaces. "Yeah."

"And?" I open the straight-off-the-press newspaper.

"I'm still processing," Winston says.

"What happened? How many clients did you take him to?"

Winston flips off his readers and crosses his arms. "I took him to see three of my major accounts. I had maybe ten minutes' notice to set it up. My clients were nice enough to let us drop by, but...well, awkward is a nice way to put it."

His voice drops. He tilts toward me. "I think the man may be in need of therapy. At every one, he got the ball rolling with dirty jokes." He shakes his head. "He do that at yours?"

I let out a long, troubled exhale. "Yep, he did. Not so much with Nellie, at St. Michael's, but with the clients we went to see afterwards he went crazy...and what was annoying is that the male contingent enjoyed it." I frowned. "I don't know whether to be relieved or insulted about that. Do you think Phil knows?"

"I think Birdie keeps himself under wraps with upper management."

I stare into Winston's calm blue eyes. "He could make the clients so uncomfortable they don't have time for us. Which could result in jerked budgets. I can't afford that," I mutter. "Should I say something to Phil?"

Winston strokes his goatee. "I think he'd weaponize that conversation... and you'd be the target." He resumes reading his newspaper.

I pull into Windsor Academy's parking lot later that afternoon to meet with the headmaster and sit in the parking lot staring at nothing, my hands on the wheel and my thoughts flapping around my brain like butterflies in a jar.

What if this pot thing has been going on for a long time? What if Horace accuses me of being an unfit mother? What if this is just the tip of the iceberg? Then what? What if the boys get kicked out? What if they're already brain-damaged? *Okay, whatever...quit spiraling.*

I breathe deep, cleansing breaths as if I'm in labor.

This motherhood thing never stops.

I tilt down the visor mirror and freshen my lipstick. If I'm headed to the muddy valley of despair, I might as well look good.

I arrive at the administrative counter in the school office, push back my shoulders, and ask for Horace.

A woman behind the counter smiles and points. "They're waiting for you."

I feel as if I am going to crack into a thousand tiny pieces. Now, in addition to clueless mom guilt, I feel late-again guilt. My palm is sweaty, and it takes a couple of tries to open the door.

Chad sits on a chair in front of Horace's desk with one leg dangling over the armrest. Peter sits rigidly in another chair. They both sneak glances at me.

Horace extends a hand over his desk. I wipe my palm on my skirt and shake his hand. Sit in the chair placed between my boys.

He scoots his chair closer to his desk and smiles. "Glad you could make it, Izzy."

I have never been inside Horace's office. The desk is large and imposing. His brag wall boasts several diplomas from prestigious universities and pictures of him shaking hands with celebrities. I notice that he is a Navy vet. The credenza against one wall holds family photos and various plaques and awards. The family cat is included in the photos.

A well-adjusted, normal family. Tears build, and I blink them away. Why didn't my last marriage work out? I glance right and left at my sons. I know so little about raising boys. I didn't even have a brother.

"Peter, Chad..." Horace begins, "We know why we're here, but I'll reiterate

39

for the record, okay?" The boys and I nod.

"We have a good relationship with the church across the street. They've been kind enough to let us use their parking lot for overflow and don't mind a certain amount of pranking. However, Windsor Academy has grown, and the relationship has become strained." Horace taps his fingers. "I'll get to the point, boys. This incident tipped them over the edge."

My heart constricts. I glare at the boys. Peter gives me a searching look. Chad grunts.

Horace continues. "I guess you realize that you were seen in the parking lot smoking pot, and before you say anything…" he points to a couple of smudged, wrinkled nubs on his desk with charred ends, "There's the proof. You're busted."

Chad frowns and crosses his arms. Peter stares at Horace, then at me. His face screws into a knot, and for a minute, I think he may cry. We sit silent for a few beats.

Peter takes a deep breath. "I just want to say I'm sorry. I am sick about it. And…and what it might mean with football. Whatever I have to do to make it right, I will. And I promise this is the first and last time I'll ever smoke pot. Honest to God."

Horace turns to Chad. "What about you?"

"So we got caught smoking pot. So what?" He shrugs. "Everybody does it. They just don't get caught."

He tilts his head toward Peter. "Yeah, the wimp here, he tried it because I asked him to." Horace glances at me.

I edge closer to a meltdown.

"Commendable, Chad, for you to let your brother off the hook. I appreciate your honesty. Now, let's talk about consequences. What are your thoughts, boys?"

Peter wrings his hands and keeps his eyes on the floor. Chad stares at the ceiling. Horace winks at me.

I am so relieved I almost faint.

The silence stretches.

"Community service?" Peter asks, his voice tentative.

His brother rolls his eyes but keeps his mouth shut.

Horace says, "What kind of community service, Peter?"

"Well," Peter frowns at Chad. "Maybe, um…painting buildings or picking up trash in empty lots or something?"

Chad puts a hand over his face.

"What's wrong with that idea, Chad?" Horace says.

"For starters, there aren't any empty lots around here, and who would buy the paint if we painted buildings?"

"Good points. What do you think about that, Peter?"

"I just wanted to throw some ideas out there, get the ball rolling…"

"How about a few laps around the track, or extra study halls, or something like that?" Chad adds.

"Do you think that is appropriate discipline for illegal activity, Chad?" Horace asks.

Chad lifts his thin shoulders. Neither son meets my eyes. They look straight ahead at Horace.

When Chad doesn't answer the question, Horace continues. "Boys, the good thing about this is that neither of you denied it. I'm impressed with your honesty. Both of your perspectives have value. At this point, I feel you could benefit from a first-hand look at the aftermath of drug addiction. I've developed a relationship with some of the NA groups and rehabs around the area, and they'd love to give you a tour."

Both boys jerk to attention.

Not me. I'm trying to shrink into the tiniest bit of humanity I can manage. Had I raised drug addicts? Was I that bad a mother?

"Sound okay with you, Mom?" Horace asks me.

My nod is weak.

Horace pulls out a few pieces of paper from his desk drawer, then walks around and hands me an acknowledgment of NA meeting attendance with Windsor Academy's imprint at the bottom and a space for the boys' and my signatures.

"Okay, guys, here's the deal. I'm going to require you to attend meetings for a while." Chad groans and slides down in his chair.

"I know it's not fair your mom has to raise you guys on her own. I know it's been rough, and you can get twisted up inside about things. But drugs aren't the answer. In fact, it makes everything—and I mean everything—worse. Which is why I want you to attend eight meetings. I think you need to hear some of the stories of these guys. And maybe you'll get a glimpse of what your life could be like if you don't get a handle on this now." He crosses his arms and looks at us.

"Sound like a deal?"

"Yeah," both boys respond in unison. Peter is teary-eyed and grateful. Chad is defiant.

I try hard not to cry. My lips wobble with the effort.

Horace directs a kind gaze toward me. "Okay, Izzy?" I mumble assent, my eyes wet. The boys cannot stand seeing me upset, so they give me quick side hugs, and walk out.

After the door closes behind them, Horace leans back in his chair and exhales. "Sorry about this, Izzy. I can't imagine how hard it is being a single parent, working a full-time job, and trying to corral these boys. I'm watching out for them, just like all the teachers here. Rest assured; consequences do make a difference."

I snuffle at him. He hands me a tissue. I wipe my face and rise from my chair.

"Kinda scared them, huh?" Horace grins.

My laughter balloons with relief.

I feel encouraged as I walk through the gleaming, locker-lined corridor back to my car.

My foot jabs the accelerator hard as I make a left out of the parking lot. Why haven't I met someone like Horace? Why?

Chapter Eight

The laptop screen springs to life. My screen background, a photo of a lovestruck couple, is my reminder that romantic dreams do come true. Somewhere, anyway.

I have dissected, disemboweled, and boundaried my sons. I'm reeling from stress and more than ready for my happy place.

For once, both Chad and Peter had paid attention. On the heels of Horace's ultimatum, their respect felt good. When had I lost it? Had I ever had it? Where is that piece of me that deserves their respect?

My laptop screen flickers.

The happy place awaits. My fingers fly across the keys.

A tingle of delight scrabbles through my brain when the site springs to life.

Online dating provides a cool, breezy oasis in the single-parent desert. The matches waiting for me blink *This. Could. Be. The. One.* Blink, blink, blink.

I'm thankful for this bright spot at the end of my day. I note the lateness of the hour and that the kids are already in bed. My schedule tomorrow is flexible. It is impossible that I have any energy left after this day.

I study my screen.

A smile creeps across my face.

Motivation outweighs energy every time.

The flattering, sexy texts lift my spirits into the stratosphere. I feel unquenchable. As if running off into the night to meet a hot, seductive stranger while two errant sons and one angel lay asleep upstairs is entirely justifiable.

The morning drive-through line snaking around my neighborhood Star-bucks is stupid-long, and since I was up until two a.m., my mood is borderline. Ten minutes and a spat of profanity later, I arrive at the window.

Lydia smiles. "Another late one, eh Iz? Triple coming right up."

I should frequent another Starbucks once in a while.

"Thanks."

She leans on the windowsill, waiting on my order, and I can tell she wants to chat. I cannot *chat* today! I will bite your head off. Please do not initiate chatting.

"Izzy, I know it's none of my business, but…"

I resist screaming and hope my sunglasses are dark enough to hide my eyes throbbing with red-veined exhaustion.

"Don't you think—and I'm just suggesting, please don't take offense—that you might be overdoing it with the dating thing?"

I mutter a generic response. Unfortunately, she dances on.

"I don't mean to intrude, but… I've been there. A single parent looking for a guy and all that. It can take over. My kids got lost in the shuffle. Just saying. After a while, I had to ease up."

She turns to retrieve my coffee, hands it out the window. "Just a thought," she says, "have a good one."

I zoom off to work, stung by her remarks. She's right, of course. I should ease off, and I will. Right after, I find the big *yes*.

I trot up the steps to the entrance just as Birdie exits. He catches my eye and shows me his big and brilliant teeth. I squint. His teeth are either false or whitened on a regular basis. Either way, they are blinding.

I don't return the smile.

"Hey, Izzy. Running late this morning?"

A wave of panic makes me dizzy.

I pause at the door, thinking that a commission salesperson's schedule is *supposed* to be flexible. "Didn't feel so good this morning. Better now."

"What was wrong?"

My brow furrows. Do I tell him the truth?

And what good would that do? No.

"Stomach thing. It passed." I wait for him to move on. He doesn't.

"Want to join me for lunch? We never have gotten to that in-depth meeting I'm doing with the sales team." His eyes hold a dangerous gleam today, but it could be my imagination. Four hours of sleep mangles one's ability to discern.

"No, no," I say, too quickly. "Got lots to do since I lost the morning…rain check?"

He gives me a long, speculative look. My mouth opens to fill the empty verbal space with an additional reason to delay the meeting, but he interrupts me.

"Izzy, you know you can't keep putting off the meeting with me forever. Let's do it in my office this afternoon. How's three-thirty?"

I resist a vicious scowl.

"Fine."

Birdie nods, and we go in different directions.

The elevator creaks and groans, accentuating my grogginess. The doors peel apart. My headache, on a scale of one to ten, has escalated to an eight. I shift my sunglasses from the top of my head to my face to shield them from fluorescent assault. With a sigh, I plop into my chair.

"Top of the mornin' Izzy." Winston is chirpy, which I credit to a satisfying night's sleep and a guiltless existence. I glare at him, shove my purse into a drawer, and bang it shut.

His hand crawls up his chest to clutch the ever-present lanyard from which his reading glasses dangle like a permanent appendage.

"Another late one, huh?"

I'm irritated by the question, but I love Winston, so he gets a pass.

"Yes. Worth it, though." I give him a half-smile that communicates regret that I am unable to do chatty and winsome.

"Tell me about him." Winston is always interested. He worries, though.

I unfold my newspaper, forgoing the typical morning chat with Darlene and accompanying coffee-trek because my morning schedule has unraveled.

I remove the sunglasses, and my eyes blink in protest. I squeeze them shut, then open them one at a time. Winston is staring at me. "What are you still doing here? Don't you have calls today?" I slant my gaze to the corner offices and note with relief that all the managers are gone.

"Well," Winston intones, "our esteemed new manager wanted a meeting." He waits, knowing I can't resist.

All I can muster up is, "And...?"

"You first," Winston says, smiling. He leans forward. His bow tie is powder blue today. His wife must help coordinate his wardrobe. Not everyone can pull off the look.

My own ensemble includes a wrinkled, cream-colored blouse, slacks, and a linen jacket. Somewhere I read that linen is *supposed* to be wrinkled, so it seemed the perfect choice. The wrinkles match my headache.

"Me first?"

"You don't have to," he says. "You look tired. It's okay."

I smile. But the quest for the perfect man overcomes exhaustion every time. I enjoy talking about it.

"I'll catch up on sleep tonight. I met a local. At least he's not a forty-five-minute drive from my house, isn't that great? His name's Cole. Isn't that the coolest name? He's in broadcast sales, and like, what a coincidence, right? We have so much in common." I describe our quick midnight meeting at a local bar and a brief list of physical attributes.

"Had you been talking for a while with this guy?" Winston asks.

"No, but we clicked right away."

"How long is *right away*?"

"Um...well, maybe two hours," I disconnect my eyes from his.

"Two hours? As in, you met him last night on the web and went to meet him?"

I pick at a cuticle.

"Izzy..." He gazes at me with those calm, blue eyes, his forehead furrowed with concern. "I've listened to these dating stories of yours for years. At first, I thought all that was harmless fun, but too many mornings..." Winston stares over my shoulder at the wall. "I'll just come out and say it. I think you

46

should give it a rest once in a while. Get perspective. And some sleep. It's not healthy."

"Perspective? What do you mean?" I am neither prepared nor interested in this conversation.

My thoughts veer toward how to get Winston to shut up, a strange and unfamiliar veer. I am perplexed, I am tired, I am irritable, and I am a single mom—a veritable powder keg waiting to be lit. Winston should back off.

And just like that, my mouth takes a relational suicide leap.

"What business is it of yours, anyway?" I snap. "I'm not a ten-year-old. I'm aware of the choices I'm making."

Winston, unperturbed, leans back in his chair and picks up his lanyard again. "Are you?"

"YES!" I screech. Assistants hovering at their various stations swivel their heads in my direction.

Great. Just what I need—an assistant-wide fall from grace. I mumble an apology.

"Izzy, this stuff is affecting your work, your attitude. Your family, too. I don't get in your face about things, do I?"

I huff out a no.

He throws his arms out. "What have I got to gain by confronting you? Nothing."

Resigned, I fold my arms across my chest and wait him out.

"I don't think you have anyone in your life that cares enough to point out a problem, Izzy. But I do. I care. I mean…I am all for internet dating, but your devotion to it is inappropriate."

The gush of honesty makes me squirm. "Can we get out of my business and back to yours?"

He shrugs. "I guess."

Good.

"So, how was your meeting with Birdie?" My tone is conciliatory.

"Ugly."

"Ugly?"

"I apologize, Izzy. I'm not in a great mood, either. The guy's attitude rubs off on me. Plus, he's too damn personal. Asked me questions that had nothing to do with my job."

My eyes snap wide open. "What kind of questions?"

"What kind of women clients I had. How many were single, that kind of thing. I hedged answering and made a joke. Then he asked me what the salespeople did for fun, where we went to drink and entertain clients."

Winston leans forward. His voice gets softer. His confidences act on me like a magnet. I lean in. We are co-conspirators whispering across the eight-inch vertical divide that slices our cubicle into three wedge-shaped workspaces.

"He's raising quotas by twenty-five percent. He made jokes about the female salespeople, which I found offensive. To top it all off, he asked me when I plan to retire. Gotta tell you, Iz, after all I've been through at this place, he may push me to retire early."

He picks up his glasses from his chest, places them on the end of his nose. I am too stunned to respond. And I have a meeting with Birdie in three hours. I feel dizzy.

Winston flips his newspaper page to the comics. "I think we're in big trouble."

"Why would they hire a guy like him? I mean, "I realize he was a faithful client over the years, but whatever possessed them—"

"Also," he said, semi-reading the comics page, "He asked about you."

"Me?" I squeak.

Winston's voice is soft. I lean closer to hear.

"He asked about the rumors he'd heard, if they were true, and if the online dating affects your job performance."

"Oh. God."

I jump up and run to the bathroom, leaving Winston open-mouthed and staring. My stomach relieves itself of all content exactly one second after I shove open a stall door and center my mouth above the toilet bowl. After throwing up, I feel better. I dash cool water on my face, sit on the floral bench in the tiny foyer in the ladies' to think.

What I do after hours isn't any of Birdie's business. I think about my track record and my ongoing success meeting quota. Why would he be digging up information about me? Has someone started knifing me in the back at the office? Does he have a vendetta against me already? Who has the most to gain by getting me out of the way?

My thoughts run rampant, then stall on one name.

Of course. Jon Hoyt. The guy who accused me of stealing his advertising revenue.

I plod back to my desk. I feel like death warmed over, and I'm fighting nausea. Moisture sprouts on my forehead. Winston keeps an eye on me as he gathers his paraphernalia in preparation to hit the street.

He could have left by now, but he's hovering until he knows I'm okay. Winston is a great hoverer.

"I'm glad you told me—I have a meeting with him later this afternoon. At least I'm, um...prepared." I smile. "Go chase ad budgets."

"Tread carefully." He walks to the elevator.

I rub my chin, thinking. How does one tread carefully around a snake?

Chapter Nine

I try to nap in my car in the alley behind the *Sentinel* building, but it's hopeless. With a groan, I un-recline my seat.

Winston is right. My online habit *is* affecting me. I glance at the clock on the dashboard. Fifteen minutes before the meeting with Birdie.

I could beg off. Tell him I'm ill.

I remember his uncomfortable, creepy gaze earlier. I can't shake the feeling of a veiled threat. I lift my hand and watch it tremble for a few seconds. *C'mon Izzy. Feel better.*

I can't get out of this meeting. He'd crucify me.

I back my car out of the shady downtown alley. A few minutes later, I'm cocooned in the decrepit elevator. My pulse pounds at my temples.

The doors hiss open on the second floor.

I death march to Birdie's office and knock on the door.

I hear his chair scoot back, then the heavy tread of his steps on the carpet. The door swings open. His smile serves up a double-decker helping of whitewashed tombstones.

"Come in, come in." He indicates a chair in front of his desk with a wave of his hand and closes the door.

"Hang on while I respond to these emails." He scoots the laptop out of my line of sight. Whatever he is working on, he doesn't want me to see it.

I cross my arms and wait. Why does this man strike terror in my heart?

He holds the reins to my job, for one thing.

I study his profile as he types. Bushy eyebrows, large, straight nose, strong jaw. He wears a large diamond ring on his right hand. A simple wedding band.

His bookshelves hold inspirational tomes by various self-made men: Donald Trump, Iacocca, Patton, JFK, Martin Luther King. There is a posed photograph of him beside what I assume is his wife. Bleached blonde, on the heavy side, lots of makeup. No kids' photos. The art on the walls depict ocean scenes featuring sailboats of various vintages. His immaculate desk is all right angles and clean spaces. I look beyond him, through the window, at blue sky, and experience the curious need to rush over to the window and jump.

My hands clutch the armrests tighter and tighter. I feel light-headed.

He sends his final email with a flourish and a bang of his fists, like a symphony finale.

I jump.

"This is good. We have our meeting."

I rub the circulation back into my hands. "Yep."

Birdie rocks gently, and his chair squeaks in that comfortable way that leather chairs have. His chair is the color of dried blood. Steepling his fingertips, he studies me.

"So. Tell me. How are things in your territory? What clients are you having trouble with, if any? Where can I help you?" His icy eyes lock on mine.

I am taken aback. Did I hear him correctly? Is he acting like a manager?

Winston's words *tread carefully* roll on a loop at the back of my brain.

I fill him in on my relationships with major accounts, my personal goals for these accounts, and steps to accomplish bringing in more revenue. Then I pick up steam and give him ideas about additional accounts and how I could leverage their budgets. A virtual yellow flag flaps in front of my eyes. I smash my lips together. Talking too much when I feel like something the cat dragged in is a trap. I should know better.

He oozes into the space my silence leaves. "Izzy, I've reviewed your history. Numbers are satisfactory, quotas are reachable, and your client relationships feel intact. All good things."

His eyes narrow. "But you can do better."

My eyebrows knit together. Why had I let my guard down? "Well. Everyone can do better, right?" I attempt a smile.

He grins. "You could use a refresher course in old-fashioned, front-porch conversation. You're stiff and frustrated out in the field. I can fix that."

I chew my lower lip. The follow-up call with Nellie at St. Michael's comes to mind. Nellie had been offended and irritated. It had taken a bit to convince her everything was going to be okay, but I had to promise never to bring Birdie with me again.

Stiff? Frustrated? Me?

Just with you, dirtbag.

I blurt out, "How do you intend to fix me?"

He leans forward on his elbows and grinds his hands together. "I think we should have a drink together to loosen you up." He winks. "I have a shitload of tricks that I'll let you in on, and this is good timing because I'm gonna be assignin' you some new accounts to bring in. I'll be your wingman."

I fall stone-silent. He mistakes this for consideration of his offer.

"Izzy, you've been meeting your quotas. All fine and good, but the buzz around is that you are so tired every day from runnin' out after men every night that you can't take care of business. Your assistant? Lonnie, is that his name? He has more than he can do, and I suspect it's because you're too damn tired to do your job." He pulls his chair up to his desk and looks me straight in the eyes. "If things don't change, I'll have to bring include Phil in this discussion."

I feel a vein begin to throb in my temple.

Oblivious to the havoc he is creating in my soul, he continues. "All the more reason we need to put our heads together."

Like a maddening drip from a leaky faucet, he keeps going. By the time he's done, I'll have to take three Ibuprofen.

"We'll get you loosened up, gal. You won't have time for that online crap if you play your cards right."

I'm sure my cheeks exhibit an angry flush. *Tread carefully, Izzy.*

I clear my throat. Wiggle around in my chair until I'm at the edge of my seat, knees tight together, hands in lap. "Getting Phil involved is a great idea.

I'd like his input on this plan as well, of course."

Birdie's smile falters, then returns. "Phil's out of town on business next week."

"Oh, that's too bad." My voice drips with syrupy sweetness. This idiot doesn't know me well enough to realize that my voice *never* drips with syrupy sweetness and that he should put himself on high, freaking alert. "We'll have to put it off a bit then, won't we? Let's table this idea until we hear from Phil. That would be my thought."

He swivels his chair back and forth, studying me under lowered eyelids.

"By the way," I continue, sifting through my words. "What I do during non-business hours is personal. I'll run this by HR, but I'm pretty sure 'meeting you for a drink to loosen me up' is inappropriate. I'll need to get the all-clear on that."

His expression reveals nothing. He is deathly still.

I rise and walk out.

I walk the twenty or so paces to my desk from his office and stumble into my chair. My body is flooded with fight-or-flight endorphins. The sales floor, except for busy assistants at their desks, is deserted. A few salespeople dribble in to close out the day per Phil's golden rule to be back by five p.m.

I watch the salespeople exit the elevator, laughing and joking with each other. Somehow, Birdie has a problem with me and not anyone else. Except Winston, and I think Birdie's comments to Winston constitute ageism, also inappropriate.

It dawns on me that Birdie has accomplished his mission—like an impossible move in checkers. Move one way, and I keep my job, but it involves going out for drinks and pandering to him—move a different way and call him out for the sexist he is… and I could lose my job.

Either way, I lose.

The end-of-day ad proofs are a welcome distraction. After five, I pull myself together and find Darlene. After a whispered, intense conversation, we agree to meet at Raphael's at five-thirty.

I'm nursing a glass of cabernet when she slips in beside me at the bar and gives me a tight squeeze. Tears bubble up.

She pats my shoulder, orders a drink. "Want some good news? Richard and I have had some hard conversations. We've scheduled counseling."

My eyebrows lift. "Wow, that is great, Darlene. A big step."

She smiles. "Yes, it's good, but clearing the air is hard. At least it's forward progress. Richard has agreed to hand off the client that's been a problem. I believe Richard is serious about our marriage, and that's enough for now. Okay, your turn."

I look at the mirror-covered wall behind the bar, which reflects hundreds of bottles of liquid solace in the soft, ambient lighting.

"Remember our conversations about Birdie?" I relate my concern about Birdie's coarseness and lack of manners. Her eyes get rounder with each revelation. I swear her to secrecy.

"This is a hard situation." Darlene taps her fingers.

"Oh, it gets worse. He's heard rumors about my dating life. Even gave me an ultimatum."

A smile flirts with Darlene's mouth.

"It's none of his business!" I snap at her. "Besides, he also wants to *take me out* to discuss sales techniques that might loosen me up."

Darlene's mouth drops open. "That's way over the line, Izzy."

"Of course it is."

Her brows pull together. "I think whatever you do, there is a trap."

"If I tell Phil, it'll be Birdie's word against mine. You know how Phil is...stiff upper lip and all that. He'll want to keep up appearances." I sip my wine. "If I stiff-arm Birdie, there'll be hell to pay—he's not the sort of guy that fights fair. I'll lose accounts, my commissions will dry up, and..." My voice trails away. I don't want to think about it.

"Seems to me you've already carved out your path, but you had no choice. He had to know where your line is. What do you think HR will say?"

I shrug. "Maybe I should have played along, given myself some time to think about the right way to respond, but...I was in shock. Maybe what I told him will get him to back off."

"Or it'll cause a war."

We sit in silence.

I push the garage door opener and wait for the door to rise. It's so slow it reminds me of the elevator at work. It's a relief that it's not even seven o'clock. I smile when I see that Peter's car is in the garage…which means everyone is home. I'm determined to carve out some quality time with my children, which includes resisting the dating sites.

My eyes adjust to the dimness of the garage. A small, white piece of folded paper tucked under the passenger side windshield wiper grabs my attention. Where the heck did that come from? Why had I not noticed on my drive home?

I hop out of the car and edge around the front bumper to the passenger side. Lift the wiper and slide out the note.

It is important to have a conversation.

I saw you at Raphael's with your friend. Time to stop avoiding me. Tyler

That creep Tyler has been *following* me?

I hold the paper at arm's length. My first response is to tear it into pieces and toss it in the trash. The more subjective part of my brain insists that I keep it in case things turn nasty. I hold it by my fingertips, take it into the house and stuff it into a Ziploc. Then I call Detective Lopez, and listen to the hold music, tense and exhausted and wondering when life will get easier.

I pull into my Starbucks drive-through, and a new girl smiles at me from the window. My lips push out in a pout. I was hoping to reassure Lydia that I'd connected with the kids last night and my family is fine. Everything is fine, fine, fine. The new girl asks for my order. A two-shot latte instead of a three. Lydia would be proud of me.

"Where's Lydia this morning?"

The young girl's eyes cloud. "Lydia had a family emergency last night. I didn't get details, but someone was in a terrible car accident."

I blink in surprise. "What happened?"

"Not sure." She slips a holder on the latte and gives it to me. "Enjoy your day."

I drive to work on autopilot. Why had I never thought to ask Lydia about *her* personal life? I hope with all my heart that she and her family are okay. She'd always been so kind to me, yet I didn't know one thing about her. How selfish is that?

I take the stairs two at a time and blast onto the second floor, beating the elevator in record time and mowing down Jon Hoyt in the process.

"Sorry. Good morning." Barring the news about Lydia, I'm amazed at how good I feel after a decent night's sleep. My brow furrows when Jon doesn't respond. He looks demoralized. "You okay?"

"Slow going the past couple of days. I'll get past it." He moves to the elevator.

"Do you have time for a chat later? Maybe late afternoon?"

"Sure." The elevator doors open, and he steps inside.

I sit at my desk, glancing around the sales floor. The staff filters in. The smell of coffee and the sound of muted conversation floats through the room. Our assistants are busy getting their checklists up on their computers. The managers huddle in Phil's office, visible through the floor-to-ceiling glass. I grab my mug and zip to the breakroom for a morning serving of sludge and Darlene.

Winston slides his chair closer to the desk and leans over the pod divide until our noses are eight inches apart. "Are we laying off the internet? Getting a little more sleep, maybe?" His eyes are playful. "There's a bounce in your step today."

I groan. "Yes, I stayed home. So what?"

He grins and turns his attention back to his newspaper. "Just an observation."

I snort my response and dash through the sales floor past Darlene's desk. She waves and smiles. The plan is to fill my cup and engage in a stroll-by chat with Darlene before my day starts.

A fresh pot brews, and a clot of starched, white-shirted, male account executives stand around waiting. They widen the circle.

"Hey, Iz...how's it going today?" an older colleague asks. I respond with a generic, "Fine."

"Hey. Can you suggest a dating app for me? Since you have so much experience..." The colleague eyes me with a smile. The rest of the guys chuckle.

Ha. Ha. This gets old.

The coffee percolates. "I'm taking a break." A lie, but I want them to back off.

"I doubt that, Iz," one of the men blurts. "How would you survive?" Their laughter is like a jackhammer to my skull.

I'd had enough of this crap over the past few years. Plus, as a general rule, I hate being teased. "I'd survive just fine, thanks," I snap.

"Birdie disagrees." The men study me.

A shiver snakes up my back. Has Birdie been spreading stuff about me? His pale, lifeless eyes flash before me. The coffee finishes brewing. "Just because someone says something doesn't mean it's true, guys. Don't believe everything you hear."

One of them chuckles. "Bet you're a slam dunk for salesperson of the year, now."

Blood rushes to my cheeks.

I stalk past Darlene and back to my desk. Her questioning gaze burns holes in my back.

I sit in my chair and jerk open my newspaper. How could a lie like that get traction? Nothing could be further from the truth.

My murderous thoughts whip toward Jon, but that doesn't make sense, either. I don't get the feeling that he'd do something so petty. Or would he? I take a sip of coffee and grimace. Why do I keep drinking this stuff? I frown and look inside the mug, where little floaty things of indeterminate origin lurk. I gag and set the mug aside. Winston is talking on his landline, so I can't even vent right now. With a sigh, I flip through the paper and check my ads, grazing the headlines so I'll have something to discuss with clients this afternoon.

I ponder Winston's comments. And Darlene's. Even Lydia. I *do* spend too much time online. It's choking out more important things.

Winston concludes his call and frowns. "What's up? Your mood has gone from cheerful to miserable in the space of thirty minutes. Everything okay?"

Sometimes it feels like Winston, and I are married.

"Have you, uh, heard any rumors about Birdie and me?"

Winston's eyes get large. He looks up at the ceiling a few seconds, then shakes his head. "What have you heard?"

"The guys think I'm hooking up with Birdie or whatever. Said I'm a slam-dunk for the annual sales award now."

He grins. "That's ridiculous. Izzy. Remember, this guy is motivated to mark his territory, and you're a threat. It's hardball with him, and he'd probably let them think whatever they want. I don't think there's any in-between."

I think about that.

Had I told Winston about Birdie's ultimatum? I spend a few minutes unpacking what I call the 'loosen-me-up' meeting. He is very still as he listens. His calm eyes act as a panic extinguisher.

"The mention of HR ruffled Birdie's feathers." He concludes, crossing his arms. "So to speak." He grins.

Winston loves puns. I give him a tiny smile. "What was I supposed to do? Let him think I'd go out with him?"

"Iz, you gotta cool it for a while with the online dating thing. For whatever reason, Birdie is watching you like a hawk." He smiles again. "I don't think your reaction to what he suggested was in any way out of line. He's an out-of-touch, failed furniture salesman trying to make a comeback." After a pause, he says, "Sure like to know what happened for his business to flame out."

"Me, too."

"Look, I know you want to find a stepdad for your kids, a good marriage and all that, but you can't give this guy an excuse to turn on you. Focus on the job and your family for a while."

I gaze at his earnest face a few moments, thinking how fortunate I am to have this man in my life. "Thanks, Winston. I've got a meeting with Jon later to see if he's involved."

Winston's eyebrows shoot up to his hairline. "You think he's mad about the Tom Burke thing?"

"We worked all that out, but Birdie's remarks and then the guys in the breakroom this morning...it made me think. What if he's the passive-aggressive type? Doesn't hurt to have a conversation."

Winston lifts a straw hat from its corner perch and tilts it on his head. "Sometimes you have to let things work themselves out." He smiles, salutes me. "Think about whose name is at the middle of all this." He strides to the elevator.

I flip another page of the newspaper, thinking. Whose name?

Birdie.

Chapter Ten

Birdie slams down the landline handset.

His eyes squeeze into small, mean slits. He pummels the armrests of his blood-red chair.

He rises, stalks to the window, and takes deep breaths. Looks out on what he considers his new domain—a new opportunity to succeed beyond anyone's expectations. Like last time.

A shadow crosses his face. His last endeavor had been a success. Except he'd made the sad choice to include his brother's wife, his sister-in-law, as a partner. He'd never forgive himself for that choice. For years he'd been told family makes the worst business partners, but she'd convinced him she'd act as a silent partner. Birdie would be in charge.

It did not work out that way. In fact, crash-and-burn better describes the carnage.

He shakes away the memories.

Through his second-story window, he studies Emerald Spring's busy Thrasher Avenue. Vehicles compete for parking on the main thoroughfare. Customers stream into boutique shops and restaurants. People flow in and out of revolving doors that front the redbrick, three- and four-story buildings opposite our office building. Ornate, black, wrought-iron street lamps embellish the sidewalks. Mature oak and maple trees line each side of the street, the result of a downtown beautification project thirty years ago. Concrete sidewalks clash here and there with root systems vying for urban space.

His gaze lifts to the horizon. Storm clouds are rolling in across the river from the east.

The conversation he'd just had with the HR director had been a struggle. In her sweet, southern way, she'd informed him that a complaint had been filed, that she was sure it had been a misunderstanding, but she needed to have a sit-down with him as soon as possible, and when might that be?

After this pronouncement, he'd tried to insinuate himself into her good graces. He'd pulled out every technique in his arsenal. He laid the charm on as thick as a good meringue. Every bit of it backfired. The call had ended abruptly. He stares at the phone on his desk. He'd slammed the handset down with so much force he was surprised it was still in one piece. He scowls. Izzy Lewis' threat had not been an idle one.

The one-on-ones he'd had with the sales team had all gone well. Hadn't they? Birdie closes his eyes and walks through them one at a time. They'd been fine. All of them except Izzy. And her sidekick… senior guy…what's his name? Winston. That's it. A forced retirement is in Winston's future. Soon.

Not everyone gets him, but it's how he's always done business—jawing with the guys down at the warehouse, making deals with a handshake and a shared joke. He rubs his forehead. Is this related to his sense of humor? His salty remarks? The teasing? He remembers the lack of response, the studied silence, even a few crossed arms and frowns. "Is that it?" he whispers to himself. "All this politically correct nonsense going around?"

He laughs, relieved. A solution is as simple as a phone call or two. Yeah, he can understand that the ladies might not take his sense of humor so well, but it's an easy fix. Lots of managers are rough around the edges. The good ones, anyway.

He rubs his hands together, thinking.

First, a casual chat with Phil to downplay it. Spin it.

Then, a planned, accidental drift by the general manager's office to lay the groundwork in case the HR complaint works its way through the system. His mind moves through each step of his strategy.

Women are too damn sensitive.

He picks up his laptop and sunglasses, much cheered. He steps out of his office and locks the door, considering where he might go for lunch. His eyes fall on Izzy sitting at her desk. He has his work cut out for him with this gal, but she is no match for him. Very few people are.

He nods at her on his way to the elevator.

Izzy ignores him.

Birdie smiles. She has no idea what's coming.

Chapter Eleven

T here's less traffic on the freeway midafternoon, and I enjoy swooping in and out of various lanes unhindered. I pull into my garage, exit the car into the house, plop my laptop on the couch in the den, and log on. The phone apps are convenient, but I much prefer to super-size the photos than try to look at the tiny thumbnails on my phone. I have an hour and a half until the kids come home from school. My heart ramps up in anticipation. I hope for several messages. Lord knows I need them. The Birdie debacle is worming its way into my head, and I'm having trouble focusing on the job.

My colleagues' comments around the coffeemaker made me realize that the war with my new sales manager is just beginning.

Client calls can wait until I sort myself out, and nothing works better than the sites. To my utter relief, there are two gorgeous men waiting for my response. I open the profiles one at a time, my heartbeat slowing. This feels like I imagine a shot of insulin feels to a diabetic.

'Astute professional seeks companionship. Prefer a career woman who values independence, integrity, and romance. I am tall, athletic, successful, and motivated to fall in love. Like poetry, good books, long walks, full moons, sunsets and jazz. Good—not great—dancer, but I can hold my own. Likes kids, and have two teen-age boys. I'm mature, but not dull; optimistic, but not unrealistic; sports-minded but open to turning off the game; educated but not stuffy; political but not narrow-minded. The lady I am looking for is attractive, intelligent, a non-smoker; interested in outdoor activities, and likes (or tolerates) dogs. Hopefully, she will appreciate a great wine and not mind if I open the door for her.'

Uh-oh. This guy sounds too good to be true.

I click back to his message, which says, 'Belle, I love your pics and description of yourself. I see that you have an interesting career, and our passions seem similar. I think you are one of the loveliest women I have ever seen. Please don't break my heart – let's talk. I'm out of the country on business in three weeks and would love to meet you sooner than later. Signed, Anticipating, Brad'

The tension in my neck and back disappear. I melt into a soggy, romantic puddle. His dog and one child are included in his photos.

My flying fingers message him that yes, call, let's talk, I'm flattered, oh so flattered, and I ask him to give me his available times to talk. It's too early in the game for that, but I'm desperate for relief. For validation. Something.

The adrenaline rush zips through me like a lightning strike. The other man's profile is okay, but not even close to Brad.

Swipe. Gone.

I stare at his photo again, then glance at the time. The kids are due any minute. I put two fingers to my lips, plant them on his, and log off.

I stand and stretch, then walk to the bath off my bedroom to freshen up before going back to work. The kids troop in one after the other, and we spend time catching up. On the way to the garage, a detail hovers at the edge of my mind. My meeting with Jon Hoyt. *Four p.m.* I text my assistant, Lonnie, and ask him to relay a message to Jon that I'm running late.

I'm amazed at the power of a well-placed compliment to bring me back to center. I start the car, hit the garage door opener. It makes a growly sound as it pulls up. Focusing on the backup camera, I pull out.

I squint as the afternoon sun blinds me. Then I see it.

My God.

Another square of white paper under the passenger-side windshield wiper. Was that there before I left the parking lot at work? Yes? No? Did I overlook it? If not, *how did he get into my locked garage?* My stomach ties itself into knots.

I grab the note, glare at it, and throw it in my purse. I'm not going to read it until after the meeting with Jon. I have enough strange men in my life. Too many.

And why is that?

I shove the voice of my conscience away.

Lonnie greets me as I step out of the elevator, his expression strained. I see by the height of the pile on his desk that he has quite a lot to do.

"Hi, Lonnie. Need me to take some of that?"

He walks his fingers through the pile and pulls out several proofs.

"Could you check these on the proofing site? That would be a help, Izzy, thanks."

"Of course. Jon around? Did he get my message?"

"Yeah," Lonnie says, one hand on his phone. "He's frustrated. It's four-thirty. Just saying."

"Thanks," I toss the stack on my desk, streak across the room through the cubicles and throw open the conference room door. Jon is tapping his fingers on the conference table. "Jon, sorry, stuff came up."

He waves his hand in a curt gesture that erases my apology.

"I'm here. What's this about?" he snaps.

I sit. "I wanted to talk to you about something I heard this morning from some of the retail sales guys."

"Okay."

"I guess you realize that Birdie, the new manager, is kind of intent on getting to know us and our account lists."

He looks confused. "Is this about the new manager? I've got a *different* manager, in case you hadn't noticed."

I am stumped for what to say next. Okay, so I'm late, and he's irritated. Fine. But is there a need to be a jerk? My attempt at a diplomatic approach flies out the window.

"Jon, for gosh sakes, there's no need to be mean. I'm trying to give context."

"Izzy, I've been sitting here for forty freaking minutes so far, and believe it or not, I have work to do."

"Yeah, well, I've got stuff to do too. I don't have time for this rumor drama crap either."

Jon blinks and leans forward. "What rumor drama crap?"

"Someone's been saying that Birdie and I are involved. It's...*so* absurd, and I can't believe it's making the rounds."

"Wait. You think I'm involved?"

I cross my arms and hold his gaze.

"I don't get roped into that type of stuff. Never have, never will. If you think I'm that kind of person, you're wrong." He makes a move to leave.

"Wait, Jon," I plead. "I'm desperate. I...I didn't know how to approach it in a diplomatic way, so...I apologize. I started thinking you might still be angry about the Tom Burke thing and that maybe..." The words sound preposterous, even to my own ears. I snap my mouth shut.

Jon, to his credit, does not storm out of the room in an angry fit, but stands his ground, staring at me with his mouth hanging open. Wincing at the full brunt of my clumsy conflict resolution skills, I hear Jon's chair scrape back as he re-seats himself.

My eyes are stuck on the floor. I watch his feet situate themselves an even eighteen inches from each other. His elbows perch on his knees, and he leans in my direction. The silence is deafening.

After a minute or two, he takes a deep breath and says, "I promise you, Izzy, that I am not that kind of person. You don't know me well, but you can count on me to *never* do something like that." He shakes his head. "If I thought you were involved with your manager, I'd say something to you, maybe, out of concern—but not anyone else. Unless, of course, it starts to affect my accounts."

We stare at each other a few seconds.

"I can promise you I wouldn't ever—" my words sputter into nonsense. I can hardly believe I'm defending myself against some outrageous rumor.

I am also thinking now would be a great time for a two-week vacation, if I could afford it. The sum total of Isabelle Lewis' conflict resolution skills—leave town.

Jon stands. "I think this meeting is over," he announces.

"Jon, I thought instead of letting my mind run down rabbit trails that I should approach you before I started believing something that wasn't true. I'm emotional about this. Maybe you can understand."

He searches my face. "Okay, never happened. And if you're dating Birdie, it's none of my business." He grins.

"He's too old for me, and besides, he's married."

"Coulda fooled me," Jon mutters.

"Why do you say that?"

"Y'know, I've been here over twenty years, and I know what goes on. I understand how management thinks and how to play the game with production. And editorial, too, for that matter. I've learned that it's best to keep your head down and your mouth shut around here. While I sit at my desk in the afternoons, turning in ads and fighting with production, and sucking up to my assistant so I can get her to do what needs to be done, I also keep my ears open. It's ridiculous how much you find out when you keep your mouth shut and listen." He chuckles. "I keep everything I know to myself until— God forbid—something happens where I have to drag it out to protect my job. But one thing I know. That dude doesn't act married."

"I saw a picture in his office with a blonde woman about his age. Looked like a husband-wife shot to me." I lift a shoulder. "He wears a wedding band."

He turns his wrist to look at his watch. It's a beauty, a Rolex, Explorer Series. As he's leaving, he turns from the door toward me and blows my mind. "What do you say we have coffee sometime, and you can tell me how that internet dating thing works?"

I try to pick my jaw up off the floor. If he'd taken a swing at me, that I could understand. But coffee? I stutter that maybe I'd like that. Sometime.

He smiles. "Take care, Izzy."

Chapter Twelve

On the way home, I remember the note I'd thrown in my purse before my meeting with Jon. I fish around in my purse and pull it out.

When I come to a full stop at a red light, I unfold the note. The typed words shout at me.

I'M WATCHING, YOU KNOW. HOW MANY GUYS HAVE YOU TREATED THE WAY YOU TREATED ME? I BET THERE ARE A LOT OF US. DON'T YOU NEED TO GET TO BED EARLY FOR WORK? WAS IT WORTH IT, THE PHONE DATE THAT LASTED TIL THREE IN THE MORNING? WHEN YOU HEAR WHAT I HAVE TO SAY THAT MOCKING GRIN OF YOURS WILL BE WIPED RIGHT OFF YOUR FACE. WHEN ARE WE GOING TO TALK? I'M SERIOUS, IZZY.

I crumple the note in horror. He'd been in my house? Watching me? How was this possible? Could he have seen me through a window? The light turns green. I don't remember the rest of the drive home.

I pull into the garage. After dinner and homework, I'm telling the police about the notes. No more procrastinating. I manage a smile for the kids' sake, and walk into the house.

Chad and Peter are at the kitchen table with their school laptops. I hear Mimi's TV upstairs in her room. I hug each son, which results in irritated looks and half-hearted attempts to pull away, but I don't care. I hug them every day whether they like it or not.

"What's up, guys? How was school?" I glance over their shoulders. "What homework are you working on?"

"Got those NA meetings tonight," Chad says. "Seven. More. Times," he says, his voice dripping with sarcasm. "We have to get homework out of the way early."

"Yeah? Good. I am one hundred percent behind Horace." I sit and look from face to face, fold my arms on the table. "So, give me your impressions about the NA meeting. And turn off the music. I will never know how you can study with that stuff banging around."

They exchange glances and smile. Peter gets up, turns off the music.

I wait.

Peter puts down his pen and shrugs. "My takeaway is that the guys have gone through some terrible things and have diseases now. Some don't even talk to their families at all. I'm not going there. Ever." He glances at his brother. "I tried it because you asked me, moron. I'm done."

I hold my breath. This is holy ground.

"Chad?"

His sigh is heavy. He throws one arm over the back of the chair and stares at the ceiling.

"So stupid," he mutters. "Pot is *not* a serious drug. It's approved in several states for um, sick people. It doesn't lead to harder drugs."

He can't quite look me in the eye. There's something deeper going on.

I take a deep breath and dive in.

"Maybe you're right, but the point is, it's illegal. Period. You've been given a second chance by Horace McAllister, but the law will not be so forgiving."

The issues fighting for attention in those tidy compartments in my brain threaten to dump out on my kitchen table. I try to scale back.

"Chad, you are smart and capable. Please pay attention to what these guys say in the meetings. You can learn from them. Be open. Talk to them one on one...tell them what happened. Maybe you can skip going through what they have."

His eyes glaze over, but he nods. Peter takes this as his cue also and picks up his pen. I get dinner going, then run upstairs to check on Mimi.

I pass by my laptop on the charger. The pull is unmistakable.

With a sigh, I open the door to Mimi's room. She's on the bed with her school laptop, typing. I walk in and smile. "Homework done?"

She gives me a look, then snaps her laptop shut. "Dinner ready?"

"In a few."

"Some of my friends are going to Stacey's house. Can Chad and Peter drop me on their way to that meeting? After dinner?"

"Which friends?"

She rattles off names I recognize, and Stacy's house is close.

"Sounds fine. Dinner in twenty minutes." She's already back online. When had she taken such an interest in homework?

Later, I stand on the front porch and wave goodbye to the kids. "See you at nine. Walk Mimi inside, okay boys?" As I walk back inside, my cell buzzes.

"Is this the gorgeous woman who calls herself Belle?"

My face flushes with pleasure. I am such a sucker for a good line. "Nice to meet you too, Brad." I'd almost forgotten about the call. He'd wanted a Facetime or Zoom, but I'd declined, thank God. I look at myself in the mirror as I walk outside to the backyard. My hair is a mess, and my makeup gave up hours ago.

I drift outside in a haze of romantic fantasy to the small deck outside my kitchen door and participate in the introductory ritual that I've polished to perfection. The information I extract determines whether moving forward is a good idea. After we chat for thirty minutes, he asks to meet somewhere. Since the kids won't be home for at least another hour and a half, I throw caution to the wind and say yes. We decide on a location.

Jittery with excitement, I race upstairs to get ready.

The night is a clear, stark black when I get back to my car after Brad leaves the parking lot. Stars prick the sky in tiny, brilliant, white points of light. I think about the deliciousness of meeting a new man. It never gets old. Well, unless the guy is a jerk or hasn't posted accurate photos. Brad had been fantastic, and I'd limited myself to one glass of wine, which helped.

'It's so clear we can see galaxies,' Brad had said as we stared at the brilliant sky.

No doubt about it, this guy had been different.

I say that seventy-five percent of the time, though.

Still.

When I'd shivered in the night air, he'd draped his jacket around me, then kissed me on the cheek. The cheek! So polite. My thoughts run 'round and 'round in my head, chasing their fluffy tails like charming little lambs, and boom. I'm lost in a sea of storybook endings. Again.

I pull the Honda into my driveway and wait as the garage door strains open. The house is dark. Good, kids are still gone. They'll never know that Mom went out. The serotonin surges wash over me like waves cresting the beach. I float into the house.

The clock on the wall in the foyer chirps ten times. The kids were supposed to be home by nine. What's going on? I throw my purse on the couch and sigh. I am reluctant to think of anything but Brad right now.

We'd parted with a hug. He whispered in my ear that he'd call later in the week. I can still feel the chills shiver up and down my spine as his breath tickled my ear. I want to lay on my bed and remember that feeling as I drift off to sleep tonight.

However.

Brad, Peter, and Mimi are over an hour late.

I run upstairs to change clothes and almost, but not quite, ignore my laptop. I groan.

One tiny minute won't matter. When I open the laptop, it practically logs itself in. One message. I click on it half-heartedly. I doubt if anyone will give Brad a run for his money.

'Belle: As I search for the perfect woman, I'm hopeful my search will yield that one woman—the *yes*—that will fulfill my dreams, help me achieve our mutual goals, and fill the void in my life. The one awesome woman who I long to smother with gifts and flowers, write love poems, become a fool. She will have my heart forever. I have to confess that I was on the verge of giving up after months of searching. Then I found you. You are all I can see, now. Your eyes, your hair, your smile. Entrancing. The things you shared in your profile a perfect match for mine. My option on this site expires soon. You cannot disappear! I don't want to be too forward, but I am serious. You have captured my heart with your profile. Meet me. Please. Read my profile. Consider. We might be perfect for each other.'

'If you agree, I will be waiting for you at Raphael's Piano Bar in River's Edge downtown. Eight this Saturday night. If you don't show, I'll take that as a no. Until then, dreaming of you.'

I stare at the screen with my hands over my mouth. Never had a message so captivated me. Why now? Brad is wonderful.

I glance at the large stack of romance paperbacks on my nightstand. Every night I read the damn things, wishing. Hoping. Clutching the stupid books to my chest after they are finished like a defibrillator.

Rolling my eyes, I grab the whole lot of them, march into the bathroom, and throw them in the trash.

It's ten-thirty. Where are my children? I change into my PJs and rummage in my purse for my phone. Missed calls from a number I don't recognize, but no calls or texts from the kids. My heart skips a few beats as I call their numbers until one of them picks up. Peter responds. "Hey, Mom."

Hey, Mom? That's it?

"Where are you?"

"Still waiting for Mimi."

"What? Why are you *waiting* for her? Isn't she at Stacy's?"

"Nope." Boys are so infuriatingly terse. After a night floating on clouds, I'm falling back to earth with a thud. "Get me a parent."

Stacy's parents sound a little put out. Mimi had told them a friend was picking her up. That it was okay with me. I'd never picked up when they'd called to confirm. I wince when I think about how I'd ignored everything but Brad. After apologizing, I send Mimi a text, bite my fingernails, and call Peter back.

"Call me when Mimi shows up. Are they okay with you hanging out until she gets there?"

I hold back tears of frustration. Where is she? She is *twelve*, for God's sake. I think hard for a minute and decide her tablet may hold a key. Didn't I save her passwords somewhere?

I run to my desk, where I keep my private stuff locked in a drawer. I gasp out a frenzied version of the Hallelujah Chorus when I find a list of her passwords.

I enter her room and marvel at how neat and tidy it is. When had she started cleaning up her room? Her tablet is on her nightstand, charging. I pick it up and sit amidst stuffed animals piled halfway down the length of her bed. Log in to Instagram, where she spends most of her time, at least as far as I know. Do I really know that? Oh God, help me find her.

Her private Instagram messages set off alarms. A lot of boys had been chatting with her. Hadn't I watched a program a few weeks ago about predators on social media posing as young boys? My heart is beating so hard I think my chest will explode. I feel sick. It would serve me right if I had a heart attack.

The phone rings. I nearly jump out of my skin.

"Mom?" It's Mimi. "I'm okay. So sorry, I didn't mean to stay out that late."

"Mimi, it's almost eleven! Where have you been? I was about to call the police. And who the heck is—" I stop myself before she catches on that I know her passwords.

"Who is who?" Mimi says, puzzled.

I grit my teeth. "You and the boys get home, please. And I expect a full explanation."

"Yes, ma'am." Mimi gets very polite when she realizes I'm about to fall off a cliff. "We're on our way."

I place Mimi's tablet back where it was, re-connect it to the charger, and smooth out her comforter where I'd been sitting.

Chapter Thirteen

I t is two in the morning before we finish talking.

I feel like Mimi had dragged me through a ship's propeller and left all the bloody bits of my body afloat in the water as shark bait.

I take a hot shower, dry off, then run a comb through my wet hair, staring blankly into the steamy bathroom mirror. I rub away the steam and think about the conversation. She'd used Stacey's house as a foil. She'd been picked up by some boy she'd been messaging on Instagram. TikTok. Something. A boy she'd never met in person.

My reaction had not been patient. Or kind.

But my *daughter's* reaction—?

I sit on the bed. Close my eyes. When had she grown so angry? Had I been oblivious to her frustrations? She'd given me no clues. Or maybe…

My shoulders slumped. Maybe I wasn't around, and she just did the best she could.

What I learned from our unpleasant—but necessary—conversation is that trying to hide my dating escapades is pointless. Her defense about meeting a stranger gutted me…she'd *learned it from me*. To be expected, I guess, but it still hurt. My lame retort had been how much older, wiser, and more experienced I was, to which she'd responded, "Oh. So that's why we have had *two* fathers so far and it looks like there'll be another one."

I'd almost bitten my tongue in half.

Plumping the pillows with my fist, I slide under the comforter in hopes of sleep.

I'd plied her with more rules, grounded her for two weeks, and taken her phone and tablet. Her words play on an endless loop.

One more thing I can't turn off.

Birdie and his expectations, Jon's coffee invitation, a potential relationship with Brad, my sons' recent drug explorations. Plus making a living and paying the bills, trying to stomach Ethan, finagling regular child support from him.

I groan, toss the comforter off and pad downstairs for a cup of chamomile tea.

I hurry past my laptop without a glance.

As the tea water heats up, I step outside. The night air is cool. Thanks to a neighborhood petition, there are no glaring streetlights to disrupt the full moon's incandescence. I wince at my struggling rose bushes, barberry bushes, and crepe myrtles against the privacy fence. How long had it been since I'd turned on the sprinkler?

Sitting on my tiny deck in the light of the silvery moon, I feel a symbiotic connection to single parents. A fellowship of suffering. A comedy of errors. I lift my teacup to them all.

The tea is soothing and delicious. It is quiet except for the night sounds—crickets chirping, frogs croaking, twigs snapping.

My head whips around. Twigs snapping?

Just outside the fence. What is that? A raccoon or fox going through the trash?

A branch cracks. Something brushes against the fence. Steps move through the grass.

I freeze in my chair, tea aloft in one hand. The sound repeats, then the definite crunch of steps across a field of acorns. I pray the gate is locked. What should I do? Panic grazes the back of my neck, crawls up my throat. I should've brought my phone out here with me.

Metal grates upon metal. The lock holds. I heave a sigh of relief and frown. Place my teacup down. We never use that gate. The bushes have gotten huge, and someone had to push through them to get to it. My mind balks at the thought of an intruder, but what else can it be? I bite a fingernail and think about prints. On the latch. I have to remember to tell the cops.

The footsteps recede. I hear them walk around the fence.

I send up a desperate prayer.

Thank God they can't see me where I'm sitting. If I move, they'll know I'm awake. Are they trying to break in?

The steps stop at the other side of the fence. Someone peers through the slats.

Clouds cover the moon, cloaking me in darkness. I hate to admit it, but it is most likely Tyler, and I hadn't given the restraining order a priority, so now what? How psycho was this guy?

I will my heart to stop beating so damn hard. *Now is the time to get a dog.* As usual, a good idea too late, but I mentally add it to my list of things to do when I am not busy being terrified.

The minutes drag by, the shadows in the yard shifting like elongated ghosts. The night, like me, holds its breath. In time, the footsteps recede. I hear them shuffle through the grass, then scrape pavement until…nothing.

I heave a noisy breath and race inside for my phone to call nine-one-one.

Yes, there was an intruder, yes I have an idea of who it might be, yes I need you to come out. How do I get a restraining order? A soft voice tells me I must file the appropriate paperwork, either myself or my attorney, and bring all the evidence I have. That a hearing will be scheduled. That a police report, yes, is evidence. That a protective stalking order will be on standby until the hearing. I tell her about the notes I'd received and that Detective Lopez is familiar. Yes, she says, we will schedule you with him.

I sit in the den and wait on the patrol cops. After I make the police report, which thankfully did not wake the kids, I drag my weary self upstairs, locate two Tylenol PM tablets, and do my best to numb out.

Chapter Fourteen

L ydia is back at the window. She smiles at me, a shadow behind her eyes.

"Lydia, I missed you. Heard you had some trouble?"

She glances at the line of cars behind me. "My son was implicated in a hit-and-run."

"What?" I take the steaming coffee from her.

"He didn't do it. Things are okay now, but it took a while to get to the truth."

"How do you do it?"

She smiles. "How do *you* do it?"

I raise the cup.

She laughs. "Honey, we'll make it. If these kids don't take our sanity."

I pull away and head toward the office, hoping for a quiet day. I don't pray much, but I make a promise to myself. I'll pray for Lydia, and while I'm at it, I'll throw myself in there, too.

I carry my latte, my purse, and my all-purpose bag into the elevator, which happens to be crammed today with an elementary school tour. I balance my coffee above their heads. As I wait for the doors to wheeze open, one of the blessed little critters' heads bumps my coffee and causes a lovely brown splotch on the front of my cream-colored jacket.

The tour guide apologizes (not the child), and I struggle through the meandering throng to my desk. I sigh, assess the damage, take off my jacket and hang it up on the rack.

Winston flips his glasses off his nose and smiles.

"Day not starting out too good, huh?"

I sit at my desk, throw my purse into its drawer. "Bunch of kids on a tour bumped my coffee."

Winston nods. "Always thought they should be on leashes until a certain age," he quips. "So what's going on? Haven't talked to you in a bit."

"I had a weird day yesterday. You won't believe this, but—"

Our conversation is snipped when all hell breaks loose over in Classifieds.

I bound from my chair to take a closer look.

"Move back, folks. Give him some room." The classified manager elbows his way through. I wrangle into the front of the crowd and see Jon Hoyt laying on the floor, hyperventilating and pale. His eyes are closed, and he's whispering. "Dizzy...so dizzy."

I kneel beside him. "Can someone bring me a wet towel or something?" A couple of people sprint toward the bathrooms. Jon is drenched in sweat and becoming incoherent. "Anyone have water?" Someone hands me a bottle. I put it to his lips. He sips. "Have you eaten this morning?"

"Dizzy," he says again.

He is close to passing out. I hear sirens in the distance.

"Hang in there," I whisper. "Help is on the way."

He gets more of the water down. Color returns to his cheeks.

People drift away. The classified manager and I sit with Jon.

Five minutes later, paramedics rush from the elevator and unfurl the collapsible gurney. They slide Jon onto a backboard and lift him to the gurney, then disappear into the elevator.

I watch, my butt growing cold on the linoleum, wondering what just happened.

Winston strolls up, offers his hand, and lifts me to my feet. "Never knew you were such a nurturing type, Iz."

I never knew I was, either.

The afternoon passes in a pleasant mix of client phone conversations, setting up meetings, and finalizing proofs. Lonnie and I catch up on equal parts gossip, personal stuff, and business, and I thank him for his assistance at work. Since my life has turned into a soap opera, I don't know what I'd do without him. He's becoming a friend, someone I can confide in.

Mid-afternoon, Phil stops by my desk. My first thought is...what ball have I dropped this time?

I can tell something is on his mind. He stutters around a second or two, exhales loudly, and looks up at the ceiling. "I have an unusual request. Can we talk about it in my office?"

I am curious, and of course, I follow him immediately. He closes the door. I sit in front of his desk.

"Jon needs some time off, and I'm looking for someone to take care of his accounts in the interim. Since you already have a relationship with one of his biggest accounts, I thought about you. It would get your foot in the door to sell his other accounts some retail space as well."

I smile at the carrot-dangle. Once a salesperson, always a salesperson. Bribes allowed.

How can I say no?

"Look, Izzy, we've got a situation. By 'we', I mean, the *Sentinel*. Jon is a functioning alcoholic. I've known for some time, but I don't want the word to get around. He's been controlling it, but..." Phil shakes his head. "Can you keep this between us?"

"He's always been such a huge producer. I never would've suspected."

"We've given him a lot of leeway. It's been comin' on for a couple years, ever since his wife died of cancer." Phil shakes his head. "Did you know he was her caregiver for five years? That alone makes him a hero in my eyes."

"Mine too." My heart does a little flip. I didn't know that about Jon.

"His manager's been keeping me in the loop. We don't want to terminate him, but this can't continue. I hope he'll respond to help." Phil shrugs. "When you commit to this, you need to understand that it may be longer than a few weeks." His anxious eyes search my face.

I'm trying to figure out where this particular Phil has been hiding the past eleven years that I have been in his employ.

This Phil is kind and understanding, and patient. I like this Phil much better than the sales-meeting Phil that gives us the hairy eyeball and lectures us about sales goals.

"I'm up for it. I'll visit Jon in the next day or two. Is he in a detox unit?"

"Not sure," he sighs. "I'd call before dropping by. He might need isolation for a while."

He slaps his knees as if a longstanding issue has been resolved. "I'll get the account list to you this afternoon," he says, the stress lines around his eyes relaxing. "And Izzy...thanks." He pops up from behind his desk and opens the door for me as I leave.

Chapter Fifteen

Pansies line each side of a sidewalk that ends at three stairs up to double glass doors upon which is etched "Emerald Spring Police Department." As I walk up the stairs, I become sweaty. A cold clamminess envelopes me. I seriously cannot believe I have to do this.

Two flags—Georgia and USA— flap in the breeze atop metal flagpoles situated in front of the building. The pansies bobbling their yellow and purple heads do not brighten my mood, though I'm sure that is what the landscapers intended.

I push open the double doors. Like most state agencies, the floor and walls are mental-institution beige. Metal chairs with stingy vinyl padding line the walls. A montage of black and white photos chronicle the succession of police chiefs since 1947.

The woman behind the information window ignores me. I approach. "Hi, there."

She frowns and slides the window open.

"I was told to come and meet, um..."I reach in my purse for his card and pull it out. "Detective Adrian Lopez...to fill out a request for a protective order and open a case file."

"Okay, have a seat, it won't be long," she says, and bangs the window shut.

The kids indicate that all is well when I text them. I slip the phone back in my purse and settle in to wait. Thirty minutes later, I shoot her a look. No reaction. I stalk to the window. She slides it back.

"Where's Detective Lopez? You said this wouldn't take long."

With effort, she pushes her substantial bulk off the chair and disappears.

It takes ten more minutes, but a middle-aged man with black hair and eyes approaches. He wears a rumpled pair of khakis and a shirt and tie that don't match.

"Ms. Lewis?" He is carrying a folder to which is affixed a yellow sticky note. He flips the folder open and scans the contents. I follow him to a small office that holds a metal desk, two chairs, a tired, framed landscape on one wall, and a filing cabinet.

He ruffles through the file, flicks his eyes across his computer screen, then gives me his full attention. "Tell me about your guy."

"I think it's all detailed in the police report," I respond, wondering why I have to go through this again. "But since the first report, I do have these." I extract the Ziploc from my purse that holds the notes Tyler left on my cars. He places it on his desk, then threads his fingers together. "Start at the beginning."

"I met Tyler on a dating site. We went out once, and I decided not to go out again. He was mad about it. I was nice, okay? There was no reason for him to get mad." I explain the incident with my neighbor, where Tyler had shown up and waited on her front porch and the hostile phone call the morning after our date. I describe the unpleasant scene with Tyler's car-towing. I go through each event, up to the point of the footsteps around my privacy fence. Detective Lopez writes on his pad.

"Okay, so the guy is less than courteous, kind of upset. Did he threaten you in any way?"

I point at the Ziploc. "He left these notes."

Detective Lopez reads them through the plastic. "Huh. Wants to talk. What about?"

"That's not the point. He left these at my house. One of them I found on my car, under the windshield wiper in my locked garage; one was placed on my windshield while I was having a drink with a friend downtown." I snapped my fingers. "I just remembered. When I was at the trolley stop downtown, he was on the sidewalk staring at me." I frowned. "He's been *following* me. I don't know or care what he wants to talk about, and I never gave him my home address. I'm careful about that." My mind whizzes back.

Did I? I had been drinking. I may have told him. I sigh and stare at my hands.

Detective Lopez lays down his pad. "Maybe we should pay this guy a visit. Do you know where he lives?"

"Not interested in where he lives."

"That's okay…pretty typical that everything we need is on that dating site and his social media. Do you feel he's a threat to your family?"

"What do you think?"

Lopez's head jerks up. He doesn't blink for several seconds. "Ms. Lewis, do you have any idea how many times this sort of thing comes through the department?" He picks up his pen and resumes writing. I squirm in my chair. After a few minutes, he puts down his pen.

"Okay, I'm opening a file. We'll see what we can find out about the guy. In the meantime, I'll get copies of the reports and these notes to give to your attorney so you can get the protective order started."

I let out a breath. Rub my eyes. It is late, and I am tired and how am I going to have time to get all this done?

"Do you have an attorney?"

My eyes fill. It's too much…and I'm *so* tired. "I'm a single parent with three kids. I can't afford a damn attorney. I don't even know how I'm going to get this thing filed." I jump to my feet, feeling the full brunt of hopelessness. "I knew I shouldn't have done this. I'll take care of it myself."

Lopez rises. Holds out his arms. "Whoa, there, girl. We'll help you. Ever heard of Legal Aid? Public defenders? Prosecuting Attorneys? We'll find someone. Okay? All you'll have to do is talk on the phone and email copies. Don't go rogue on me."

I cover my eyes with my hands. The detective extends a tissue. "I'm sorry about what you're going through, Ms. Lewis."

"Izzy," I squeak out. "Call me Izzy. Short for Isabelle."

He smiles. "I'm putting extra patrols around your house for the next week. We've got it, Izzy. Go on home. You have my cell number. Get some sleep."

By the time I punch my garage door opener, it is close to nine p.m., and all I want to do is crawl into bed.

The TV is blaring in the den, and one son is asleep on the couch. I move through the kitchen to the hallway and trot upstairs. Mimi's door is open. She's reading an actual book. One with pages. This restores a glimmer of hope.

"Sorry, I'm late. Did everyone get dinner?" A chorus of assents floats back to me from various parts of the house. I sigh in relief. Maybe tonight, there will be no crisis to manage.

Chapter Sixteen

All day Saturday, I think about the man that has invited me to Raphael's. On one hand, I'd love to take him up on the 'adventure' aspect; on the other hand, everyone in the world is telling me to stop taking risks online.

I chuckle. If we worked out, it would be the story of stories.

Logging off, I promise myself to keep it that way. Besides, I have a lot of housework to catch up on. I push away the unpleasant sensation of rejection attached to the fact that Brad has not followed up on our meeting. I'm not fond of initiating contact, and though tempted to call or text him, I don't. I'd define my online dating style as 'catch-and-release'. Looking for that perfect, yummy candidate.

I pull out my vacuum cleaner and vent my frustration on the carpeting. There's an *endless* selection of men online. Not the end of the world if I don't hear from Brad. The vacuum roars across the carpet as I work out the kinks that Brad's silence has caused.

As the vacuum sucks up stuff from my floor that doesn't belong there, I apply the same principle to my thoughts. Have I been so single-minded about finding someone that I've developed an obsession?

I mutter soft profanities.

Vacuum. Do laundry. Be a normal person with three kids and a house to look after. Pretend nothing weird is happening. My eyes fall to the envelope that contains the restraining order that I'll take to the courthouse tomorrow to file.

With a grimace, I admit to myself that the mere appearance of this envelope is a big, red flag. If I hadn't been serial dating, this never would have happened. Is the online dating thing doomed? Who else has these issues? All I hear from people that date online are *success* stories. Maybe they keep the hinky stuff to themselves.

I unplug the vacuum and re-plug it into an outlet in the den, and promise myself that when I have the money, I will buy a Roomba. Then I run upstairs, collect laundry from each bedroom in a laundry basket and lug it downstairs.

Next, I dig into the morning dishes and work until the kitchen is tidied up. Not sparkling clean, but good enough. Ethan wanted the kids this weekend, and though they grumbled about it, they went. I have the house to myself.

I congratulate myself that I caught up on housework.

I run upstairs to throw on something other than pajama pants and a T-shirt. I'd promised to visit Jon in the hospital. This is the day.

An hour later, I am navigating miles of antiseptic hallway, my nose wrinkling at the smell. I locate Jon's room and knock on the door. "Come on in, everyone else has." Jon's voice is strong, clear, and irritable. I step in.

"I take it you've had a lot of company?"

His mouth twitches. "Yeah. But it's been real nice. Kinda talked out, though." He sits up, re arranges the pillows behind his back. "Hey, I heard you were the one that took care of me when I was on the floor." I nod and shrug. He stretches an arm to the table beside his bed, picks up a small dark form. The candy bar I'd stuffed in his pocket. "You responsible for this?"

I smile. "You were supposed to eat it for energy, but you passed out before I could get it into your mouth."

Jon's expression gentles. "I saved it. Reminded me that people can be kind." His eyes rise to mine. "Want to thank you for that," he says, his voice brusque.

"Anybody would have done it, Jon, I just happened to be there." Jon looks a little the worse for wear, but content. "What happened, anyway?"

Jon drops his head and studies the metal table by his bed. It holds a plate with gelatinous wads in various colors, a small carton of milk with a straw, a box of tissues, and dahlias in a vase.

"Well, not to rationalize, but it's been hard the past couple of years. When Marie died, a stiff drink to numb the pain turned into two or three. A steady diet of vodka is not good for one's health." He grins. "Doctors and nurses tell me I gotta stop. I mean *really* lay it down. They said if they hadn't gotten an IV in me and pumped me full of meds, I could have—well, I wouldn't be here, I'll put it that way. My liver's on life support, and I have to quit drinking."

"Sorry, Jon."

"So, I'm laying here trying to figure out how to do life without booze."

"It'll be okay, Jon. There are so many support groups."

"Phil is pushing a group on me. I'm thinking about it."

I blink. "Phil?"

"Yeah," Jon responds. "Phil's been sober about ten years now." He waves one of his hands. "We're a sad, little club, us drinkers."

My regard for Phil catapults into the stratosphere. "I never knew that."

"Nope. He doesn't talk about it. But he's like a pitbull when it comes to helping people. He can sniff out the ones that are sinking. He's talked to me before, but it took a trip in an ambulance to wake me up."

This comment resonates deep within my soul. I fold my arms across my chest.

"We never did have that coffee date to talk about your online dating stuff." He grins.

"Yeah, well, that's not going so well right now. Long story."

"I'm getting outta here in a week, they're assigning me to outpatient counseling and I'll be off work a couple of months, I think. Let's shoot for a meet-up."

I cringe at the same terminology I use for my own 'addiction.'

"I'm gonna need some activity to keep my mind off drinking?" Jon continues. "Just for coffee or a walk or whatever."

"Sure, Jon. I promise. You just get better. Focus on you."

"Phil's commanded me to take the time off. No arguments." Jon shrugs. "I hear you'll be taking care of my accounts. I'd like to prep you on them before you leave, okay?"

We set a date to get together the first part of next week.

As I walk down the hall I have a hard time getting his comment out of my head. "Took a trip in an ambulance to wake me up." My life is so out of control I am wondering what it will take to get it back on track. I would like to avoid an ambulance if possible. I hike my purse on my shoulder and find the elevator.

Later that evening, I'm waiting on the kids to arrive home from their various activities when my hands start an argument with my head. My head is doing a pretty good job of resisting logging onto the sites, but my hands are about to rip off my arms and float to my laptop by themselves.

In the time it takes to blink, my fingers are dancing across the keyboard. When had my hands developed a mind of their own?

A surge of pleasure zips up my back and down my arms when I see four messages. I reassure myself that it is *impossible* to become addicted to online dating.

Bradley is back in the picture. He'd love to see me again. The next one is a new guy, and after scanning, I swipe left. The third one goes straight down the tubes as well. The fourth one is the guy pounding on me to meet him at Raphael's, appealing again to my adventurous spirit. I sink into his compliments like a warm bubble bath. I read what he's written twice.

This man intrigues me. At least what he has *written* intrigues me. His photos are kind of artsy, profiles with dramatic lighting, and I cannot tell how old he is, or even if he's attractive. But I want to meet him anyway. Why? Do I feel the need to find out if he's real? If the things he says are true?

My lips press together. I stare at the ceiling. Is it wrong to desire a man that delights in me? Who finds me irresistible and fulfilling? Who doesn't make me feel like a failure or a disappointment...or something to push away?

This guy is pushing my buttons so hard that it feels like fate.

The kids burst in downstairs, yelling for me. I log off the site with one word: "Okay."

Chapter Seventeen

Traffic is light for a Monday, and I make it to my desk in record time.

The weekend had passed with pleasant, boring mom-stuff. I'd begged off Mystery Man's request for a Saturday night meet and we'd agreed on another evening. I'd even managed to stay off the sites. Which was a good decision, because the minute I sit at my desk I am bombarded with the double workload.

Jon's coordinator had put a note and action items on my desk, a courteous gesture that makes things easier for me. I hit the streets early, leaving Winston puzzled and pressing his lanyard between nervous fingers. He is concerned that I'm not taking care of myself, and he is correct. I wave a quick goodbye and hop in the elevator.

Later in the day, as I pull up to the fourth automotive dealership in a row, I think about how well Jon has cultivated these relationships. My final stop, Ardmore Chevrolet, is a relief since Tom and I already know each other. My workday's end is within reach, which makes me insanely happy.

The receptionist directs me to the service department.

I walk across miles of pavement, past hundreds of bright, shiny cars, down a well-manicured, landscaped hill with a pond, and across a large concrete-scape to the service department. I pause in front of the door to catch my breath before I experience a tachycardia event and tug open the glass door.

"Tom around?" I ask. "He told me to find him back here. Have you seen him?"

The mechanic points toward a man on a golf cart studying his cell phone. "There he is. Just like he always is, every Monday. Where's Jon?"

Golf cart? I fill him in on my stand-in status and join Tom.

He says, "Get on."

Before I can respond, Tom says, "Jon didn't tell you about the photo updates?"

Nope.

"I heard he was out a few weeks. Hop on. I'll show you."

We zip off, and I hold on for dear life. Tumbling off a golf cart in front of the GM of a prominent Chevrolet dealership would do nothing to enhance my professional image. Especially if my skirt flaps up over my face. Slacks, next time. Wear slacks.

After figuring out automotive ads all afternoon, I drag myself back into the pod. Open my desk computer and grimace at all the changes needed. I'll have to work until God knows when.

I rake my hands through my hair and rub my face.

"You look like someone ran you over with a truck," Lonnie says helpfully.

I roll my eyes. "Yeah, well, I've earned it. I spent the day riding around on a golf cart, taking pictures of cars, looking up *VIN* numbers. Before today, I didn't even know what a VIN number was."

Lonnie blinks. "Wow."

"My knowledge of cars stops at the entrance to the service department and the nice people that tell me they'll take care of everything," I snap.

Lonnie smiles. "You wanted a piece of that automotive business, right?"

I gaze at my crammed inbox. Probably be here 'til midnight, since Lonnie is not one to volunteer for overtime. I'll have to sit with the night production crew and figure out these changes.

An hour of steady work later, a tall shadow falls across my desk. I glance up from the tedious copy in irritation.

"Need something?"

"Loaded question," Birdie says and laughs.

I wonder if this guy ever has a clue. About anything.

"Well, I'm somewhat busy here, as you can see," I say in an effort to persuade him to leave me alone.

He looks over my shoulder. The smell of cheap cologne and his head about three inches from mine make me uncomfortable. I back up my chair.

"What's this?"

"Jon Hoyt's ads. Phil asked me to take his accounts while he's off. I thought you'd know about it already."

He crosses his arm, scowls. "When did this conversation happen?"

Wait. Isn't Phil Birdie's boss? What is this reaction about?

"You want me to get Phil?" I ask, the picture of innocence.

"No. I'll talk to him. Are you getting your own work done?"

"Looks like a lot of overtime for a while." I shrug. "No big deal."

It *is* a big deal and may kill me, but whatever. Paint me as the dedicated, long-suffering employee. One that deserves a raise. And a promotion.

"At least it'll keep you offline." An evil grin splits his face. I resist puking.

"It'll put a dent in my evenings, for sure," I mutter, willing him to fly away.

"Let me know if I can help." A token offer, and we both know it. He leaves.

The moon is bright and full by the time I leave the office. A shiver of premonition ripples up my back when I pull into the garage beside Peter's car.

I know my kids stayed home tonight because I'd talked to them earlier. Clutching my purse to my chest, I inch out of my Honda.

Rakes, trimmers, and a gas blower hang on hooks. An aging lawnmower sits in a corner. Metal shelving covers the back wall, every inch loaded with athletic equipment or beach paraphernalia for our trips to Tybee Island. My nose picks out smells of lawnmower gas, lawn debris, the oil leak we can never resolve from the kids' car. I scan the shelves, the floor. The storage room door at the back of the garage is closed.

Was it closed when I left this morning?

My heels striking the cement garage floor in the middle of the night remind me of old Law and Order episodes. The ones where Eames and Goren discover a body beside a car in a puddle of blood.

I should stop watching those shows.

My eyes graze Peter's eight-year-old Toyota.

I blink. My pulse rockets from zero to sixty.

Not tonight, my mind screams. Oh, please. Not after this long, exhausting day.

My chin trembles. My feet glue themselves to the floor.

I mutter reassurances to myself. Swallow the knot in my throat. Before I pull the note off the windshield of the Toyota, I click a photo.

I lift the windshield wiper. Pull out the small, folded square of paper. Hold it away from my body with two fingers like a rotting piece of garbage.

I dart into the kitchen and shove the deadbolt home.

Detective Lopez's number rings and rings. I lay a trembling hand on my chest.

"Yeah?" Cough. "Lopez."

I picture him beside his lovely wife in bed, torn from a peaceful sleep, and feel horrible about it. Maybe I should end the call. No. He'd recognize the number, anyway.

"I got another note." I cannot stop shaking. My voice is scratchy.

"Izzy?"

"I'm sorry to call this late—"

"That's okay," he blurts. I'll get a patrol vehicle out there. Can you wait for them and get down the particulars? What does the note say? Listen, Izzy, we've analyzed fingerprints on the initial note. Verified that it's this Tyler you've told me about. Tomorrow he gets a rude awakening."

"I don't know what to do." Tears slide down my cheeks.

"Read me the note."

"It was on my kids' car." The tears fall harder. "My *kids*, Detective."

Detective Lopez is quiet a beat. "You weren't home, then?"

"I had to work late. And the garage was locked, my kids know to lock it after they're in for the night."

A beat of silence ensues. "Let me get a uni over there. I'll call right back."

We end the call. All I can think about is the storage room. It has a window.

Is it locked?

I don't know. My mind spins. I need a weapon. I slip over to the sports equipment on the shelves and find a bat. It feels solid and intimidating. I hold it up with my right hand and open the storage room door with my left.

The darkened room emerges bit by bit as the door creaks open. Light from the garage spills into the room, illuminating old cans of paint, a broken lamp, and boxes. I push the door open further. The window is on the back wall, shards of cobwebs hanging from the edges. Moonlight shimmers through the filthy window. I grope for the light switch. Great. Bulb must have burned out.

To my utter and profound relief, the room is empty. I lean the bat against one of the boxes and look around for something to stand on. The window is high on the wall, and I am unable to reach the latch.

Two crumpled boxes stacked one on the other are underneath the window. I stand on them to check the window.

It slides open easily. My throat constricts.

How long has it been unlocked?

I latch the window. Step off the boxes.

Tyler. He'd gotten in through the window and out the same way. He'd used these boxes.

My cell buzzes. Lopez. "The window wasn't locked," I tell him.

"A cruiser is on the way. Put the note in a baggie. I'll get an analysis of the prints tomorrow. He's trespassing and in violation of the restraining order. Just make sure you lock the door to the garage from the kitchen, also. Most people don't, you know."

"What happens now?" I viciously shove the squashed boxes away from the window with my foot.

"Has he mentioned harm or displayed a weapon?"

"No. I blocked him from everything. Email, dating apps, all my social media. And my phone."

"That's why he's doing this. Can't get to you along the usual channels. Look, we can get the guy on a misdemeanor. But that's a slap on the wrist. We think he's done this before. If it's within the last seven years, it's a felony."

My hands grow clammy. I'm having trouble holding the phone. "He's…

93

done it before?"

"Yes, but we don't have specifics yet. Right now, all we've got is violation of a restraining order…that is, if you've gotten it filed."

I think about Jon's client list and the horrible timing of Phil's request for me to take over for him until he is back on his feet. "Didn't have time today, and thanks for talking to Legal Aid for me. I'll get it done tomorrow."

"Good. We can't arrest him unless that's in place."

My body screams for rest. "So I'm *helpless*? How am I supposed to deal with this?"

"When our officer arrives, tell him what happened, but also get on record any changes to your lifestyle you are experiencing because of this guy, Tyler. Are you sleeping? Are you changing your routine? That should be a matter of record to take to court. I'll have your house patrolled the rest of the night. If you have lights where the storage room is, leave them on. Leave all the exterior lights on if you can. These cowards do their sneaking around in the dark."

"Sorry, it's been a long day, and I come home to…this."

"I understand," he says. "Are the notes escalating? Do they feel like a threat? Tell the officer, make sure it's documented."

"I took a picture of it on the car."

"Send it to me."

With one last look at the storage room, I exit and close the door. Make a mental note to call a locksmith tomorrow to get a deadbolt put on it. I walk back into the kitchen for the note. Open it and read it aloud to Lopez:

STILL LOOKING FOR A TIME TO GET TOGETHER. I WAITED FOR YOU OUTSIDE THE SENTINEL BUILDING THIS AFTERNOON, BUT YOU NEVER CAME OUT. I HAD A NICE CHAT WITH YOUR BOSS, BIRDIE. ONE EVENING OF COFFEE, IZZY, THAT'S ALL I ASK. EVEN YOUR BOSS THINKS IT'S A REASONABLE REQUEST.

I hear Lopez breathing on the other end of the call. "My boss?" I manage, my brain fried. How creepy can a guy be?

"It's overreach, for sure," he agrees, "but not illegal." We end the call.

It's now one o'clock in the morning. I trudge upstairs, thankful the kids had slept through the whole thing. Slip out of my clothes, kick them into a corner, and fall into bed with a groan. *Birdie?* Was that a fortunate happenstance for Tyler, or had he sought out my boss on purpose?

I am *so* screwed.

Chapter Eighteen

My landline rings. I stare at it like it's going to bite me.

"Izzy."

"Hey. How're things?"

Jon.

I sigh in relief. Lately, the only calls I get are straight from hell.

"I'm plowing through. I have new respect for you, Jon."

His laughter lifts my spirits. "Do you want to meet somewhere? You can let me know what's going on with my accounts. You might need my help."

"The only way you can help is to come back and take over these accounts. I've never worked so hard in my life."

"You get used to it. I've worked out a rhythm."

We make arrangements to meet later in the day. My mind meanders to Brad, who's asked me out again. My lips curve into a smile.

Things aren't all bad.

Lonnie drops into his seat, and we chat a few minutes. The sales floor is empty, the sales staff long gone in search of those elusive advertising dollars. I gaze at my cleared desktop with satisfaction and plan an afternoon working on my own accounts. I'm looking forward to a lunch break when Birdie approaches. I force a grin.

He smiles, and as usual, his eyes do not. His icy, flat gaze scrapes up and down my form. I suppress a shudder and wonder if I should call him out on this disgusting habit that seems to affect every woman in his line of vision.

"I've received end-of-the-month sales reports. Your numbers look good, Izzy."

"Thanks. Glad you approve."

When he lingers, I give him a questioning look.

Birdie clears his throat. "Wanted to mention that your friend Tyler was hanging around the front door a few days ago, looking for you. He asked several people if you were inside, including me."

I grip the sides of my chair. The note had confirmed as much.

He continues, unfazed, as if my stalker lingering at the entrance was the most normal thing ever. "Our chat was illuminating."

I am unable to formulate a complete sentence. "He's not a friend. He... he..." I swallow, hard. "I've reported him to the police."

"Then why the hell was he standin' outside the newspaper building askin' everybody where you were?"

"It won't happen again." The terror of the note and squashed boxes in my storage room rushes back. I don't trust Birdie enough to dump the whole story, and right about now would be a great time for Detective Lopez to materialize. Birdie would believe an investigator, but I doubt he'll believe me.

He squints. "I have a feeling this is one of your messy online-guy situations, and what happened falls smack-dab into the category of negative workplace issues. If you think this kind of thing is gonna go unnoticed, then think again. I am on excellent terms with the HR Director now, by the way." He smirks and crosses his arms over a light blue shirt and a tie adorned with tiny, grinning porpoises. The crevices on his face grow deeper as he smiles.

He walks away, and I am left with the unpleasant feeling that he'd just set a trap.

"Hi, Izzy," the hostess smiles, "you here to meet someone tonight?"

I nod. "Yes, there should be someone waiting for *Belle*." I smile a secret smile. After Birdie's threat, a quick meet-up with Mystery Man is a perfect distraction. I pat my hair into place and scan the restaurant.

"He must not be here yet, but I'll let him know. He'll ask for Belle, right?"

"That's it," I smile and pick out a seat at the bar.

I force some distance from the day. What a jerk Birdie had been. I am tired, but also looking forward to an evening that will take me away from it all. The romantic rush of endorphins is already kicking in. I focus on meeting someone who has no history with me. Someone with whom I can pretend, for at least for an hour or two, that life doesn't include a stalker, a creepy boss, and single-mom-kid issues.

The tantalizing aroma of linseed oil on seasoned wood, flamed steaks, and fruity drinks tickles my nose. The jazz pianist in the corner is playing "Til There Was You," and a few people are conversing on stools around the black Steinway.

How did this guy know Raphael's was my favorite place in Emerald Spring? And what the heck am I doing meeting a man for the sheer *adventure* of it, anyway? Don't I have enough on my plate? The bartender works his way over.

"What'll it be?"

"House cab is fine."

"Coming right up." He smiles and turns away.

There is just one man at the bar. He is sitting in the darkest corner, drinking a beer. Keeping to himself.

My drink arrives.

I accept the glass and swivel my stool so I can see the entrance. The guy I'm supposed to meet must be running late. I check my phone. No text. I've been here, done this...some guy I'm meeting is late and doesn't let me know. I have a rule. Fifteen minutes with no text or call, and I'm gone. My watch says Mystery Man has eight minutes left.

The lone man sitting at the bar slips from his stool and emerges from the dark corner.

I glance at him, then at my watch. Where is my date?

The man walks in my direction. I suck in a breath.

He pulls out a barstool beside mine and sits.

He puts his elbows on the bar and threads his fingers together. I feel heat building at the top of my head.

"You're upset. I get it. Our last discussion was unproductive."

I glare at Ethan. "Can we talk about this tomorrow? Or never, maybe?

I'm waiting for someone."

He smiles. "Who?"

My ex-husband and father of my kids is a tall, rotund giant of a man. He puts one foot on the floor, the other on a rung of the tall stool, and swivels back and forth. His grin tells me he has a secret.

"Stay out of my personal life, Ethan. We've had this discussion several times. What is it with you?"

His grin stays in place. "Our discussions have changed nothing." He tilts in until his lips brush my ear. *"Belle."*

Dread slithers through my body. How could he possibly know my dating app name?

Wait. I slit my eyes at him and the shit-eating grin on his face.

The hot, interesting, amazing guy I'd met online? The one that checked off all the bullet points on my list of non-negotiables? The one I'd drowned in my life story?

It was Ethan. All along, it was Ethan.

My hands shake. My cheeks burn.

"What do you want?" My mind scrabbles to remember everything I'd told him online. Had I dumped out how I felt about my first marriage? Why we'd divorced? Said anything about his parenting style? Had I talked about my job? Oh, dear God…what had I *said?*

The smile falters. His dark eyes, in the murky light, are unblinking. Reptilian.

His lips press close to my ear. "For Chrissakes, you're headed off the deep end. It's got to stop. Now."

I rub my ear where the moistness of his lips touched. Doesn't this fall under the realm of predatory? Harassment? Impersonation? What are privacy laws regarding this kind of thing? A thousand questions blast through my mind. I can't feel my lips.

He throws a few bills on the bar. "I think I've made my point, *Belle.* Stop this freaking online habit, or there'll be a thousand reasons to jerk the kids from an unfit mother."

Suddenly, I hear the voice of an angel.

"Izzy? That you?" Detective Adrian Lopez stands before me with a trim, brunette woman who I assume is his wife. I have never been happier to see anyone in my life. I swivel my stool toward them with a relieved smile.

"Detective Lopez, how are you? Nice to see you tonight." I say, too loudly, but who cares? I'm trying to make a point.

Ethan's brow furrows.

"I'm good, Izzy." He puts an arm around the woman by his side. "This is my wife, Marion. We do Raphael's about once a month."

I murmur niceties to Marion, thinking how wonderful it must be to have an actual, honest-to-God, normal marriage. At the same time, I telegraph distress. Lopez is smart. He'll wonder why I don't introduce Ethan.

Detective Lopez glances at me, uncertain. I turn to Ethan. "Detective Lopez and I met a few days ago when I requested a protective order on a person that has a problem with boundaries. He even came to the office," I tell him, with a smug tilt of my chin. Hoping he will pick on the mild threat, I continue my narrative in my head...'and *you* impersonated someone to lure me to a restaurant, you freaking weirdo.'

"Tyler?" Detective Lopez pulls out his notebook.

I bobblehead. "Yes."

"Tyler was waiting *outside the office* for you, Izzy?"

"I haven't had time to tell you about it."

With an apologetic glance at his wife, he pulls out a notepad and jots it down.

"Anything else?"

Ethan jumps in. "I'm sure it was a joke. Izzy's famous for her adventures, you know. Awkward situations are a consequence. She needs to back off the adventures." He scowls at me.

Detective Lopez's eyes harden. "And you would be?"

"A friend," I murmur quickly. He didn't need to know that Ethan is my ex. I don't want him to get wrapped up in my ex-husband woes, I want him to get rid of Tyler.

He addresses Ethan. "This is not a 'joke.' This man has trespassed on Izzy's property more than once. He is unstable and a threat." He angles himself toward me. "Call immediately if he shows up around the offices again, okay?"

I promise him I will.

"Good to see you. They're holding our table."

They disappear into the nether regions of the restaurant.

Ethan rubs his thumbs together. From living with him for eight long years, I recognize this as anxiety.

I get the feeling Detective Lopez might have made a dent in his little stunt to intimidate me.

My hopes are short-lived.

"Izzy, what the hell are you doing? This is dangerous, and it's affecting the kids. He sips his beer, his hand lingering on the bottle. "They share things with me, you know."

At this point, I'm looking for an escape route. I text the kids and tell them I'll be home in twenty minutes. I promise God if He will get me out of this mess, I'll be a better mother. I'll only get on the apps only once a week. I'll start going to church. Clean my house more often. Whatever. My pulse hammers my temples.

I give him a hard look. "It's not my fault that some of the guys I meet turn out to be psychos." This comment meets its mark. He scorches me with his eyes.

"I want you to get my point. You came out here to meet a guy you thought might be your soulmate without blinking an eye." He chuckles. "Like you always do. I'm worried about the kids. They're like sponges. I don't want them to end up…well, with another loser."

I don't make the obvious comment that he was the first loser I married. "We've worked it out okay. Can we keep it that way? Message received, but wow. Really? I think what you did is called catfishing? Gaslighting? Something." I give him a hard stare. "If you don't back off, I'll report it."

Ethan tilts his head, folds his arms across his chest. "To the Lopez guy? Izzy, does it even occur to you that if you get this Lopez involved, he'll contact Family Services, anyway? What you're doing is not good for the kids. Can't you see that? Wake up. You're acting like a slut."

I stare at the floor. I am not a slut.

Ethan finishes his beer and declines another.

"I've talked to your boss. Birdie." He frowns. "What kind of name is that, anyway?"

My eyebrows shoot up. *"About what?"*

"Online dating issues. Oh, and our custody battles." His voice is quiet, sinister.

My chin quivers. "We haven't been in court in five years. What are you talking about?"

He chuckles. "Let's see here." He starts ticking off points on his fingers. "The threats you've made that you won't let me see the kids. Your ongoing battle with being an appropriate parent." He clears his throat. "I have a file. You know, like when a manager documents reasons to get rid of an employee, he needs proof. Well, I have proof."

My blood runs cold. He's making up stuff in his head, but a judge won't know that.

"Ethan. I could lose my job."

"Oh, come on. I kept it tame. Concerned ex-husband worried about his wife. He assured me he had only your best interests at heart, and he'd keep the chat just between us."

I gape at him, shake my head. "You're not *worried* about me, Ethan. You just don't like not getting your way. That's all you've ever care about. Control. You don't want the kids. You don't even like them! And it's not me keeping them from you. They don't *want* to go. So take your list and shove it up your ass."

He shrugs. "This stops now. Quit running out at night when the kids are asleep, or I'm taking you back to court."

"So because you can't control what I do, you have a chat with my boss?"

"Someone has to teach you respect, Izzy. We are co-parents, after all. The fact that you met me like this...that alone is enough to get you on Georgia Child Protective Services' radar." He stirs the ice in his glass with a straw. "And your boss's radar, too. Oh. I forgot. You're already on his." He grins.

I feel sick to my stomach. The reason I divorced this man years ago rears its ugly head once again. He is a manipulative, evil jerk, and I need to cut him totally out of our lives. When and if I can, I will.

I start seeing stars and grip the bar. I am so wobbly I almost fall off the barstool. Ethan reaches out. I shove him away and make a dash for the exit.

When I emerge on the sidewalk outside, I gulp deeply of fresh air. Ethan is right behind me. As fate would have it, I am not even surprised when Jon Hoyt walks by, pausing to glare at me.

"Weren't we supposed to have a meeting at four-thirty?" he barks.

I glance at Ethan, who looks at Jon as if he's some sort of scraggly dog I rescued. I introduce Jon as a co-worker. "I'm so sorry, Jon. I got busy and forgot."

He looks at Ethan standing there with a smirk on his face. "I can see that."

"It's not what you think."

"Your personal life is none of my business, Izzy." With a shrug, he walks away.

I whirl around toward Ethan. "My personal life is none of *your* business, either."

His eyes spark with anger. "We can let our attorneys duke it out, Izzy."

Chapter Nineteen

By the time I pull into my garage, my emotions have flat-lined. How long is a person supposed to keep fighting with life, anyway? When is it time to throw in the towel?

My eyes adjust to the gloom of the garage as I sit in the car, trying to make sense of things. Impossible. I drape my purse on my shoulder and walk inside, making sure to leave the garage light on and firmly lock the door from the garage to the kitchen.

The house is quiet and dark. My footfalls cause the flooring underneath the carpet to squeak as I check each bedroom. Mimi is on her tablet in the middle of her mob of stuffed animals, Peter's still at his basketball game, and Chad is snoring on the couch in the den. I walk into the kitchen and fix myself a quick bite.

Holding a pickle in one hand and a turkey sandwich in the other, my singleness crashes in on me. I let out a sob. With a frown, I swipe at the tears. "Stop it, Iz. Self-pity accomplishes nothing."

My teeth tear off half the pickle. It squirts juice all over my face. I throw the damn thing in the sink.

I zip through today's highlights. Forgetting the meeting with Jon today had been a severe misstep. I need all the allies at the office I can get. Tomorrow, a meeting must take place.

What if Birdie dumps everything Ethan told him right onto Phil's lap? How can I explain? *Should* I explain? Maybe nothing will happen. Maybe I should leave it alone. Birdie will use the information, though. I'm sure about that. He'll either tell Phil about it with a wink and a nod, or he'll keep it to himself and blackmail me later.

Thanks, Ethan, you complete loser. Can I mitigate this situation? If I try to head off any misinformation spewing from Birdie, I'll come off sounding like a paranoid maniac.

Which, of course, is exactly what I'm becoming.

I grind off a huge bite of sandwich and start chomping. My phone vibrates on the table. I stare at it. Lopez.

"Hey, Izzy, sorry to call so late, but my wife and I just got home, and I wanted to touch base," Detective Lopez says.

My brutalized heart soars.

"Nice to meet your wife tonight."

He chuckles. "Yeah, she's a keeper. Always patient when I run into someone I know from work. So, that guy you were with...something was off about him. You seemed uncomfortable."

My mind races. Should I tell him about Ethan's catfishing scheme? He's already working on one problem-guy situation for me. What will he think if I throw another one at him?

"Izzy, I could tell you were having a hard time. If this was another guy that's...well, another guy you don't want in your life, just let me know."

My thoughts circle the drain. Should I tell him the truth?

I bite a fingernail.

Not the whole truth. Maybe a little bit of truth.

"He's my first husband, Detective. He's intrusive sometimes, and we'd had a hard conversation. It's difficult sharing custody."

"Okay. Got it. Perfect explanation for why you were uncomfortable." He chuckles. "Hope things work out. Have a good night."

I thank him for his concern. Then I rinse my dishes, put them in the dishwasher, and head upstairs. Open my laptop. Five messages tonight. I roll my eyes heavenward and thank the good Lord for small blessings.

I click on the first one, then hesitate. Didn't I just get blindsided as a result of this? I locate the message that turned out to be from Ethan. I trash the message, my face scrunched with the same disgust reserved for cockroaches and black widow spiders.

I block him, but I doubt it's necessary. He won't do it again. Not after the nice detective had been so point-blank and protective.

My phone buzzes with a text. Brad. I smile.

Hey Izzy, Hope your week is going well. Looking forward to Saturday, hope you are too. Do you like sushi? Get back to me. Yours, Brad.

My smile covers half my face. The knot in my stomach loosens. I feel protected by Detective Lopez and validated by Brad. Still, I reach for the laptop and read the messages. I am so tired I can't keep my eyes open, yet something deep within me needs feeding. One of them wants to chat. I spend the next hour chatting up a new guy. I stare at the clock. It's getting late. Another chat request pops up. My heartbeat speeds up. I shut my laptop and put it out of reach. Don't these men ever sleep?

The laptop taunts me.

Tugs at me.

Maybe I should put it in another room. My phone, too.

I pop a couple of Tylenol PM and try to sleep.

Chapter Twenty

"Everyone have breakfast?" I reach for the cereal boxes on the top shelves of the kitchen cupboard, pull out a bowl for myself and fill it with flakes, thankful for a decent night's sleep. Though it was just five hours, it was a disaster-free, restful five hours.

"Yeah, Mom, we got breakfast," Chad says.

I pour milk on the cereal. Find a spoon.

"Homework done? I apologize for getting home too late to go over it with you." I sit at the table and join them. Peter gives me a dark look, finishes his cereal. Mimi chatters in her typical way. Chad is oblivious and in his own world.

"So what's up today, everybody? Any plans after school?"

"Football practice," Peter says. "Every day this week, Coach told us, and I'll get a ride for Chad and Mimi if you need me to." I log into the calendar in my head that Chad and Mimi will need to ride home with Annie's kids this week.

"Okay."

Chad eyes Mimi. "What's up for you, dork?" She makes a face at him. "Wait," Chad says, "I know. Books and more books, right?"

Mimi rolls her eyes and says, "You can't even read."

"Can too."

"Stop it. Mimi and Chad, hitch a ride with Annie this afternoon. I'll let her know she's taking you home this week. Text me if anything changes, and I'll come get you from work, okay?"

I wave goodbye as they zoom down the street in the Toyota that somehow keeps running in spite of 100,000-plus miles on the odometer.

As I pass the mirror in the foyer, I check my reflection. I have important discussions pending, and I am dressed accordingly. My flat-ironed hair falls to my shoulders in a shiny sheaf. My subtle eye makeup screams *innocent until proven guilty*. My lips are a dusky, liquid rose. I have on black slacks, a patterned blazer, and a creamy silk blouse. Sensible heels.

I plan to march into Birdie's office and tell him I know about his conversation with Ethan. Then, in so many words, I'll tell him to back off. If this approach doesn't work, I'll start looking for another job, in which case I'm already dressed for the interview.

The perpetual shiver races up my back when I step into the garage, and I wonder when this will quit happening. I fob open the Honda, throw my purse and bag inside, get in, and lock up. Maybe the stalker hadn't threatened physical harm, but the emotional harm lingers. With a frown, I start the car.

As I back out, a cruiser glides by. The patrol cop nods. All is well, the nod says.

My shoulders relax.

I speed off toward my morning latte, radio blaring. As I wait in line, Brad's number pops up on my Bluetooth.

"Hey, gorgeous."

"Good morning," I chirp, and pull up one car closer to the window. He responds with typical pleasantries, confirms our date this weekend, and tells me to have a great day. A goofy grin lingers on my face.

Lydia's familiar visage beams down at me in the car. "The usual?"

"I have some important stuff going down today."

"So, a triple?"

Winston is thumbing through his newspaper when I land in the pod.

Lonnie is flying around the cubicles, and managers roam the floor in herds, like buffalos seeking grazing pasture. A nice hum of voices fills the room.

When I trot to the breakroom, Darlene is head-down and busy at her desk. She lifts her eyes and waves at me. Her smile gives me strength. I square my shoulders. I'm not sure how to untangle this huge mess with Ethan and

Birdie, but I'm on my way. I head back to my desk with a bottle of water instead of coffee.

My body is already as taut as a violin string.

"Locked and loaded," I mutter to myself, sipping the water. "Ready for battle."

"What battle?" Winston says when he overhears.

"I don't know if I can get through it all in five minutes. Pray for me, will you?"

His eyes widen. In all the years we've worked together, I have not once asked him to pray.

"I have a few things to say to Birdie."

Winston's eyebrows take flight. "I want the scoop after."

"I have to get some stuff off my chest. Big time. Before I lose my mind."

"Got it. You've have my support, always, you know that."

I smile. "Thanks." I hop up and make a beeline for the ladies'. Darlene is at the sink with a vase, arranging the daily dahlias.

"This is the last of them," she says, shaking her head. "I hate it when they finish blooming. How are you? You good?" She sets her vase on the counter, crosses her arms, and leans against the wall.

"I haven't had time to share the latest with you." My chin quivers. "I have to get Birdie arrested...or fired...or *something*."

"What has happened?" She takes a step toward me. I back away. If she touches me, I will blubber, and I want my power outfit devoid of tears and snot.

"I'd tell you, but right now, I have to fix it. I don't want to lose my...my... mojo."

Her eyebrows draw together, and I rush out.

I decide to grab a little more coffee after all and circle back to the breakroom. The coffee nook, as usual, holds a white-shirted, tie-bedecked contingent of managers. They must be on their second cup.

I'm in no mood for chit-chat with a full complement of caffeinated managers. I stand outside the circle and study the linoleum, hoping at all costs to avoid Birdie.

"Mornin' Izzy," Birdie sings, his smile blazing like blanched bones at high noon. Obviously, he's taking the path of pretending he never talked to Ethan, that it's their little secret. I squint at him and mumble a response. Phil shoots question marks at me with his eyes and sips from his mug.

One of the managers pulls the carafe from the coffeemaker and lifts it in my direction. I extend my mug and manage a few throwaway comments before I race back to my cube and lunge into the safety of my chair.

It's now or never. To live with this situation will prolong the inevitable. If I wait, it will get worse. Fear grips my brain. What if I get fired on the spot? How will I support my family?

I'll have to punt, but this meeting must happen.

Phil stops by my desk. "Something going on, Izzy?" Like Winston, Phil has a sixth sense where I'm concerned. I take a deep breath. "Do you have a few minutes?"

His eyes twinkle. "A *few* minutes? Izzy, you and I both know it is never a few minutes with you." He smiles and gestures for me to follow him into his office.

Phil closes the door after me and sits behind his desk. "Floor's yours, Izzy. You've got about twenty minutes. Go."

After stumbling through a few emotional drips of information, I become Niagara Falls.

I tell Phil about the online mystery match that had lured me out. I tell him about my shock when my ex-husband stepped out of the shadows, the result of a fake profile. His threat to try to get custody. I tell him Ethan had talked to Birdie. I tell him about Tyler stalking me...that I'd contacted the police. I tell him about Birdie's inappropriate demeanor with clients. I tell him about reporting him to HR for the 'I want to take you out for a drink and loosen you up' idea.

When I finally stop, I cross my arms and stare at my lap.

Ten seconds of silence follow.

Phil sighs. "Jon called last night."

I hear muted traffic sounds outside Phil's second-story windows, and a few sparrows warbling from the treetop branches are visible through the window. Dark gray clouds skitter across the sky.

"He's concerned. He called to tell me he'd seen you come out of Raphael's with someone last night and that you missed a meeting with him to be with this man." Phil shrugs. "I think there's a point where everything needs to be dumped on the table. What he told me lines up with what you're telling me."

I bite my lip. "Ethan catfished me. I'm thinking about making a police report, but he uses the kids to manipulate me. This was not a random date, Phil."

"What got you there, Izzy?"

My forehead wrinkles. I know where he's going. It isn't Ethan's fault that I'd showed up to meet him...it was mine. Still, he misrepresented himself online. Isn't that a crime?

Phil continues, "I'll be honest, Izzy, Birdie's shared his concerns. The rumors worry him." He waves one of his hands in dismissal. "He hasn't told me about your ex, or talking to him. But..." Phil strokes his chin. "Ethan, you said his name was?"

I nod.

"Huh. He called me, too. Left a voicemail." Phil thinks about this a few seconds. "So now we have an ex-husband that has it in for you and some wacko that hangs out around the front entrance."

"That guy is demented. I even have a protective order now, because he left strange, little notes at my house. You can call Detective Lopez if you need proof."

"I get it, Izzy," Phil said. "But look at it from my perspective. I'm sorry that this guy is a problem, but he *cannot* become a problem for the newspaper. Your online dating habit is gathering predators. Not to mention, um, detective, did you say? Really?"

My gaze lowers to the carpet. My fingertips tap out a nervous rhythm on the armrests of my chair. Maybe this had been a mistake.

"Izzy, it's affecting your work. Plus, you've got Jon's clients to take care of. I can't risk it. What if one of these guys decides to show up at a client's place of business? They'd jerk their ad budgets in two seconds if one of my account executives creates problems. Your sales numbers haven't dropped yet, but if things continue like this, they will."

I sit in front of Phil's desk, numb. Hadn't he heard me tell him all the crazy things Birdie had told me? The threats? That I'd been grappling with a criminal? Did he have no mercy?

Phil slides his fingers along the side of his mug. "You've brought some pretty serious allegations against Birdie. What I want you to do is go see Human Resources and fill out a report, or add to the current one you filed. Document what you told me. Have them send me a copy. I'll initial it, and we'll put it in his file. In the meantime, business as usual."

"*Business as usual?*" I warble, my voice catching in my throat. "How in the world do I do business as usual? The guy is—"

"The guy is my new *sales manager*, and he is innocent until proven guilty. In the meantime, what I want you to do is what you always do—sell and service your accounts. And for the foreseeable future, Jon's accounts. Report to me. I'll tell Birdie that you're reporting to me until we sort this out. Agreed?"

I resist the urge to leap into the air with joy. A minor victory, but an important one— Phil didn't dismiss my comments as frivolous. He believes me, or he wouldn't have pulled me out from under Birdie's thumb.

"One more thing."

I grip my hands together in my lap and lean forward.

"We haven't had this conversation."

We lock eyes. The mission has begun, and Phil and I are on the same team.

The walk back to my desk is buoyant. My feet barely touch the ground. *I have an ally!* I focus on my schedule for today. I push the waiting fresh newspaper aside, my mind humming with ideas. *I have an ally!* And I don't have to report to Birdie— maybe ever. I feel as if ankle shackles and handcuffs have been unlocked and tossed in the trash. *Freedom.*

My landline rings.

I cautiously pick up the phone. "Izzy, *Sentinel.*"

"Izzy?"

"You got her. What's up? Who's calling, please?"

"Izzy, this is Mrs. Dubois, Chad's second-period teacher. I wanted to give you a quick call. Chad has been absent a couple of days."

My back whipsaws in the chair. "Absent? Are you sure?"

"Oh yes, dear, quite sure. I checked with the receptionist, and he's not been checked out. I also talked to a couple of his other teachers, and he was not in their classes either. Wondered if you were aware. Chad's instructors tell me he's not doing his schoolwork, and he's been distracted and moody."

My heart jackrabbits in my chest. "Thank you for the call. I'll figure this out and let you know." We end our discussion. I stare at Lonnie, dumbfounded.

His eyebrows scrunch together. "What?"

Chapter Twenty-One

C had's cell goes straight to voicemail for the eighth time in an hour. I call the school administrator before I lose my mind. She may have a different slant on things.

The administrator in the front office verifies that Chad had not been in for two days, and I ask if she'll pull Peter out of class for me. I hear her scribble a note and give instructions to someone, then steps receding down the hallway. She asks if I'd like to wait, or would I prefer Peter give me a call, and I think to myself, woman, if you were dying a thousand deaths because you do not know where your kid had been for two days, what would *you* do?

I tell her fine, that's fine, have Peter call me. She knows nothing about Chad and in fact, doesn't know him at all, so it's a dead end. I give her my number.

As I dial Chad's number again a few minutes later, I see the school's number pop up. "Peter?"

"Yeah, Mom, what's up?"

I have trouble catching my breath. "Hey, um…do you know where Chad has been the last couple of days?"

"Uhhh…" Peter begins, then stops.

"You know something. Tell me."

He clears his throat. "Mom, I *don't.* He wasn't at school yesterday, but lots of kids skip. The first day he showed up at the car as usual when I was getting Mimi after school. This morning on the way to school, he didn't say much. I thought he was in class, but I guess he must've gone somewhere after the bell rang."

"Honey, I don't know where he is."

"I think maybe I have a clue at least. The other day he talked about needing some time to think, get his head straight."

My brow puckers. "Get his head straight? From what?"

"Well," my thoughtful son responds, "you know Chad, he's a deep thinker, and he wanted to get perspective, he said."

"Okay, perspective. Good. Now, son, think...do you know *where* he might go to get this perspective?"

After a brief pause, he responds. "He loves the river. You know, the good memories we've had on the north side when we watched the Fourth of July fireworks from Festival on the River? There are tons of overlooks. Maybe that's where he went." He pauses. "I bet that's where he is. I mean, how else would he go somewhere without my keys? The *bus*," he says, tripping over his words. "The transit bus comes right by the school twice a day, and I know that's one of the stops!"

"Okay. Thank you, honey. If he shows, call me. Can you ask around, some of his friends, and find out more? He agrees, and we end the call.

I run all over the office like a crazy woman and finally find Lonnie leaning over one of the women in production, basking in her attention. I pull him away.

After I give him a breathless, anxious summary of events, his eyes darken with concern. He agrees to take up the slack. I crush him in a hug of thanks and dash down the stairs to the parking lot.

On the drive up the winding, narrow road to the Bluffs Office Complex, a rambling cluster of offices and scenic vista areas high atop the Savannah River, I call Detective Lopez.

So far, I have a stalker, a boss who is possibly a jail-worthy pervert, an ex who is using my kids as a bribe to get his way, and now... a missing child. *Maybe he is not missing.* I repeat this to myself all the way to the scenic overlook Peter suggested. *He is not missing, he is not missing, he is not missing, he is—* My Bluetooth kicks in.

"Hi, Izzy." A faint reluctance colors the words. I wonder how many other cases run him ragged like this.

"You have time to talk to me a minute?"

"Sure. What's up?" I hear the rustle of papers in the background and voices over loudspeakers. The squawk of a police radio. Laughter from people that have no missing children. I think about the ugly chairs and the beige walls. I think about the antagonistic receptionist.

"It's my son, Chad. I can't find him."

The rustling of paper stops. "When did you last see him?"

I give him details and wait. I know him well enough by now to know that he will process the information like a computer and spew out a plan. He has a logical, well-ordered brain, the perfect antithesis of mine. I force myself to be quiet and listen instead of dissolving into tears.

"Alright. Where are you going right now?" I tell him. "Once you are up there, give me a call if you find anything. Your son saw him this morning, right?"

"Yes, and I saw him at breakfast. He seemed quiet, but nothing out of the ordinary."

"Well, kids this age do this all the time. I bet he'll be home after school. Anyway, I've got some information down, and I'll keep this out until I hear from you. What was he wearing?"

"Gray hoodie, jeans, red tennis shoes." The lump in my throat is strangling me. "He has medium-brown hair and brown eyes," I squeak out. "The kind of golden-brown eyes that a stuffed bear has." I put a hand over my face.

"Got it. Also, have your other kids talk to their friends or mutual acquaintances. Have you checked his social media?"

"This kid doesn't let me see his feeds. Peter's doing that, I'm sure. I'll check in."

After I end the call, I floor my accelerator and don't slow down until I reach the top of the Bluffs. I exit the car and look around. Memories of dragging lawn chairs to watch the fireworks wash over me. The kids had streaked all over the place in happy abandon on the grass, then settled in their chairs as fireworks split the night with explosions of color. I remember their squeals of delight, the claps of little hands. I can almost smell smoke from the fireworks lingering in the air. "Mommy," Chad had cried, spellbound. "It's so beautiful. I want to remember this night forever!"

I try to pray, which comes off as more of a sob, and stride down the path to the overlook. Benches are scattered around the area's perimeter. I stand in the center and rotate. I scan the parking lot bracketed by brilliant-red maples, office buildings in the distance, the Savannah River, roiling and churning, its banks straining at high water levels, a trailhead, and caution signs about the steep trail. I walk toward the trailhead, the most logical place, I think, that my son might be in his current state of mind. On the trail somewhere.

Decorative wrought iron borders the cliff's edge. I inspect each direction in meticulous detail. After ten minutes, something catches my eye as I stare down the trail and at the fast-flowing, murky river below.

About halfway down a vertical drop, in the midst of scraggly undergrowth and rocky outcroppings, is something red, like a small flag planted on the side of the bank. My breath catches in my throat. I jerk out my phone. Detective Lopez said he'd come.

I sit on the overlook bench, my thoughts rising and falling with each lap of the river. Then I burst into tears.

Twenty minutes later, I have tried Chad's number another ten times and indulged in some strict soul-searching. When had I become so disconnected from my kids? Other parents didn't keep tabs on their kids 24/7, right? I check in with them all day long with texts or calls. Isn't that enough? I concentrate on Chad. Scenes play in my head like a movie on fast-forward. Rushed, hectic, erratic. Like my life.

Chad's image in the scenes is hazy. Small. He sits in a dark corner. His face is sullen and angry. I'd meant to sit down with him and talk a hundred times, but something always got in the way. Tears leak down my cheeks. The scenes rushing through my mind slow to a snail's pace, and I see night after night of Chad on the couch, sleeping in front of the TV. I'd been glad that he didn't need me for something. But what if he'd been depressed? Or high? On who knows what? All I thought about was that at least *one* of the kids did not need my attention, thereby freeing me to click away in my hunt for *The Yes,* which will hopefully release me from being responsible for *everything.*

Chad, my troubled, brilliant, rebellious son, please forgive me. Forgive me for not taking the time to give you the attention you need. The attention you deserve.

Gosh, I am so tired. Endlessly tired.

The panorama before me is beautiful. Emerald Spring's skyline glints in the sun. Barges chug down the river, and a few speedboats whip by. The sun is almost directly above, and fluffy clouds dot the sky. The breeze lifts my hair. I feel a chill and wrap my arms around myself. If I'd focused on Chad like I was focusing now, he wouldn't be missing. *He is not missing!*

I scream through the silence of the still morning at the top of Overlook Park. My voice reverberates down the trail across the river.

My cell buzzes.

"Mom? I've gone through all his socials and talked to his friends. He didn't tell anybody he was going to be out, and his social media is the same old stuff. It didn't give me any information. He hasn't posted in a couple of days, though."

I push my hair out of my face. "Thanks, Peter." He asks if I need him to come, and I tell him to finish out the day and take care of Mimi, and I'll update him.

A motor purrs into the parking lot and stops. The car door opens, and steps crunch toward me. Detective Lopez is on his cell, binoculars in hand. He's wearing a bomber jacket and a shoulder holster that I get glimpses of when his jacket flaps open.

"Hi." He takes in the view, the trail, the landscaping, and benches. "Do you think your son comes here often?" He steps to the overlook. "Where's the red you talked about?"

I walk to the edge and point. "His favorite tennis shoes are red."

He aims his binoculars. His fingers adjust the sights. I hear his steady breathing. He lowers the binoculars. "It's a tennis shoe, Izzy."

That's the last thing I remember.

My eyes flutter open to a bustle of activity.

I lay on a bench, Lopez's bomber jacket bundled underneath my head as a pillow. A red strobe alerts me to the ambulance parked on an incline a few feet away. I hear muffled shouts from the bank of the river. My foggy mind clears, and I leap up. *Chad!*

Detective Lopez barks orders into his phone. Police and emergency personnel gather at the edge of the overlook. Three of them hold a huge steel cable that disappears over the edge. Patrol cars fill the parking lot. A knot of stoic EMTs wait by a mobile gurney on an aluminum frame covered in white sheets. One of them notices me and jerks a thumb. "She's awake."

Detective Lopez mumbles something into his phone, ends the call, and strides toward me. My balance is not the best. I'm stumbling around, mumbling my son's name. "Easy, Izzy. You fainted." I stare at him, too afraid to ask.

He smiles, pats my shoulder. "Chad's okay."

The dam breaks. I wrap my arms around myself. "Oh God, Oh God, Oh God," I whisper.

"He's kind of out of it, so we're taking him to emergency to get him checked over. You can ride in the ambulance. He had a fall."

I close my eyes and breathe.

A few seconds pass before I speak.

"Thank you, Detective." I wave my hand toward the bench, which still holds the crumpled coat, "for all of it."

"Listen, after he gets to the hospital, you'll be met by a social worker that will ask you some questions. Be prepared. It's routine, but she'll want to know about your home life to determine if he needs counseling or whatever, okay? Try not to be too emotional. They look for, um..." he cherry-picks his words, "*signs in a home.*"

If this is a warning, I'm confused.

Signs? A social worker? Signs of what?

"Call me after he's home. Let me know what's going on. I'm still checking out some other things that you probably need to know about. For now, go take care of your boy." He nods toward the edge, where the disembodied voices are getting louder. "They're bringing him up now."

Never had I seen a more beautiful sight than my son tucked into a makeshift sling, helped over the precipice by the police, and handed to the paramedics. I cover him in hugs and kisses while the paramedics stand by. His arm is in a sling; his face is covered with scratches and bruises. His hoodie is torn, his hair matted with blood. His eyes are unfocused.

"Mom," he says, and tears start at the corners of his eyes. "Mom, I'm sorry. Don't worry 'bout me. I love you, Mom." The words are slurred.

I stare wide-eyed at the EMTs.

"Ma'am, your son needs a scan. You can ride with us, but we need to go soon." I release my death grip on my son's arm and follow the gurney to the ambulance. I glance over my shoulder and see Detective Lopez's tail lights disappear down the hill.

The river grinds its way west into the sunset. The water ebbs and swells with laps of sun-kissed gold. The sky is bathed in ethereal pinks and oranges, and birds circle overhead. I register the beauty, but it bounces away. My mind is a jagged block of ice.

"Now! Ms. Lewis, get in."

I look at the sky one more time before I climb into the ambulance.

Two hours later, after Chad is comfortable in his hospital bed with a bottle of water and two packages of Twix, I check in with my life. Lonnie assures me all is well on the home front, but my clients need some attention tomorrow. He says Jon's automotive clients are fine, too.

Peter and Mimi gush with relief when I call. I know this awful episode will take time to unpack as a family, but I can't think too far ahead. Right now, all I can do is the next thing in front of me. I assure them I'll be home soon, give them a few chores, talk about homework, tell them to lock all doors, and stay home. I call Jon Hoyt, apologize for missing another meeting, and explain.

Just as I think I might have time to take a breath, a social worker from Georgia Family Services walks in.

I gaze at my son, whose chest rises and falls as he breathes into an oxygen mask. He is covered in a hospital-issue, thin, white blanket and hooked to an IV. He's had an MRI and a tox screen. Results are forthcoming.

I do *not* want to know what Chad has been taking.

A certain amount of denial is understandable. Even allowable, under the circumstances.

"Ms. Lewis?"

I stare at the woman, all soft and yielding in her light chocolate skin, sensible shoes, and warm brown eyes. Is this an assessment? Is Ethan getting the last word after all?

I feel like I am carrying a backpack loaded with bricks as I struggle to my feet. This woman has entered the holy ground that contains my son. I have nothing but outrage to offer her.

"Ms.," I correct her.

She extends her hand. "Thelma Wells."

Her handshake feels like a concerned neighbor asking if she can coordinate meals. But it's a ruse. I've been prepared by my new best friend, Detective Lopez, who has insinuated government intervention if certain signs are present. I look at her through this filter.

"Ms. Lewis," she continues, "I'm here as a service of the hospital to see if you need anything or if there is a way to help." She smiles.

I don't smile back.

Her smile falters. "Um, so what happened?" she continues.

Why is this any of her business? The outrage bubbles closer to the surface.

"He fell," I manage through clenched teeth. "This is not a good time, Thelma."

She assures me with flaps of her well-endowed arms that she knows her timing is unfortunate, but explains that in these situations, it's best to chat right away.

"Chat?"

"Of course. We...we like to make sure we have the right information in our reports."

My eyes slit. She is on dangerous ground, and I am on the brink of insanity.

"Information? Reports? What. The. Hell. *Are you talking about?*"

121

She continues, "We have to fill out these reports. It's government mandated."

Oh. *That* helps. Just what I need right now. To placate some freaking, uninvolved, intrusive government agency.

"You have got to be kidding me," I hiss. "My son was injured. He is trying to recover. I am not talking to you. Please leave."

Instead of leaving, she lowers her voice to a whisper and eases closer. Her scent is clean and light.

"Ms. Lewis, I am a Special Investigator with the Child Services Unit. We require contact if a child presents with a serious injury. If you don't tell me what happened, I am required to report that you are uncooperative and argumentative, and you may be looking at spending hours at our offices waiting for an interviewer. Give me a few sentences, and I'll be on my way. I can see you're overwrought and concerned. You need to be available to your family. I'll check back and get details later."

I stumble through an abbreviated story. Thelma takes notes and leaves. I cannot imagine a worse job than the one she has—sifting through terrified, anxious parents to look for warps and tears in their parenting skills.

My son stirs.

"Mom?" He focuses on my face.

I smile and take his hand. "Yep, right here, honey."

He rotates his head, taking in the IV, the medical trays, the pokes in his arm. "Guess you'll know pretty soon."

My eyes round. "What do you mean?"

"What I've been taking."

Drugs. He means *drugs*, my mind screams. I shove aside the implications. I can't think about this right now.

"We'll work this out. Just sleep."

His chin trembles. His hands shake. "I've been doin' them for a while. I know it's wrong, but it's a way I can feel happy. Like there's nothing bad going on. Like we're a normal family."

I look away. I can't cry anymore. The tears have dried up inside me, leaving behind a vacant stare. Chad exhales, then the sedatives kick back in.

Chapter Twenty-Two

Hours later, lying in bed unable to sleep, my mind rehashes the day's events for the hundredth time. One would think the hamster in my brain would tire of the exercise wheel after a while. Tomorrow, I will down gallons of coffee in order to make it through. Maybe a *four*-shot latte in the morning. Lydia will be speechless.

Three a.m., and I'm still wide awake.

Great.

Might as well do the milk and cookies thing. I throw off the comforter and pad down the hallway, where my laptop sits. I stop. Stare. My fingers twitch.

Milk and cookies don't hold a candle to online hotties.

I glance at Chad's empty room. Cocooned in a warm bed at the hospital, I'm relieved he is safe, but it doesn't help my heartache over the whole episode. If all checks out, I might be able to bring Chad home tomorrow. Horace tells me Chad can complete his assignments at home until he's ready to come back.

I think about that.

I have no idea what this child's future holds. Rehab? The tox screens had identified opiates. The thought of my son on drugs is overwhelming. Why? How? When did it start?

I hold my forehead. *Not now. I can't.*

With small, shuffling steps, I walk to the accent table that holds my laptop and log in to a couple of the dating sites. When I see how many messages I've racked up, a wave of anticipation ripples through me. My son is lying

123

in a hospital bed, and I *still feel* the thrill of a new guy. Maybe I'm the one that needs intervention, not Chad.

However.

It's not like I'm drinking myself into oblivion or hopping into bed with strangers, or taking drugs. It's a harmless trip down fantasy lane in the dark quiet of the night. A mind-numbing happy pill when life falls apart.

The adrenaline rush starts in my brain, tingles through my chest, then ends in a pleasurable surge of endorphins.

I click on the first message with a happy expectation.

"Belle, after reading your profile and looking at your pictures, I feel you will make all my dreams come true..." What a loser. Who wants to be the reason someone's dreams come true? Besides, I hate clichés. I click on his profile anyway, just to look at his picture, which confirms my first impression. Ahh, no. He ends up in the swipe trash. I click on the next one.

"Belle, sounds like we should talk. We have a lot in common. I'm a sales rep by day, an actual person by night. After work, I morph into an interesting, fun guy instead of a numbers-driven, irritating drone. Can I get an amen? I see you're a rep, too. What do you sell? I see you have kids, me too. Love being a dad. Not fun being one that flies solo, but hey, it is what it is. Read my profile. Let me know what you think. Reach out. Road Warrior"

With a smile, I click on his profile. I gasp. He's gorgeous. Dark hair. Sparkling, dark eyes that seem to look right through me. Strong, confident jaw. Great smile. His full-length pic shows him in professional attire, including a sport coat, white shirt, and khakis. I wonder if responding in the wee hours of the morning seems too forward?

Certainly not.

My response: "Road Warrior, you sound fun and interesting. I, too, morph into a semi-interesting person after work. I love being a mom, but wish I had more time to focus on being one. Tell me about yourself. What do you sell? Where's home for you? And...let's be honest with each other... how current are your pics? Thought I'd beat you to it. I bet we could share war stories about online dating. Look forward to hearing from you, Belle."

I read my response over a few times and decide it is fine. Middle-of-the-road. Not too interested, not too uninterested. The flip side of the line about war stories should communicate that he better match up to his pics. The leprechaun experience is still achingly fresh. My palm drifts across my mouth as I yawn and stretch my arms toward the ceiling. I have to be at work in three hours. Maybe I can catch some sleep if I hurry. I click on the remaining profiles, but after Road Warrior, it's hopeless. My mind spins at the prospect of chatting with him. As my head hits the pillow, visions of his sculpted jawline and killer smile dance in my head.

Maybe it will give me some relief from the jarring, repetitive visual of my bloody, injured son emerging from a bluff overlooking the Savannah River.

The next morning is a blur of filling in the blanks about Chad for Peter and Mimi, homework reminders, lunch packing, dishwasher emptying, and throwing long-neglected laundry into the washer. I scramble around the kitchen after the kids leave for school wiping counters and trying to attain some semblance of organization, since I'd been on autopilot for the past few days. The debris of our lives sits in corners, hides under coffee tables, lives in closets, or piles up all over the kitchen. Shoes. Dirty socks. A notebook. Dishes in the sink. Overflowing trashcans. We can't find the TV remote. I am desperate for order. If I can organize even one tiny space of my world, it will help.

I pick up and scrub and put away and take out trash until my arms need a break.

I leave a text on Chad's phone that I'll be at the hospital in an hour. His phone is the first thing he sees in the morning and the last thing he checks at night. When had he traded his beloved stuffed puppy for a cell phone? Had I noticed? Was it two years ago? Three?

After a shower, I throw on jeans and a T-shirt and drive to the hospital.

Chad's door is open. He is sitting up in bed. The IV is no longer in his arm. He looks better. His eyes light up when he sees me in the doorway. I rush in and give him a hug. "How are you feeling?"

"I'm okay," he says. "Dad came by."

My eyebrows rise. "When?"

"Earlier. Before he had to go to work. They let him see me even though it was so early."

I ruffle his hair. "Well, that's good."

"He asked me a lot of questions."

The skin on the back of my neck prickled. "Like what?"

"How much you go out at night, that kind of thing."

I look away. "What'd you say?"

Chad adjusted his position and winced. Looked at me with a stern expression, as if he were the parent and I the child. "Mom. You go out all the time. I never know when you get home. For all I know, you could've stayed out all night."

"Not every night," I protest. What was I doing? Did I expect Chad to protect me, or keep my dating life a secret? Maybe. But...this is sick. Am I asking my kids to lie for me now?

A bedraggled shame fills my chest.

"Okay, Mom," Chad says, his voice thin.

I stroke his arm. "Feeling weak?"

"It's not that..." He looks away.

I blink. The opiates. He's detoxing. "Chad, what were you taking?"

He stares at the bed, crosses his arms. "Oxy." A sheen of sweat breaks out on his forehead.

"OxyContin? The pain pill?" I am a babe in the woods where drugs are concerned.

"The kids at school get 'em. It's hard to say no." He shrugs.

"Don't they...cost something?"

"I use my allowance, Mom."

I wish I didn't know. Why do I have to know this? As I marinate in the fresh revelation, the door to Chad's room opens.

"Hey." Peter approaches Chad's bed. I get misty-eyed as they hug. A long time.

Peter pulls up a chair on the other side of the bed.

"It's Friday. Why aren't you in class, honey?"

Peter lays his hand on his brother's arm. "I called in. They understand. I think Chad's my priority right now." He pauses. "We need to be together, Mom. As a family."

"You okay, bud?" he asks.

"Gettin' there."

The boys understand each other in that silent, non-verbal way of the the male species that I will never, ever understand.

Peter leans back in his chair, flicks his blond, straight hair off his forehead. I drink him in. Peter is sixteen, tall for his age, with striking blond hair and Caribbean-blue eyes. After-school football training has filled him out, and he's earned respect as a valuable team member. Peter has strict standards about who he dates but has a hard time fending off all the attention he gets from love-struck high school girls. He cruises through all this adoration with humility. I am so proud of him.

Peter gets up and closes the door.

"Noise getting to you, honey?" I ask.

He returns to his chair. "Need to talk to you about something."

I wince. These words have become my own personal pandemic. My tenuous hold on emotional equilibrium is decimated by this simple phrase. "Okay," I mumble.

"Before all this happened with Chad, I heard a noise one night and got up to check it out. Mom. It was Mimi. Sneaking through a window in the den."

I suck in a breath. 'Need to talk to you about something' is a harbinger of doom. Every time.

"She had a bunch of makeup on, Mom. I was like, what the heck, Mimi? She got mad and said you do the same thing all the time."

My eyebrows jerk together. "Do the same thing? What does that mean?"

"Run out at night to meet guys."

"Wait. Back up." Mimi is twelve, for God's sake. How could she run out to meet guys?

"Mom," Peter said, his tone gentle. "You know she watches YouTube and hangs out on Insta and TikTok all night long, right?"

"I didn't know," I lash out. I feel betrayed. Not to mention a complete train wreck of a mother. "Where did she go? Did someone pick her up? How did—"

"An older guy. He contacted her by DM through Instagram."

My heart rams my ribs. I feel faint. "Is she okay? Did you take her to school before you came here?" I ask in a tiny, terrified voice.

"She is, Mom. She is fine, and she's at school. I had a talk with her. She says since you do it all the time and her dad is never around that, she thought she deserved someone to make her feel pretty. Like you do."

I slump in my chair. Had I given her the impression that unless I had male attention, I wasn't pretty? Or wanted? Or validated?

Of course I had. Not on purpose, but that doesn't matter. The consequences of my choices? That's what matters.

Chad's face is ashen.

Family is messy, yeah, but mine is a nightmare. I stare at Peter. "How did she get out? I mean, I always set the alarm…wasn't it engaged?"

He shrugs. "She's learned some kind of YouTube method to trick the alarm, anyway. So it won't get set off."

A tremor races through my chest. Yes, I am terrified for Mimi, but that psycho Tyler could've waltzed right into the house as well.

Peter puts his hand on my shoulder. "It's going to be okay, Mom. I talked to her a long time. She heard me. She knows it was stupid. I told her you were going to get it together."

I study his face. He is too damn young to have to deal with things I should have already figured out. That any responsible parent would have figured out, or at least set aside on behalf of the kids. My jaw clenches.

"I will," I whispered. "I *will* get it together, Peter. And I'll have a long talk with Mimi." I rub my cheek. "Do you know the guy she went to meet?"

"She wouldn't tell me." He walks back to his chair beside the bed. "Sorry, bro," he tells Chad. "Mom needed to know. Might as well clue in the whole fam, y'know?"

Chad clears his throat. "Mom, I know you won't like this, but I…I was thinkin' the same thing when I went out to that trail on the Bluffs. I mean…it feels so unfair. Like nobody cares about me. Mimi feels that way, too."

I guess if I'm going to get dumped on, it's best that it all comes at once. I close my eyes. "I love you so much, Chad. A million times a million."

Chad rolls his eyes. "Why do you think I do drugs, Mom? At home, you're never there, and at school, I get in trouble all the time. I didn't even think you'd notice I was gone." He lifts his bony shoulders. "At least when I'm high, I don't feel anything." He looks at Peter. "I'm the loser son. Gym King here," he motions toward Peter, who frowns. "Is the perfect son."

"Chad! You two are different, that's all. Different gifts and talents. Different personalities. I never meant to...I never knew you felt that way, honey. What can I do? What do you need? Please. Tell me what I can do to make it right."

A tear slips out. He slaps it away. "Just be HOME. After work, I mean. I know you have to make money and all that, but what good is it if...we never see you? We don't need another stepdad, Mom. If you're doing that for us, you shouldn't."

I smile a quivery smile at the boys.

The topic changes, and I use the opportunity to find a waiting room to have a good cry before I call Detective Lopez and check in with him.

I have to make some hard decisions. Whatever the cost.

Chapter Twenty-Three

I feel like a thousand bucks as I sail into the *Sentinel's* parking lot after dropping Chad. This is the day that Chad returns to school and the start of a do-over for his mom.

We'd made a lunch date for today. I'd resisted logging on for three days, and I am hopeful that I can keep it up. It feels amazing not to drag around all that guilt, and also amazing to sleep through the night.

I'm grateful.

Chad hadn't gotten deep enough into opiates to need a detox unit, thank God, but Family Services gave me names of outpatient facilities. Between Horace at Windsor Academy and Thelma, the Family Services busybody…it looks like we will right this ship.

I do not discount the fact that it'll be up to me to steer. Add to that, I have my own brand of detox to undergo.

At any rate. Onward. Through the fog.

The office feels alien after being absent four straight days. Even on weekends, I'm on call and may run in a time or two to take care of something. It's a twenty-four-hour job sometimes, but I'd been clear. No contact until Monday.

I fling my purse in its drawer and plop into my chair. Winston gives me a look.

"Where you been?"

"Righting my ship, Winston."

He smiles. "Cool."

First order of business: reschedule meeting with Jon.

His response is terse, but he agrees to a time.

I schedule afternoon meetings with my accounts and scan some of Jon's ads before they go to press. Darlene materializes at my elbow. Her movements are short, jerky. She's biting her lower lip. She glances at the corner office.

I close my eyes and rub my forehead.

Oh, please, God. Where is your mercy?

A non-event-life is my goal from now on. Go to work. Go home. Raise kids. Clean house. That is all.

"What is it, Darlene?"

"Birdie is on fire," she murmurs. "I heard your name mentioned earlier, around the coffee nook. I don't know what it's about, but he's having a hissy fit about something."

We make a date to meet after work at The Saucer Shop, a familiar watering hole in the River's Edge District. As I watch her retreating back, I am not sure if knowing Birdie is 'on fire' helps or hurts.

Lonnie widens his eyes at me and makes a face.

I laugh.

"Sounds like he's in a mood," he says, flipping through proofs. "These are going to press in thirty minutes. If you need changes, tell me now."

"I'm good."

"How's your son?"

"He's great, thank you. All is well."

He puts an elbow on his desk, his chin in his hand. "What's going on?"

"Oh, nothing. Trying to get together with Jon has been a nightmare. He's not happy about it, and Birdie resents that I've been handling accounts other than my own." I smile at him. "That's all it is."

Winston puts his head down and whispers, "Incoming, twelve o'clock." Birdie barrels toward me, his mouth a firm, hard line.

He stands beside my desk, his whole body vibrating like a tuning fork. "Need you in my office."

Winston glances at Birdie, then me. "Izzy. I reserved the conference room to have a sit-down about that ad that's about to go to press. You need me to reschedule?"

Bless Winston. He senses danger. He is my protector at all costs. We are a team, and we'll lie, cheat, or steal for one another. I paste a confused look on my face, fold my hands, and look up at Birdie.

"Birdie, can I circle back? Winston and I, well, we're on deadline." I let the unspoken priority hang in the air. Printing deadlines trump irritated management every time, and he knows it. A blush crawls up his neck.

"It's urgent. The minute you're done, get in my office." With that, he strides to his office and slams the door.

"Looks like we need to have a meeting, right?" Winston grins.

My laughter is shaky. We walk to the conference room.

"Hope this room isn't reserved by someone else," he quips.

"Yeah, no kidding. I thought Birdie's eyes were going to bug out of his head. Perfect timing, Winston, thank you."

"My pleasure." He sits. Threads his hands together on the table. "What's going on?"

I start at the beginning, including the counterfeit emails, the snarky comments around my desk, the off-color jokes, and insinuations. My stalker. That Birdie had talked to him. That my stupid ex had talked to him, also.

"I swear, Izzy, you should write a book."

My eyes glaze over. "I know. It's pathetic. And, oh, you won't believe this either, but Detective Lopez—"

"*Detective?*" he blurts. "What detective? Is there a crime in there somewhere?" I fill him in on the stalking charges and the protective order, omitting Chad's situation. I don't want to offload too much drama on Winston. He has a nice, peaceful existence at home and a sweet wife who loves him. The man has never experienced a heart-stopping crisis in his life that I know of. How I envy him.

"I can't believe you've been going through all this alone, Izzy." He rubs the top of his head and focuses on the ceiling as he thinks things through. "So where are you, I mean, the thing with your ex? That...well, he's threatening you. What are you going to do?"

"I don't know. We've been good, I thought. I'm not sure what happened."

"He ever get remarried?"

"He has a girlfriend."

Winston gives me a look. "Izzy, you're an attractive, strong woman. The mother of his children. Do you think that he's still...?"

I put my hands over my ears. "Don't say it! I can't take any more. He's getting just as creepy as the stalker." I take my hands from my ears. "He even tried to call Phil, but I got to Phil before he picked up. Birdie's probably already told him about their conversation." I frown. "What a load of BS. Ethan's not worried about me. He doesn't want me back. He wants control. He's just mad that I'm not following his directives. Why do you think I divorced him? He hasn't changed, and he doesn't really care about the kids. The custody suit is a scare tactic."

Winston lets his arms fall by his side and shakes his head. "How can I help?"

I ignore the question. I'm on a roll. "Anyway, when I left Raphael's, guess who I ran into outside?"

Winston holds his breath. "Who?"

"Jon."

"Jon Hoyt?"

"I'd missed another meeting with him, and here I was with a guy on the street when I was supposed to be talking to him in the conference room."

"This is killing me, Izzy. It's like...you're a magnet."

"For what?"

"Trouble?"

"Yeah. Well." I push up off the chair. "It's got to stop. One way or the other. Thanks for the rescue today. At least he's had time to settle down."

"And I'm all caught up," Winston beams.

With a roll of my eyes, I'm off to Birdland.

Lonnie motions me to my desk. I take a minute, get him sorted out, then square my shoulders. With a deep breath, I stride to Birdie's office.

Open the door.

Holding up one finger, he motions me in. "Let me finish this email, and

I'll be right with you."

The chair in front of his desk is new and uncomfortable. I listen to the click-click-click of his typing. He uses the hunt-and-peck technique, but he's quick about it.

After a couple of minutes, he plops his elbows and clasps his hands atop his perfectly ordered desk. His icy and penetrating eyes rake my length. I return the insult with an icy stare of my own. I am a mother who has experienced the restoration of a missing fourteen-year-old son. Hear me roar.

"Phil informed me you report to him, now."

I hold his gaze, silent.

"I want to know why, Izzy. And I want to know *now*."

I feel my brain flip into overdrive. The stress of Chad, Jon's accounts, dealing with Birdie, the stalker, my ex—all of it is tearing at the thin shreds of my self-control. Foremost in my mind is the lunch date I'd promised Chad today, and no snake from hell is going to trap me in his office and keep me from that. I struggle to keep the words going through my mind in check.

Birdie slams his hands on the desk. "What. Is. Going. On!" he thunders.

I blink in surprise.

Does he think this is okay? I cross my legs and wait. Anything I say is useless until he calms down, anyway.

He projects himself across his desk like a lizard crawling out of its hole. His voice drops to a whisper. "If you think you can go behind my back, you're dead wrong. If I don't get the respect of this office from you, you're without a job. Period."

In my mind, I say, 'we'll see about that, asshole,' but I don't say this aloud because I don't want the stink of his breath in my face.

I shake my head in disbelief. He is so inappropriate that I have trouble forming a coherent sentence.

Red veins crisscross his eyes as he stares. The intent is clear.

I am the enemy.

I fold my hands in my lap. "HR will be happy to document your concerns. Remember, I'm not your responsibility anymore, and they'll be very interested in your version of what you construe as disrespect. You might clue Phil in, too, before you have a meeting with HR." I give him a look. "You can't be too careful."

His eyes never leave mine. He grips the armrests of his chair and sits stiff and upright. I walk out.

Once I'm outta there, I grab my purse and bag and jerk open the door to the stairs and run down them as fast as I can. I don't stop until I'm locked into my Honda. I force myself to take deep breaths and drink a bottle of water. The look on Birdie's face was worth it, but what had my swan dive into hostile territory done to my future? My paycheck?

For once, I didn't care.

I acted appropriately. He didn't. End of story.

Twenty minutes later, I'm in my kitchen fixing Chad a sandwich. I stuff notes and all kinds of fun things into a lunch bag and put Birdie out of my mind. I'm going to make Chad's first day back at school special. He will feel loved, no matter what, and I will focus on the blessing of getting him back in one piece. After my love offering is complete, I race to my Honda and drive to meet him at school, where he will receive his lunch special delivery.

After Peter drops off Chad and Mimi before he runs back to football practice, Chad is exhausted. He goes straight to his bedroom. My steps are hushed on the carpeting as I tiptoe upstairs to check on him an hour later. I knock on his door and push it open. Afternoon shadows ripple through the blinds that cover his window.

"Oh, hi, Mom." He yawns, stretches. "Come on in. I slept for a long time, huh?"

His eyes are clear and direct. He's taken a shower. I'd been wondering if his disjointed attire and hazy demeanor had been a phase, but according to the blood panel, it was a mix of pills and pot.

"Want to come downstairs?"

He agrees and walks behind me. I sit in my favorite recliner, and he sits on a loveseat opposite. The antique clock on the wall ticks a steady beat. White bookcases tuck in against facing walls that hold family photos, pottery, and faux succulents. I love this room. It's intimate and cozy and the perfect place to unpack what's been going on with Chad.

My words bump against themselves. "Your...the...uh... tox screen was troubling."

"Yeah. It would have been."

"How long?"

"A couple years."

I am stunned, but too exhausted by everything to respond with the shrieking that should accompany such an announcement. "I need an explanation, son."

He stumbles through a series of events that I'd downplayed in his life. The rejection from a couple of school events. The teachers that had underestimated him. His increasing fear that Mom is unavailable. His dad's rejection. Our financial burdens. My late-night treks.

Chad shrugs. "Mom, you don't think we *stay* asleep when you are gone, do you? We know you're out a lot. We all think about...well, what if someone got in? What would we do? We don't know where you are..." his voice trails away. "Of if you'd answer your phone."

My sigh is deep. "Chad, you know I'm in a high-stress job, plus I try to keep up with the house, getting you guys to your school events and everything else. Online dating is efficient. I didn't think you'd know I was gone." Lame, even to me.

"So when you're gone, and Mimi has a nightmare and calls for you, then me or Peter get to take care of her." He glares at me. "She needs *you*, Mom."

I feel a distinct burn in the pit of my stomach. "I get it. I do, honey. Let's get back to you right now, though."

He gingerly crosses his arms and looks away.

"So, Chad, how serious is the drug issue? Are you going to need help staying away from them? Because you can't just...try them, you know. It becomes this huge thing. A trap. We need to deal with it now."

Chad gives me an evil grin. "How serious is *your* huge thing, Mom? Is online dating a bigger problem than you think? Are you gonna deal with it? I'll deal with mine if you deal with yours."

I grunt. "It's not the same thing at all, Chad."

"*Every night*, Mom. When's the last time you didn't go out? Except for when you just had to stay in for something with us or whatever, it's every stinkin' night. I'd call that a *problem*."

This conversation had not turned out like I wanted at all. And now, here I sit in the uncomfortable searchlight of my son's accusations. He needs some kind of deal here, and I need to decide.

"If I make some changes, will you stay away from drugs?"

"They're not that fun anymore, anyway." He looks at me with a small spark of hope. "How about you?"

"How about if I agree to limit it to weekends?"

Chad gives me an exaggerated eye roll. "Sure, Mom. And what if I just smoke a little weed on the side? Limit it to weekends?"

"Chad. You scared us to death. Please, if you're feeling isolated or something I'm doing bothers you, talk to me. I'll listen, I promise. And I also promise...to make more time for you. I'm sorry I've been distracted. That I haven't noticed that you're...that you're..." The tears start.

I walk over to Chad and wrap him in a hug. He may be fourteen, but he still needs his mom. Now more than ever.

He mumbles he's going to go play video games. I watch his back recede up the stairs. His pajama pants are decorated with small, yellow, SpongeBobs.

As I pass my laptop in the upstairs hallway, I snap it shut.

Chapter Twenty-Four

"How's it going?" Lydia asks as she hands me my morning latte. "Not wonderful." I glance in the rear-view at the twenty-odd cars behind me. "Better go. I'm holding things up." I lift my latte in salute.

"Hang in there, Izzy," she says.

"Yeah, hang in there, Izzy," I tell myself as I drive away, interpreting her well-intentioned words in a much darker way—a noose around my neck.

The music I'm playing scrapes my raw nerves. I turn it off.

What am I supposed to do about Birdie? How am I supposed to work in a hostile environment?

The freeway is an ocean of writhing metal, and I pound the steering wheel in frustration at the traffic. "Move, dammit!" Chad pushes to the forefront of my brain. He'd been suspiciously cheerful this morning. Which is what oxy does. It creates a false serotonin rush. Is he still using?

The first chance I get, I'll search his room. Is this my future? Searching my kid's room every day? Waiting for the inevitable relapse?

I'd told Peter and Mimi that we need a family conference after school, and they agreed. My stomach fizzes at me as I think about it. I don't know how much stress one person can take, but I have a feeling I've reached my limit.

By the time I pull into the parking lot, I'm tense and irritable and praying that I won't run into Birdie. I take the stairs two at a time, jerk open the door to the sales floor, and ease inside. Lo and behold, there he is, right in front of me, the Bird in all his thuggish glory. Diamond cuff links. Perky pocket kerchief. Blazing smile. His hatchet job on me deftly buried under the compost heap of business as usual.

"Morning, Izzy." His expression is speculative.

I walk to my desk. Not quite a full ignore, but close. He continues down the stairs. I sit at my desk in confusion, thinking about how all this pressure building in me will find release. Can I keep a lid on it until I'm done with the workday? I pull out my purse drawer. My blood freezes in my veins.

A note.

I close my eyes, put a hand on my chest, and glance around the room.

Assistants dart from cube to cube, laughter erupts from the corner office, and a pleasant hum of activity indicates little chance of danger.

With trembling fingers, I pick up the note and unfold it.

My frozen lips crack into a smile. It's from Darlene. An encouraging note with one of her beloved scripture references. I seek her out with my eyes. She grins and gives me a thumbs-up from the back of the room.

I love this place. It's my second home.

I glare at Birdie's office door. Except for him. He doesn't belong here.

Winston arrives, stands at the coat rack, shrugs out of his light jacket, and inserts it among the others. He then places his hat on the shelf on top of the rack, winks at me, and walks around to his spot in the pod.

He rubs his hands together as he sits. "Getting colder out there."

"Winston, I still can't believe your timing yesterday." I peruse the newspaper. The soft, broadsheet pages rustle with each turn.

"You've bailed me out on more than one occasion, too," he says as he unfolds his newspaper, flattens it with his thumb, and turns to his favorite section. The one with the comics and the crossword puzzle.

He sips coffee from a Jiffy Mart cup. "So, how's the search for the perfect man going?"

"Winston, I don't know. Maybe we shouldn't talk about it anymore."

Winston's eyes snap from his newspaper to my face. This comment is a big departure for me, he knows.

I pick up my ringing landline.

"Izzy, *Sentinel*."

"Hi, Izzy, Detective Lopez."

139

I go quiet a beat. When had a call from him ever *not* been bad news? "Hey there."

"I'm checking on Chad. How is he?"

My shoulders droop with cautious relief. "He's good. We've had some serious conversations, and I'm getting the kids together tonight to talk through stuff. He's being honest with me."

"Getting a kid his age to talk is an accomplishment. Congrats." He clears his throat. "There's something else."

I palm my eyes.

"Seems your Birdie went by Elias Costanza when he lived in St. Louis. He had a wholesale business that outsourced manufacturing to Columbia and Mexico." I hear papers rustle and imagine him squinting at tiny lines of type. The rustling ends, and he says, "Name of the parent company was Cacciatore Manufacturing."

"Cacciatore?"

"Means 'hunter' in Italian," Lopez explains. "Probably a last name."

I feel my eyebrows pull together. "Okay. So, is this important?"

"Yeah, could be." He pauses, and I picture him playing with stuff on his desk with his hands. When he's thinking, he fondles things on his desk, like Winston's lanyard habit. "He's had a couple of arrests in St. Louis. Nothing that would stick, though. Also, and this should interest you, some misdemeanor sexual harassment charges. In addition to his lack of polish where the ladies are concerned, I'm wondering about the wholesale furniture business. Three locations shut down a year ago. I found fraud charges resulting in a fine and probation, but I'm sure there's more to it."

"He's definitely a predator," I say, thinking about the name of the business. Birdie hunts things down and shoots them; that's how it seems to me. I frown.

Winston looks at me over the rim of his coffee mug.

"Keep an eye on that guy. Call me if things get out of hand. How's the stalker? Staying away like a good boy?"

I smile. "No notes, no calls. I almost feel rejected."

Detective Lopez chuckles. "Lock doors and windows, keep exterior lights and alarm on. Make it a habit every night to check." I mumble assent, assessing the warm fuzzies coursing through me. If Lopez was single, I'd scoop him off the market so quickly his head would spin.

"Izzy, the hard stuff won't last forever. It's temporary. You'll find your way through this, and you'll come out on the other side a winner."

I love this guy. Wish my dad had been like him, but my father worked long hours, and when he was home, he watched television with an intensity that I always hoped would shift to me. It never did. After I end the call, Winston folds his arms over his chest in anticipation.

"What?"

"Anything you need help with?"

"Why, do I look worried or something?"

He scrutinizes me. "Something."

I roll my eyes. "I'm just getting it together before I head out into the wild."

Winston smiles. Touches his lanyard and leans in. "Into the wild?"

"That's what I call my world outside the office. It includes clients, kids, annoying challenges, and whatever else life decides to throw at me. You know. The things I can't control."

Winston puts his index finger on his chin and repeats the phrase, his voice soft and thoughtful.

I decide I need a walk to the ladies' room and bump into Jon on the way. "You're back! How are you?"

He is awkward and fidgety. A little reparation is in order. "How about I take you to a welcome-back lunch?"

His smile is tight. "Okay, but my treat, because you've been taking care of my accounts."

At eleven-thirty, Jon waits at my desk as I wrap up a busy morning. I feel like a juggler in my own circus, balls dropping all over the place. Unless I want to watch my commissions sail out the window, I need to catch up on face-to-face time with my accounts. I don't have time to do lunch with Jon, but I want us to get along, so I'm taking the time, anyway. "Okay," I smile. "Let's hit it."

Jon and I wait in front of the elevator. The doors slide open, revealing…
who else? My best friend and nightmare, the Birdster. He gives me the
side-eye and strides to his office, slamming the door behind him.

I look at Jon and shrug. "He has a thing about slamming doors."

"Nice guy." Jon grins.

The deli is packed with a comfortable crush of twenty-somethings that live
and work in the artsy area around River's Edge, administrative types of all
ages from the many businesses that office downtown, and tie-and-suited
financial types from investment firms.

We take our orders on trays and sit at a four-top in the corner. It's hard to
hear.

I hang my jacket on the back of my chair. Sit and pick up my sandwich.

"I've had compliments about your work with my accounts. Thanks," Jon
says.

"They're nice guys. I couldn't believe everything they expected me to do,
though. And you do it weekly. I'm impressed."

"There are shortcuts."

"Don't worry about me going after any more of your accounts," I grin.
"Way too much work."

Jon nods. "The automotive industry is tough. It's changing, but…some of
the female reps don't work out."

I scan his face. "Why?"

"The younger ones sail in there and act like the reels they watch on
Instagram and TikTok. Boom. The account asks for a different rep. They
don't want the complication." He pauses to chew the sandwich, then bites
into a dill pickle. "A few said some not-so-cool things about you."

Customers walk by our table. A child cries. Someone laughs. It is crazy
loud. I lean in so Jon can hear me.

"I can't remember doing anything to—"

Jon interrupts, "Izzy, I don't think you're aware of the signals you send."

My eyes slide to the wall behind him, and I bite into my sandwich, thinking.
As a single professional woman calling on male clients, do I default to the

same games as when chatting up someone online?" My forehead wrinkles. I put down the sandwich and fold my elbows on the table.

"Okay. What?"

"C'mon Iz. You're single and looking…you have this air about you." He shrugs. "Guys mentioned it, that's all."

Wow.

Jon swallows a bite of sandwich. Sips a Coke. "No big deal. But I think you should be aware."

I frown. "How do I come off?"

Jon assesses his answer. "Needy. Woman on the hunt." He shrugs. "Some of those car guys are on the hunt, too. In the wrong way. I don't want you to fall into a ditch, that's all."

I look at my plate. What am I supposed to be feeling right now? Do I come off that way to everybody?

"So noted, Jon." I clear my throat. "Listen, I want to apologize for the last meeting I missed. I wasn't giving work priority at that moment."

"No kidding," he smiled. "Did it work out? The guy, I mean?"

Should I tell Jon about my hovering ex? About the threats? About how that whole episode made me feel and I that I'd wanted to sink through the sidewalk when I saw Jon that afternoon?

Nope.

"My ex. He's an idiot. It was a mix-up."

After a beat, he says, "Okay. I forgive you. You've got your hands full with Birdie so I should cut you some slack."

I smile. "I knew I was in trouble after the ride-along, but I hoped for the best." I push my plate away, crumple my napkin and toss it on the table. "Not anymore. He likes to impress people with dirty jokes and sexist commentary and passive-aggressive threats."

Jon grunted. "Heard about that."

"Well, it didn't stop there. He asked my assistant Lonnie about my personal life."

"What kind of things? It's one thing to pry into an employee's home life; it's another to ask about public domain information. You know, you're pretty open about your online dating journey on social media. Maybe he saw something."

I feel bright red hot spots form on each cheek. "I know people talk about it, but I didn't think it would be like…a favorite sport. Lots of people date online." I wither a little under his gaze. Touch my hair. I'd taken special care today to look presentable. For some reason.

"Not like you. You're world-class." He chuckles. "Look. Any guy gets that Birdie's a joke."

I spend the next few minutes filling Jon in on the sly intimidations, the threats if I don't spend time with him, so he can 'loosen me up.' Filing a report with HR about it. His cold silence afterward. I tell him about Phil's decision to take me out from under Birdie's wing temporarily, and oh, by the way, I've been dealing with a stalker and have an Emerald Spring investigator's personal cell number in my phone. When I notice Jon's eyes start to glaze over, I stop piling on.

We don't speak for long seconds. I squeeze my hands together and look away. Insecurity drifts through my chest. Had I overshared?

Jon strokes his chin. "If I were Phil, this information would inspire some serious conversations with his latest new hire."

He stares at the wall, then at me.

"However, I gotta tell you that online dating stuff is *not* your friend. The jokes around the office paint you as a woman on a quest. From Phil's point of view, your reputation could color the facts about Birdie's behavior. Just saying. You have a reputation, too. Maybe you should hold off for a while."

"The dating apps are an escape for me," I snap. "Some people read books, others drink or take anti-depressants. I log on and forget the world for an hour or two. I don't have *time* to go to the gym, run marathons or join book clubs. How else am I going to meet anyone? Online dating is an efficient process, and searching for the right guy is a good and healthy desire."

The words sound hollow.

Jon stares at me like he can't believe what he's hearing. "Sure, for some people. But Izzy, don't you get it? It's an obsession with you."

"Is not," I protest.

He greets someone he knows across the room, then re-focuses on me. "I get it. We all have our release mechanisms. I did my own acting out when Marie died. Losing her was like a concussion that took over my life. I started drinking too much and couldn't stop. I'm working through it, as you know."

I think about Phil and his grace toward Jon as he struggled to find his legs again after losing the most important human being in his life.

"That day, in the office, when the ambulance came? Was that your wake-up call?"

"Pretty much. Other stuff happened too, but that event sealed it. I made the decision to change."

"So…how?"

"Phil got me to an AA group. I would've done it sooner, except I never recognized I had an issue. I figured I could stop drinking anytime I wanted, but listening to other men that have gone through the same things shook me up." Jon shakes his head. "I don't want to end up in a hospital bed waiting for a liver."

He pulls a coin out of his pocket and extends it to me.

"Here."

The coin feels warm in my hand. On one side, it says, 'God, grant me the serenity to accept the things I cannot change and the courage to change the things I can.' On the other, it says 'One Day At a Time.'

I am humbled. I don't know what to say.

"When I woke up in the hospital with all that booze out of my system, this was in my hand. Phil had put it there. It's a touchpoint for…this new life I'm building." He smiles. "Sounds like you could use a touchpoint about now."

My hand closes around the coin. "Thanks, Jon," I whisper. "It means a lot."

His smile is reassuring. "I can ask around, see what the temperature is in the upper levels, Izzy. I'll see what I can find out for you." He scrapes his chair back and rises. "Ready to walk back to the office?"

Chapter Twenty-Five

I am buried in ad copy when my cell rings. I lift my head and take a breath. I'd driven all over town meeting with clients, and quitting time has snuck up on me. I stare at all the work I'd produced with pride. Having Jon and Phil on my side has acted as a catalyst. Getting back to my pre-crisis self feels amazing…but I still answer the phone as if it's got rabies.

A brisk, warm voice responds. "Hey, Izzy, this is Thelma. From the hospital? How's Chad doing?"

My forehead creases. Oh, yes. Thelma. Family Services.

"Chad's good," I say, measuring my words. "We've had serious discussions, and they will continue."

"How is he responding?"

Courteous is one thing but intrusive is another. "Is this the action plan, Thelma?" I growl. "Are you planning to dictate how and what to discuss with my son?" I grip the handset. "We're *not* best friends or anything. What is this about?"

"I know this difficult, but after talking with Chad, the agency and I have suggestions. We run into these situations all the time, and there are ways to cope."

"Cope with what?" My hands curl into fists.

"Single parenting, of course. In your case, co-parenting."

"I'm on the edge of my chair."

She pauses.

My tax dollars at work. I tap my fingers on my desktop.

"Isabelle, there's something else. Your ex-husband, Ethan, has made some serious allegations."

My jaw drops. I take a few seconds to ingest the information, then get sizzling, boiling mad.

"How the hell did he get involved?"

She is quiet.

"Oh." I pinch the bridge of my nose. "*You* called *him* because I'm being investigated. Call it what it is, Thelma."

"I'd hoped it would not come to this." Her voice is somber. "Ethan made some good points. It's not an option, Izzy. We'd like you to attend a support group of our choosing. The other option is to discuss who the kids could stay with while we sort this out. "

I am stunned into silence. Detective Lopez's words boomerang back to me: "They look for *signs*, Izzy." Awareness dawns. Ethan had given her an earful. I'm sure of that. All I need now is for Tyler the Stalker to torch my house. Then life would be complete, and I could say goodbye to my kids, because Ethan would get custody and make the whole thing my fault.

Maybe it is.

I drop my head. Of course it is.

I find my voice and sputter, "*Mandated?*"

"I wouldn't call it a mandate. More of a free pass to sanity."

"Free?" I squeak. How did she know to touch on one of my worst fears—the one that underscores the entire life of a single parent—running out of money.

"Yes, free," Thelma says. "Won't cost you a dime. The recovery program for single parents is well-attended and successful. You'll be talking about your struggles in a confidential environment with like-minded women. Sharing issues as a single parent brings a lot of strength, Isabelle. A lot of healing, too."

I slump in my chair in defeat. "When?"

"Day after tomorrow. Once a week. Honey, you'll thank me for this."

Before I can demand not to be called 'honey' by this turncoat, she gives me the address and time, and I jot it all down on a sticky and stuff it into my purse.

Maybe it'll get lost in there, and I'll have a good excuse to skip.

"Another thing, Isabelle," she pauses to select her words, "you'll be getting a follow-up visit sometime over the next couple of weeks. A spontaneous visit. We will want to talk with the kids."

I sit up straight in my chair, my face stone-cold, granite.

An awkward silence stretches. She clears her throat.

"As you may be aware, your son is worried about how much you go out at night. The hope is that when I talk to your kids again over the next few weeks, this concern will be neutralized. Am I clear?"

"Very. Clear." Or, more accurately, pissed. My kids can clip my wings, but this woman should not have the right.

I hear scribbles on paper. "I'll be looking forward to hearing about how the first meeting goes? Please call?" I assure her, with all the sarcasm I can muster, that I will be delighted and slam down the receiver.

The pile on my desk mocks me. It will take another hour or so to clear before I can head home. How am I going to fit in a weekly meeting?

I attack the pile on my desk.

Within an hour, I race down the wide linoleum highway to production, skid to a stop in front of one of the production team, and sit in her cube to go over a few things. I call the kids, assure them I'll be home by eight. I feel bad about not going straight home, but after that phone call, I need a good dose of Darlene. I snag her from her desk, and we walk to the parking lot together.

It is still early, and the after-work crowd hasn't filed into The Saucer Shoppe yet. The red trolley rumbles by, and a few tourists look into the windows. The restaurant is a big tourist attraction, and people can buy 'I visited the Peach State' plates to take home with them.

"You can't be serious." Darlene frowns as I fill her in on my pathetic life. "What is coming next? I cannot believe it." I laugh at that, because what she knows is just the tip of the iceberg.

"Oh, sweetie, there's more, but this state agency thing is killing me. I don't know what to think. I'm a good mom, make a decent income, don't sleep around, and make sure my kids are happy, right? That damn Ethan." I pick up my wine glass. The wine slides down my throat and ends in a warm glow somewhere around my naval.

She ponders this question a few seconds.

I study my wine. My lipstick prints march around the edge of the glass. I take a minute to consider Darlene's questions.

"Maybe Chad and Ethan brought up red flags on their list." I shrug. "All I know is I have this stupid recovery group to attend at the end of the week."

Darlene smiles an indulgent smile. "Sometimes we get so caught up in our own lives we are not able to see clearly. I know for me, and for Richard too, we were stuck. Our group has been a life-changer, and maybe this will be one for you, too."

I stare at the wall. Decline another glass of wine when the server comes by.

"Secrets are like cancer. Richard and I had to be honest with each other." She tilts her head. "Maybe it's time to be honest with yourself."

"So that's the primary thorn in my side right now, Darlene. The other one ranks up there pretty close. Birdie."

"Did I ever tell you what Richard found out about him?"

I shake my head.

"He said Birdie has a long string of sexual harassment charges. That's the rumor, anyway."

My expression hardens. "Would've been nice if management had checked out that little detail before hiring him."

"So have you told Phil? About how Birdie tries to manipulate you?"

"Yeah. He was good about it. But please, just keep this between us, okay? For all I know, Birdie's planting seeds with the rest of the team about me."

We acknowledge the time, murmur our goodbyes, hug, and part. I am less tense when I ease onto the freeway, and thank God for friends like Winston and Darlene.

Chapter Twenty-Six

Birdie listens to the voice on the other end of the call with a guilty glance at the kitchen, where his wife is preparing dinner.

"I've found Izzy, and I'm following her now."

Birdie curses under his breath. "I don't need minute-by-minute updates, Tyler."

Three seconds tick by.

"Do...do you have any more instructions for me? I mean, you said to follow her, but should I approach...should I ask her...?"

"Dammit, Tyler. Are you an idiot? Of course, don't approach yet. All I asked for was surveillance." Birdie put a hand over his eyes.

"I just need you to wait until she leaves and follow her home."

"Okay. And then what?"

"Watch. See if she goes out."

Four seconds tick by.

"What if I get arrested?"

Birdie clenches his cigar in his teeth. "You won't." A lie. He will alert the cops the minute Tyler oversteps. The poor guy had been easy to manipulate. The reasons to get rid of Izzy are stacking up, and he chuckles when he thinks of how a sensitive comment planted here, and there can blow holes through a reputation. Phil won't have a choice. He'll be forced to let her go. The break-in might even get coverage in the newspaper. Now that would be icing on the cake! And ironic as well, since he'd lost his own business that way. Public scandals are a treasure when used properly.

He puffs long puffs of the cigar. "That it?"

"She got a protective order against me. Did I tell you that? It's a little more complicated than getting inside. If I get caught—"

"I didn't know." Smart girl, Birdie thinks. "Call me when you get inside or if you see something through a window. That's all I need. If you don't want to do it, don't. I'll figure out something else." He ends the call.

"Dinner's ready, Birdie," his oblivious airhead of a wife calls out.

"Be right there, hon."

She leans against the doorframe. "So when are they going to announce? I'm so proud of you."

Birdie basks in the look she gives him. "These things take time."

She walks over, puts her hand on his shoulder, her eyes bright. "Advertising Sales Director Birdie Costanza, of *The Emerald Spring Sentinel*. It has a nice ring to it. I never knew you had it in you, honey." She walks down the hall into the kitchen.

Birdie snuffs out the cigar. Leans back in his chair and threads his fingers behind his head, thinking about how far he'd come.

Two years ago, when his own scandal had begun, she lost all respect. Eventually, he lost his business, and she treated him like something to scrape off her shoe. It had taken time and hard conversations to get her to stay. 'Proud' was a word she hadn't used in a long time. It had been a long road, but she'd forgiven him for the tiny amount of money he'd embezzled. What's fifty thousand these days anyway? Pocket change. Probation. A payment schedule. A blip on the landscape. The other charges slid away without enough evidence to convict. A bankruptcy had pretty much mitigated any loss. Once again, he'd emerge the victor.

As always.

It's a gift.

He reels his mind back to his current scheme.

Phil is oblivious.

Upper management will carefully ask Phil to resign due to the scandals surrounding one of his star employees, his favorite gal-pal, Izzy. Lonnie, who is resentful of her as all hell, will corroborate the story he'd been cultivating. Lonnie, a young, ambitious man who resents Izzy and is hungry for power, is quite useful as a snitch. If the plan falls into place, the current ad director will become a liability. After all, look at his choices in sales personnel. Had they been credible? No. It will take time, however, to plant a convincing narrative in the proper channels. If it works, the sales staff will eventually be under his jurisdiction, and then…well, the sky's the limit.

Not a bad retirement scenario.

Chapter Twenty-Seven

I hum along with 'Coffeehouse Classics' as I weave through morning rush hour traffic, sipping my latte. Chad, Peter, and Mimi had been in better moods than usual this morning, and I attribute it to intentional family time.

The results are astonishing. I'm determined to make this choice more often.

As I pull into the parking lot, I spy the homeless man who had thrown my quarter back in my face a couple of weeks ago. I dig around in my purse and come up with a five-dollar bill. I plant it in his hand. He stares at me with suspicion.

"You're welcome," I say and cross the street to the double-door entrance of the *Sentinel*. I avoid the elevator and take the stairs, wondering what awaits me on this brand-new day. I anticipate good things.

Please, God. Only good things.

I pull back the door to the second floor and smile at the receptionist, a mother hen surrounded by her flock of assistants. They turn and mouth good mornings, then return to the bubbly receptionist's endless stream of updates.

Winston is perched at his desk, newspaper flattened into submission. A Starbucks cup is on his desk. I notice his fresh buzz and goatee trim.

"Morning, Izzy." He says without lifting his attention from his newspaper.

"The Starbucks smells terrific. What's up?"

"Wars, rumors of wars, stock market decline, more government mandates." He shrugs. "The usual."

I smile. Winston is a political conservative, and I am a vote-for-the-man-not-the-party person.

My eyes rove around the sales floor. "And in other news?"

Winston lowers his voice, tears his gaze from the paper. "Birdie came in early. He didn't look happy."

"Does he ever look happy? I so look forward to the day when I. Don't. Care."

"I understand, Iz. I'm sorry."

I open the newspaper and the smell of ink blossoms. "I'm hoping things will come to a head soon. Maybe...he won't work out. I can dream, right?" I take a sip of coffee and study his tie. He'd chosen a normal necktie instead of bowtie today.

"Winston, what are the red things on your tie?"

"Sharks." He gazes at me with those calm eyes of his.

"Why are they red?"

"Sharks are drawn to the smell of blood in the water." He glances at Birdie's office, then sticks his nose back in his newspaper. "Thought it was appropriate."

Birdie's office door jogs open. His overly pale visage appears. He catches my eye and motions me in.

I curse under my breath.

Winston flips his reading glasses off his nose and begins to move his fingers up and down the lanyard.

Like the proverbial dead man walking, I trudge the ten feet of carpet to his office door. I flinch when he closes the door.

"I have a problem, Izzy, and I need your input." His expression is unreadable in the curtains-drawn gloom of his office. Since I now report to Phil, I'm not sure why my presence is required.

"Okay."

He smiles. "Your friend Tyler is still hanging around. I don't think you want Phil involved in this, so I thought you and I could put our heads together. Come up with a plan."

A big gotcha. I think about how to respond. I'm not sure he's on solid ground with this, and I'm certainly not.

"Tyler is emotionally unstable, and I've taken care of it with a protective order. Standing around the office is public domain, right? He's out on the sidewalk, and he doesn't know when I'm here, so my protective order won't apply, will it? If you have a problem, you should make a police report for a record, I'd think. On behalf of the newspaper. Have you talked to Legal?"

Birdie presses his fingertips together and scowls.

This isn't going as he's hoped.

I suppress a grin.

He clears his throat. "Let me be clear. If Tyler sets one foot in this office lookin' for you, it will be immediate grounds for dismissal."

Alarm bells clang through my brain. He's setting me up.

"That's Security's job. I'd suggest alerting them." I jerk out my cell and text a photo of Tyler to Birdie's number. "There. Share it with Security."

He is unfazed. "Maybe it would be a good idea to get Phil's take on this."

The insinuated threat fogs the air between us.

Birdie doesn't know that I've taken Phil into my confidence. I feel like a cornered informant with a crooked cop. It occurs to me that he's just like Ethan. I frown and jam my arms across my chest. No. Ethan is worse than Birdie. Or maybe they're equal.

"I've checked the HR regulations, and "harassment" or "stalking" is defined as immediate grounds for dismissal, in case you didn't know," Birdie says, condescension dripping from his lips like a leaky faucet.

My temper flares. "That regulation means that no *employee* should stalk or harass. It isn't talking about a situation like mine."

He looks at me with contempt, then swivels his chair to his screen, dismissing me. "It can be interpreted both ways. Have a good day, Izzy."

Winston looks up when I return.

"Your face is white as a sheet, girl."

"I hate him," I mutter.

Winston murmurs comforting things, but I can't hear them. Did he mean that Tyler was outside *this morning?*" I cringe at the thought and pull up Detective Lopez's number on my cell. My fingers hover over his number.

I'm sure he doesn't want to talk to a hysterical female at this hour of the morning about a 'what if.' I abort the call.

Lonnie approaches and slides into his cube. "How's it going?"

"It's going." My gaze slides to Birdie's office.

"What's he done this time?"

I smile at Lonnie. He's been such a trooper these last few weeks. I give him the basics, but stop short of dumping it all. Lonnie is an assistant, not a colleague, and I don't want to be responsible for the spread of rumors. Although I doubt Lonnie is that kind of guy, there's a lingering hesitation when I talk to him. I've been burned enough to pay attention to certain signals.

That's my hope, anyway.

Chapter Twenty-Eight

Piccolo is a great neighborhood restaurant and bar ten minutes from my house. Tonight, I meet the latest online tingle before going to the meeting that Georgia Family Services requested. Well, *requested* is not the right word, but whatever. Meeting this guy may constitute a final act of defiance, but I don't care. I'm looking forward to it.

My Honda jerks against the curb. I correct my angle and park. My heart skitters in my chest. Patting my hair into place on the way to the entrance, I walk inside and sit at the bar.

This time feels different. I acknowledge nerves, but also the desire to get home to my kids before the blasted meeting starts at eight p.m. I'll have an hour-long first meeting with this man, then I'm out. I find myself almost wishing for a no-show.

My eyes adjust to the dim lighting. Airy, light hardwoods cover the floors, and plantation shutters adorn the windows. The tables have live flower centerpieces.

Piccolo is touted for its great food and friendly staff, but its main appeal is the great wine selection by the glass. I can live without sumptuous decor, but the wine list has to deliver. I order a French bordeaux. One glass, and that's it. My gorgeous guy is now fifteen minutes late. When I finish the wine, if he doesn't show, I'll leave. My support group will have to forgive me for being a tad tipsy.

A brief shaft of light splits the dimness as the door opens and shuts. The hostess minces to her station, asks if the man would like restaurant or bar, and he points toward me. I wave and smile. On a lust-worthy scale of one to ten, the guy rates a strong nine-and-a-half. The hostess is disappointed as she relinquishes him to me.

Sorry, chickadee.

I light up like a firefly as he approaches, forgetting my new leaf that has been turned over. It is hard for me to keep my jaw from dropping. He gives me a side-hug and cheek-buss.

"You are every bit as pretty as your picture." He beams and looks around the room. "Nice place. What are you having?" I tell him. He orders a fruity, girlie drink. I forgive him. Some things can be taught.

His drink arrives. I am tongue-tied due to stress, guilt, exhaustion or a combination of all three.

I clear my throat. "They have a great wine list here; that's why I suggested this place." I resist telling him I live right around the corner. "So, what are some of your favorite spots?"

He gulps down his drink in two swallows, orders another. My brows knit together. I am adjusting on the fly. I suppose the talks with Birdie, Phil, Jon…and Darlene…have draped a big, fat, wet blanket across my typical dating operatives. The fluttery eyelashes, seductive commentary, trilling laughter have vanished. I frown and drink more wine.

He clutches his empty drink glass like a rosary. "I live in Driftwood, y'know, up north of Emerald Spring? I don't get to the city lights much, just to work, then it's a forty-five-minute drive home." His new drink arrives, and he surrenders one glass for another. "I have two boys, and they take up a lot of my time."

"Kids do usurp a social life, don't they?"

He gazes at me with a smile. "I'm not sure what 'usurp' mean, but if it means 'sucks,' I agree." He kicks back the second drink.

"Usurp means to preclude." Too late, I realize that he won't know what that means either. "So…you're a sales rep, too. How's business? It's tough for me out there."

Casual conversation. Getting to know each other. No commitment. I sip my wine and glance at the time. Men love to talk about what they do for a living. I'll give him another twenty minutes, then bounce.

He grins. "Now, that's kind of a secret."

A secret? Really? Interesting.

"You CIA or something?"

He places his drained glass on the bar with a clunk and circles his index finger at it. The bartender nods and begins preparing another. The guy downed two fluffy drinks in fifteen minutes. Shouldn't he be throwing up or something by now? The bartender brings the drink over, glancing at me in what I construe as brotherly disapproval, before he sets it down in front of the man from Driftwood.

After a big glug of the drink, he pats my hand. "Don't you worry your pretty little self about that. Let's just say I sell something that's necessary to our survival as a nation."

"Don't I get the least, tiny, little hint?" I prod, curious. If I am going to hammer the last nail in this guy's coffin, I want to go out in a blaze of glory. I know better than to hook up with a conspiracy theorist or an apocalyptic weirdo. Anyway, he'd patted my hand. I'm not fond of men who pat my hand like I'm five years old.

He winks. "We have a patent on a device that will revolutionize the energy industry. Just takin' a little while for some folks to catch the vision. We utilize methane gas."

"Um. You mean the, uh, cow thing?"

"Cattle have four stomachs. Can you guess what that means to the climate? We can harness the methane just like we harness the wind."

The irony of meeting a man online that harnesses cow farts for a living is overwhelming. The laughter gurgling up my throat erupts as a snort, and it'll graduate to a full-on hysterical laughing fit if I don't get out of here.

The early dinner crowd arrives. I decide leaving is the better part of valor. Which is sad because the guy's looks could stop traffic.

I huff out a sigh, slip off my stool, hoist my purse on my shoulder, tell him it's been nice but, I have work to do, and hope he has a nice drive back to Driftwood. He is pleasant enough, but I see question marks in his eyes. He'll have to fill in the blanks himself, because I am done. I motion the bartender to bring my bill, then pay my tab. Give him a long, sad, goodbye hug. His abs are hard as rocks. Ah. Well.

I laugh all the way home. Why do the great-looking ones have the most deficits? It just isn't fair.

I unlock the garage door to the kitchen with relief, glad I can cross that one off the list, and the fleeting thought occurs (again) that I should consider taking a break. I push the thought away. Like I said, fleeting.

I run upstairs to change, run back down to give mom-hugs all around, and prepare a light dinner for the kids. They catch me up on their various activities, and I counter with a full-throated, diplomatic explanation of why I must attend support meetings.

Their enthusiasm is daunting and vocal, but then again, the roller coaster of the past few weeks is unlike anything I've ever known. Nothing surprises me at this point, and at least they're happy about it.

I throw on jeans, bulky sweater, and boots. I drag lipstick across my mouth, fluff my hair with my hands and hop in my Honda, caressing the dashboard. Who doesn't love a Honda? I plug in the address on my GPS, which takes me through west Emerald Spring to Peachtree Road. After a few minutes, I spy a group of low-slung, whitewashed stucco office buildings and pull into the parking lot.

To the side of the entrance is a free-standing sign that says, *"There is strength in shared support. All welcome."* I fight an overwhelming desire to rocket back to my car. Home is where I belong. *Home.* With my kids. I'll ignore the apps, promise, I tell myself.

Not without help, myself says back to me.

According to Thelma, if I don't open this door, consequences will drop like dominos.

I pull open the door and walk inside.

A cute woman with shiny, dark hair and wearing large, red glasses smiles. She sits behind a desk loaded with books and information. "Welcome."

I thrust Thelma's card under her nose and blurt out my name.

"Oh, yes, I got a call from Thelma today." She pulls a group of documents together and paper clips them. "Here you go. This'll explain why we do

160

what we do. The meeting starts in five minutes, right down that hall." She points, then says, "After the joint introduction meeting, you'll divide into smaller groups. You'll be in the love and relationship group, Isabelle."

"Love and relationship?" I repeat, confused. "I thought it was a divorced women's support group?"

She tilts her head. "Thelma and I feel this is a better fit. She consults a notebook. "The online dating? That's the primary issue, right? Love and Relationship is a sub-group of the Codependency group."

I frown. Issue? It's a release, a soft breeze, an escape from the harsh reality of my life. Issue? It's so much more than that it's—

"It's such a trap," the woman interrupts.

I frown. Had she read my thoughts?

"You'll be surprised how many women have a lot in common with your struggles, Isabelle."

She waves me down a hallway into a large meeting room. Struggle? Online dating is a lot of things, but it's not a struggle. Not to me. This is a mistake. Curling my arms around my waist, I walk into a large meeting space. Rows of metal chairs have been set up in front of a small stage. People chat in clusters around the room. There are refreshments and bottles of water. Nobody pays any attention to me. I feel about as comfortable as a turtle without a shell. Pulling out my phone, I stare at it, willing it to have a text that my kids need me. Something.

But there's nothing.

I walk to the back row and sit.

No one sits beside me or comes to talk to me. My shoulders hunch. My nerves are frighteningly raw. This is not working. I pop up, wiggle out of the row, and pick up speed as I approach the exit.

"Izzy?"

I pause my escape with extreme reluctance. Turn around and look right into Jon Hoyt's face.

Jon's eyes crinkle at the corners with his grin." I'm glad you're here. This is a great bunch of folks. What group are you in?"

"Love and Relationship."

Jon nods. "You'll love it."

I grimace. "Sure I will. Whatever. I'm here under protest."

He is quiet.

I groan. "Between my ex and Family Services that got involved when my son had an accident...I had no choice."

"Izzy," Jon begins, his voice kind. "Sometimes we can't be objective about the help we need."

I look away. We are quiet a few seconds.

My reticence slips a little. "'We'll have war stories to share at work, anyway," I joke.

Jon considers the line. "We'll have *progress* to share, Izzy. You'll see." He glances at the people starting to filter into chairs. "Want to sit together?"

And just like that, a new journey begins. With a roll of my eyes, I follow Jon.

The lights come up, and a man steps to the podium and welcomes us. He congratulates we peon newcomers as if stepping through the door the first time is tantamount to winning an Olympic medal, and encourages us to keep coming back. Announcements are relayed, and the lights dim. A hushed expectancy fills the room. A couple of people walk to the podium.

I'm not totally on board, but at least I'm willing. With a sigh, I glance at Jon. He elbows me and grins. I'm grateful for his support.

However.

I still have time to dash out to my car and disappear.

One man shares his struggle with addiction, another shares how becoming a part of his group has changed his life, a woman walks up and talks about how she'd fallen into sex trafficking. All I can think is that I didn't belong here with this group of people that can't manage their lives...who disclose choices that almost destroyed them, or their families.

The large group concludes, we are given directions to our small groups, and Jon tells me to 'have a good group', whatever the hell that means. I walk down a narrow hallway and stop in front of the door. What am I doing? Panic floods my nervous system.

The door swings open. I back away. A short wisp of a woman with silver, wiry, Brillo-Pad hair, merry blue eyes, and an infectious smile motions me in. "Welcome."

I step back a pace. "I'm, uh…Isabelle…Izzy for short."

"Welcome, Izzy-for-short." She chuckles at my expression. "We don't bite, promise. Come on in and meet the girls." Women of all ages sit on metal chairs, chatting. Their smiles are warm and inclusive.

I let out a breath and sit.

The leader closes the door, shares group guidelines. When it is my turn to introduce myself, I stutter out a few words. I have no idea what to say or what to expect.

When all these women shout, "HI IZZY!" I am stunned. I feel overwhelming acceptance, but my resentment at being forced to do this trumps the acceptance. "I'm here because I want to find a good guy to marry." I shrug. "What's wrong with that, anyway? Isn't this a good thing to want?"

The circle goes quiet.

My eyes dart around the circle. "I could lose my kids. Or my job." My voice drops to a whisper on the last few words. Tears well up in my eyes. I see a box of tissue in the middle of the floor, and realize that its placement there is on purpose. I pull out a tissue and sit back down. "Anyway, that's it, thanks."

To my surprise, they applaud. This causes me to extract another tissue from the box on the floor.

After an hour of listening to other women share the evisceration of their lives by their clueless choices in partners, I am an emotional wreck. The transparent sharing of their lives triggers an avalanche of insight into my own disasters. Regret squeezes my heart so hard I feel nauseous. The leader of the group approaches me afterward.

"You alright, dear?" I look into her kind face and mumble that it's hard.

"It'll get easier. Until you embrace the consequences of your choices, you can't forgive yourself. That's the first step. It hurts, but in a good way. Just keep coming." She gives my back a little rub, then dashes away to offer the same sweet reassurance to other women. Women just like me. With the same good desires and the same dumb choices to get there.

I think about Darlene. She is the only other person who'd been this honest with me. I wonder if I can keep it up. My hand seeks the coin in my pocket that Jon had given me. As I rub it, I feel the stirrings of change.

Chapter Twenty-Nine

My bed feels warm and soft.

I lay on my back with my hands behind my head, reliving the evening.

To think that there are untold numbers of women just like me is mind-boggling. Women who are so desperate for male companionships that they sacrifice time, effort, money—even their kids. Their stories swim through my mind as I drift to sleep. Chad, Mimi, and Peter had pounced on me the second I got home. They wanted details. As I related the evening's events, the primary reaction I saw on each face had been relief.

Pure, unadulterated relief.

Tears slip out. I hadn't known how deeply my dating life had affected them. Can they forgive me? Can I forgive myself?

All I know is that something big is happening. Something pivotal.

Sleep won't come

I toss and turn and finally throw off the comforter.

The hushed darkness as I walk downstairs is intimidating. Pausing on the stairs to listen, I hear nothing but the whir of the heating unit as it revs up and the hum of the refrigerator.

Still spooked about the whole stalker thing, I walk through the house, checking windows, the alarm, the garage. Detective Lopez called earlier in the day to let me know he'd had a sit-down with Tyler, but there hadn't been enough evidence to arrest. The latest notes had no fingerprints on them, and Tyler denies leaving them. They'd let him go. This fuels an anxiety spike, which in turn, fuels my desire for my favorite stress reliever.

Warning flags flap in my mind as I pull my laptop from the charging station and log in, but I ignore them.

As fate would have it, there are six reasons to make contact. The validation slakes a deep thirst in my soul. The desire for validation is palpable. My stress takes a back seat. My fingers hover over the keys. Who should I contact first?

In a split second of what the group tonight called *sanity*, I drop my head and ask God to intervene.

At that moment, the home alarm shrieks. Two seconds after that, my cell buzzes. I leap from my chair and answer. My hands are shaking.

"Ms. Lewis, your alarm has signaled us that there may be an intruder. We've notified the police, who should be arriving in approximately three minutes. Are you okay?"

"Yes, yes, but I need to check my kids' rooms."

"Ms. Lewis, keep us on the line." Holding the phone, I spot-check the security app as I walk upstairs. Whoever or whatever it was, isn't showing on the footage.

"I am walking to their rooms now," I whisper and enter each room. Peter is up, dragging on his pants. Chad stands at his bedroom door, rubbing the sleep from his eyes. "Cops are on the way. Let's check on Mimi."

I open Mimi's door. The stuffed animal menagerie is on the floor, her bed rumpled. Her window is open, the curtains softly billowing. Her bathroom door is closed. My mouth drops. Had she gone out through the window? Had someone taken her?

"Mimi!"

The fan in the bathroom stops, and she opens the door.

"Mom?" She steps out, her intense, hazel eyes wide. Sun-streaked, blonde hair twists in unruly waves over her shoulders. I motion all the kids into her room and lock the door. We plop on the bed as a unit.

"The police will be here any minute. We just need to stay together." I stare at her open window. "Mimi, did you...do that?"

Her hands fly to her face in embarrassment. "Oh gosh, I wasn't thinking."

"It's okay, Mimi." I run my hands through my hair, take a deep breath. Not exactly the way I'd have chosen to interrupt the temptation to shop for men, but whatever works. I call the company and tell them to cancel.

"Okay, guys, back to bed now, but lock your doors, okay?" They agree and leave. I hug Mimi, tell her to be more careful, and over my daughter's shoulder, my eyes fall to her desk, upon which sits her school laptop, open to a familiar profile.

I squeeze my eyes shut, then look again. My mouth drops open. "What's this?" She looks at the ceiling and crosses her arms. "Okay, so I stayed up too late. What's the big deal?"

"Well, for one thing, you'll be dead tired tomorrow." I peer more closely at the profile and to my horror, see that it's Tyler! Panicked, I sift through the messages.

"MOM!" Mimi tries to jerk the laptop from me. I push her away.

"What the heck are you doing?" she cries.

I scan through the communication. "Do you know who this guy is? Do you have any idea?!"

"It's none of your business!" she yelps. "I have my own life. He's a nice man, and he helps me. He's like a big brother."

I look at her in disbelief. "You have two awesome big brothers." At a loss for words, I quickly find her settings and block him. Then I turn to my daughter, who sits hunched into a ball on her bed, her back toward me.

I hate myself with a raging hatred.

Nothing is worth this. *Nothing.*

It's not an accident that I'd seen this; it's a wake-up call before something horrible happens.

"Mimi, I'm not leaving this room until we talk."

Winston is well through coffee-and-newspaper time when I arrive at the top of the stairs. I'm running late and emotionally drained from my talk with Mimi, but at least I'm here. Only ten minutes late. A miracle.

Unpacking Mimi's baggage had been intense and punctuated by crying and wailing and a sleepless night. For both of us.

I glance around the sales floor, hoping Phil is in the coffee break area with the other managers. The coast seems clear, so I run to my desk, drop my purse in the drawer, and shut it with a bang.

Winston doesn't miss a beat. "Phil's in the back, so he won't know when you arrive, and I haven't seen Birdie this morning." He says this with his eyes locked on the newspaper, then looks at me and smiles. "Don't understand why commission salespeople have to arrive at eight-thirty on the dot, anyway."

I smile. "Me either. What's going on?"

He thinks a minute. "No calamities that I know of. Yet."

"Maybe one will come along any minute now."

One of his hands drifts to the ever-present lanyard. His fingers work at it relentlessly.

He leans over the divider and whispers, "When, exactly?"

I lean toward him until we are almost nose-to-nose. "Watch and see."

He grunts. "That doesn't tell me anything."

"If you see the HR Director wandering in and out of Phil's office or Birdie running around, something's happening."

He responds, "Birdie is on full tilt. What's going on with him?"

"Not sure. I'm going for coffee, want any?"

Winston grimaces. "I'm fasting from the stuff."

I grin at him, dash to the back, make a pit stop at Darlene's desk before I fill my mug.

She looks away from her computer screen. Rubs her eyes. "Morning. How are you?"

"That support meeting I was dreading? It turned out to be good."

Her face lights up. "I'll be glad when life gets back to normal for you. That's such a great step."

I give her a quick thumbs-up and continue the next few paces to the coffeemaker. My nose twitches at the slight scent of male cologne, a hint that the managers have huddled around the coffee.

The upper-tier professionals of the advertising department of *The Emerald Spring Sentinel* form a casual loop. As I approach, I notice that Birdie stands outside the circle—a subtle nod to his indiscretions that are dragging themselves into the light of day.

Vindication feels amazing.

A chorus of good mornings greets me; a few cups lift in salute. We banter about my accounts, a refreshing alternative to bantering about my online activities. My self-confidence, which I had apparently misplaced, is renewed. I feel a comforting camaraderie with this group today.

Out of the corner of my eye, I notice a man walking from the production department into the sales department. When he passes by Darlene's desk, he stops and asks her something. She points, then drops her hand. Jerks her chair around to look at me with rounded eyes. I put my mug down, slow and careful. My world narrows.

I stare at the managers in a convivial circle around me. They have no idea that a train wreck is imminent. *Phil.* Where's Phil? I spot him chatting with the production team in the back offices and breathe a sigh of relief. Maybe I can head this off.

I forego the coffee, slip away from the breakroom and walk toward Tyler. My hands ball into fists. How should I handle this?

The frames proceed in my mind like stop-motion photography. He takes a step. I take a step. He takes another. I take another. Tyler approaches Winston, who rises and extends his right hand for a shake. The men clasp hands. I watch Winston internalize who the guy is, ratchet through what could happen, then turn his head toward me.

I raise my arms to each side, my eyes wide and despairing. He nods in understanding and continues chatting with Tyler. I hear him ask him where he's from, how he knows me, and more. The words reach my ears in sluggish sound bites.

Stay calm. You can do this.

Like an epiphany, I know what to do. I approach, walk to my desk and act as if I don't realize who he is. Instead of exhibiting the shock and awe going on inside my soul, I paste a wide smile of surprise on my face. "Tyler! What are you doing here? Did you have business with the *Sentinel?* Do you need our help?"

He swivels his head from Winston to me. His eyes are vacant, and his clothes are rumpled.

I swallow the lump in my throat. "I've gotten all the notes, Tyler. I've been meaning to talk with you."

He frowns. "I sent *one* note. That's what I told the detective. Don't you believe me, either? I didn't send the last two."

My eyebrows jerk together in confusion.

"They never enforce those protective order things, you know. You didn't have to do that."

Winston gives me a look. His hands stall on the lanyard.

Phil and Birdie, and the classified managers walk from the back toward Phil's office. Tyler grimaces at the sight of Birdie.

I frown. Winston's eyes are wide.

My breath comes in shallow gasps. In a burst of understanding, I know what that dark cloud around Birdie means. Why I'm the target of his crap. I get Tyler to focus. "How do you know Birdie?"

He blinks. Once. Twice. His distress is obvious.

I glance at Birdie, sweat sprouting on my brow. Thank God he hasn't noticed Tyler.

"That's what I wanted to tell you," he whispers. "Birdie thinks I'm helping him get you fired." His eyes slice toward the corner office, where the three managers have settled in to chat. "He thinks I'm his little errand boy, a 'useful idiot,' to quote Lenin."

My chin jerks into my neck. I glance at the conference room. "Winston," I hiss. Is anybody in there?"

"Not that I know of. You..." He points toward the room, his jaw working. Want to take him in there? Alone?"

I drag Tyler by his sleeve. "Let's go."

Winston leaps up. "I'm going with you."

The three of us traipse into the conference room and shut the door. I push Tyler into a chair. "Start talking." I take out my cell, set it to record.

He rubs his eyes. Leans an elbow on the table. "God, I'm so tired. I haven't slept." He looks at me with road-map eyes. "I'm not a stalker Izzy. Look, yeah, I wanted to meet you, and I was mad when you blew me off. When I found out where you worked, I…well, I went on the website and saw that jerk's photo." He frowns. "I went a little nuts. Believe me, I was going to leave you alone, but you needed to know about him. Everything I'm doing right now…it's all about him."

My lips part in surprise. Winston is riveted.

"Birdie is scum. My mom was an investor in his furniture outlet stores. She'd been in the business thirty-five years. Her whole savings was tied up in that chain, and when he was charged with embezzling, it might as well have been a kill shot. Birdie, and by proxy, the outlet stores, became toxic. Mom was his business partner. You couldn't ask for a nicer or more honest woman." His voice drops to a whisper. His eyes are on the floor.

"What happened?" I glance at Winston. For once, he's not taken hold of his lanyard.

Tyler's nostrils flare. He sweeps his arm to one side. "They had a meeting. She tried to reason with him. She lost over a *quarter of a million bucks*. Right down the drain. Birdie laughed at her. Said he was protected, and it was up to the courts." Tyler frowned. "That would've taken years. Mom couldn't wait that long, and she couldn't afford an attorney. Birdie had mortgaged his assets in some kind of con, and the equity was gone. You know what Birdie told her?'

Winston and I can't breathe, much less speak.

He snorted. "To file bankruptcy, that he wasn't her *social security*."

He straightens. His chin quivers.

"A week later, she died of a heart attack."

I gasp.

He gives me a flinty stare. "So yeah, this guy? He's cancer. All I wanted was to tell you this story. So you could tell your management that maybe…" He shrugs. "Maybe they don't need an employee that murders a business on purpose." His head drops. "And people."

I feel terrible for him. But still. There are questions.

"Tyler, did you come to my house and walk around the backyard? Around the fence back there, and try to get in?"

171

He frowns. "I didn't."

My heart speeds up.

"Did you open the window in the back, get inside and plant a note on my kids' car?"

"Of course not," he spits out.

I think about the police investigation. The fact that there had been no prints on the final two notes. "Did you contact my twelve-year-old daughter?"

He groans. "She reached out to me. I'm sorry about that. She must've seen your site open or something? I don't know how she found me, but she managed to create a profile for herself and chat with me on one of those apps. She told me who she was and asked me questions about online dating and that sort of thing. I couldn't tell you. I would have, but...the protective order had become a problem, and I doubt you would've listened." He shrugged. "Or believed me. I told her to talk to you about what she was doing. I did not encourage a relationship, I promise you."

"She told me she liked you because you were like a big brother."

He smiles and reaches for me. "Izzy, I..."

I hold out an arm. "No. Just...no."

"Okay." He straightens in the chair. "Listen. I'm not who you think I am. I'm a heartbroken son who wants justice for his mom. All Birdie got was a fine and probation. No jail time. There were others, too, that invested in those stores, but not like Mom. That was all she had. Dad died ten years ago. She was counting on a future without having to struggle, y'know?"

"What did Birdie want from you, Tyler?"

"He was setting me up as the fall guy. I didn't do half the stuff he wanted, I just acted like I did. But he wanted me to spy on you and report back." Tyler smiles, crosses his arms. "He thought we were a team, and I figured I'd let him think that way. Birdie is real interested in online hook-ups; plus, I think he's got a thing for you.

I wince.

"Worse, he's after your job."

"Why? If I have a good year, he gets rewarded for it."

172

Tyler shakes his head. "He doesn't stop until he sucks the life out of whatever blocks his path. He thinks one of those things is you."

My mind is blown.

"We probably need to get Tyler out of here, Izzy," Winston says. "Until we figure out next steps."

Tyler shakes his head. "I apologize for my reaction when you didn't want to go out with me again. It's been a helluva two years." He stares at the floor, threads his fingers. "When I saw Birdie, it was like...fate, y'know? He has no idea who I am. I saw it as an opportunity for justice and went with the flow. I wanted to see where it went and how I could..." His eyes darken. "Then he gets all buddy-buddy and suggests I go after what I want." Tyler rolls his eyes. "As far as he knew, I was there to get you to go out with me. So he tells me to 'go after what I want'. Like he's my freaking life coach."

"Tyler. If what you say is true, he's implicating you in serious stalking charges. I mean, the protective order is not a joke. It's a real thing. And I got it because someone else planted those notes and made us think it was you. I think he's setting you up."

Tyler goes pale. He licks his lips.

"He had me follow you, Izzy. I didn't, though. He thinks I did."

I frown. "Why?"

"He wanted to know your activities...I think he wanted to catch you going out...partying, who knows? He wanted photos, too."

"But...if you didn't plant the notes, who did? And who scared the crap out of me at night creeping around my backyard?"

"He got somebody, I guarantee it. That's how he operates."

"Who let you in the building? You came in the back, through production. It takes a code to get in."

"Birdie gave me his code. I didn't know people had separate codes."

I glance at Winston. The time of Tyler's entry could be corroborated.

"You wouldn't have had to do that, you know."

"I only did it to so I could finally tell you all this. I wanted to slip in and try to get your attention and talk a few minutes. That's all." He laughs. "Now I know how right I was about him."

A soft knock sounds on the door. "Izzy? You in there?" Birdie opens the door. When he sees Tyler, he frowns. "Who's this?"

Tyler closes his eyes, shakes his head. "You're such a dumbass, Birdie."

"What did you say to me? Who are you?" Birdie barks.

"I'm the one who's going to take you down, you sick piece of shit." Tyler explodes from his chair and head-butts Birdie's stomach. When Birdie doubles over in surprise, Tyler wraps his hands around Birdie's neck and squeezes.

Winston springs into action. "Someone call Security!" he yells through the open door.

Tyler and Birdie tumble out of the doorway onto the salesroom floor. Winston tries to pull Tyler's hands apart with no luck. I watch Phil's shocked face through the glass walls of his office. He bursts out of his office and barrels toward us. Sales reps pop up from their cubicles.

Tyler screams curses at Birdie, all the bitterness and grief from his mother's death pouring out through his hands, still locked around Birdie's neck. Two burly male security guards explode from the stairs and run across the room. Each struggles to pry Tyler off, but his rage, passion, and desire for justice have given him a superhuman strength. "You killed her!" he screams. "You killed my mother! You're going to hell where you belong!" Tyler's face is blood-red. Veins protrude from his neck. The guards point their weapons and command Tyler to let go. Birdie's face is turning blue. His tongue protrudes from his mouth, and he's struggling to breathe.

The cops burst onto the floor, take in the scene, pull their weapons. One cop races across the room, yelling at people to get down, get down, get down! The other moves in on Tyler.

Detective Adrian Lopez walks into the space, pulling up the rear. He stands with legs wide, hands in pockets, watching. He takes in the scene, clearly puzzled.

Tyler relaxes his grip. With the advent of two robust guards plus Emerald Spring PD aiming weapons at his center mass, the fire in his belly dwindles. He lets go. Birdie drops to the floor in a dead faint. Tyler falls to his knees and puts his hands behind his head.

I hear the soft counts of CPR compressions as one of the cops works to resuscitate Birdie. Phil hovers around the perimeter, alternating between wringing his hands and glaring at me.

Winston is his calm, inscrutable self. Standing apart, but watchful and ready to jump in when necessary. I know Darlene is in the crowd somewhere, but she's so tiny I can't see her over everybody else. Across the room, as far as possible from the action, stands Lonnie. Why isn't he over here watching this bizarre thing unfold? I squint at him.

Lonnie can't look me in the eyes.

It's him.

He's the one Birdie's been using to drop notes and skulk around and...*wow*. He's acted so interested in my life the last few weeks. My naiveté is gag-worthy, yes...but Lonnie's stupidity is outstanding. His job, and maybe his whole life... are toast after this. When Birdie starts breathing again, the cops help him to his feet. Phil dances around like a deranged monkey, flapping his arms, yelling instructions at people, doing his best to mitigate anything he can. Which, of course, is impossible. He has no idea what is going on.

I sink into an exhausted puddle on the floor.

The elevator doors open, and out bursts the general manager. He strides toward us, scowling and determined. I close my eyes. I don't even want to think about all the garbage that's coming down on my head after this.

Detective Lopez approaches and squats down beside me. "What happened?"

"It's complicated." I see Lonnie sneaking past the ruckus, heading for the stairs. I pop up from the floor and stride over to Winston, whisper in his ear, then return to Lopez. Winston walks toward Lonnie, reaches out for his elbow. When Lonnie struggles, he twists his arm behind his back and makes him walk toward us. Detective Lopez gives me a look.

"You might want to talk to Lonnie." I pull out my cell and wiggle it. "I recorded an earlier conversation that you'll be interested in, too. I'll text it to you." I tuck the phone back in my pocket. "For context."

Detective Lopez runs a hand through his dark hair. Looks at Phil maniacally, trying to calm things down, the general manager in his grey suit, stiff and tall and glowering. Birdie and Tyler in cuffs. Birdie is yelling that he's been attacked and screaming for an attorney. Lopez shakes his head and tells a uniform, "Put the younger guy in an interrogation room. I'll be there soon." He glances at Birdie. "Shut up. An ambulance is on the way. We'll take your statement at the hospital."

I feel cold. My lower lip trembles. I'm worried about my kids and need to call them. Do I still have a job? What is happening? My mind blanks. Winston puts a fatherly arm around my shoulders after releasing Lonnie to the patrol cop. "Iz? You up to a visit to the station? They're going to want to talk to you."

I stare into Winston's reassuring gaze, breathing in his strength. He squeezes my shoulders and smiles. "Ok," I whisper.

"Ride with me," Detective Lopez says.

Chapter Thirty

I follow Detective Lopez, looking over my shoulder at Winston. Darlene is beside him. She puts her hands together in the classic prayer gesture, which makes me smile. I know both of these wonderful friends will be praying for me. Phil stands erect, his hands behind his back, his mouth a thin, firm line as he watches us leave. No telling what's going through his head.

I'll take all the prayers I can get if they'll save my job.

We ride the elevator down and walk outside. My whole life passed before my eyes the moment Tyler lunged for Birdie, and out here, nothing has changed. How is that possible? A pristine, blue sky holds cotton candy clouds. A few hardy leaves cling to the trees, tiny orange and red flags fluttering in the breeze. We get into a state-issued, unmarked, four-door sedan and pull away from the curb.

I text my kids and tell them I may be late tonight.

This time the colorful pansies that line the walk to The Emerald Spring Police Department entrance do their job. My spirits lift a little at the sight of them.

Detective Lopez and I stride up the sidewalk. A flash of recognition sparks in the eyes of the ill-mannered receptionist as we enter.

"Roberta, would you take Ms. Lewis to one of the interrogation rooms, please?" He looks at what she hands him through the window. "Izzy, I'll be there in a few minutes. Tell Roberta if you need water or a Coke or something." He smiles, leaves me alone with her. She tries, but fails...to

177

smile. Why do I have that effect on people?

I follow her ample backside down a hallway covered in linoleum that reeks of lemony antiseptic. We pass the same dust-colored walls and the same garish posters advertising Bulldog Auditorium's latest event. We arrive at Interrogation Room C. She pulls a key from her pocket and unlocks the door. I sit in a metal chair. I decline something to drink, and she leaves.

It's cold in the room. Rubbing my arms, I get up and pace. Back and forth, back and forth. I wonder why I'm in an interrogation room instead of his office. I fume and pace for fifteen minutes.

Detective Lopez opens the door. "Hey. Let's go to my office now, okay? I'm sorry to park you in here, but I needed time to listen to that recording and jot down a few questions."

I follow him to his office and sit in a chair that has actual padding. He notices me rubbing my arms, pulls a jacket off the coat rack, and hands it to me. I smile. "Thanks."

He folds his arms on the desk. "If I had any clue at all about where the truth is in this mess, I wouldn't have brought you in, Izzy."

"Do you believe Tyler?"

Lopez rubs his chin. "Have to admit, it's plausible. My patrol guys tell me Birdie denied knowing him the whole ride to the station. He's demanding a lawyer, which is his right, and complaining that he's a victim of police harassment or something." Lopez grins. "Don't think innocent people demand a lawyer right out of the chute."

I frown. "He *does* know Tyler. People saw him talking to him outside the office. There are witnesses. And you got the connection about his mother, right?"

He nods. "Okay. Give me the date people saw him out front. We'll ask around." I jot down a date and approximate time on a notepad he swings in my direction.

"And how did you say this Lonnie is involved?"

I shrug. "It's a hunch."

Lopez grimaces. "I brought him in on a hunch?"

I frown. "Isn't that what you guys do? Ask questions?"

"Better if we have a little more than a hunch, that's all."

We sit quietly a few seconds. I rub my eyes. "I'm worried about my job."

"I would be, too." He taps his fingers on the desk. "How about we have a meeting with your boss, uhh...the one above Birdie. What's his name?"

"Phil." I think about that. Would he come?

"Let's call him."

The wait until Phil answers feels like ten hours. Worry clouds my mind. What if Phil has already made up his mind? It could take months to find another job like this one.

"Phil," he barks. Lopez puts the phone on speaker.

"This is Detective Adrian Lopez. I have your employee, Izzy, in my office. I'm wondering if you could make time to join us."

Silence.

I put my hand over my eyes.

Lopez shrugs, looks at me as he waits.

"I'll be right there."

The call ends.

Lopez smiles. "There ya go. Let's keep your job."

After I introduce him to Lopez, Phil sits on the matching metal-and-gray vinyl chair beside me in Detective Lopez's modest office. Phil sips the coffee Roberta brought him and asks Lopez about the point of this this meeting.

"The more information we can gather, the better. We need to cover all the bases, and of course, you offer a unique perspective."

I smile, wondering if he's memorized this response and how many times he's used the term 'unique perspective'.

Phil looks at me. I notice the dark circles underneath his eyes. He doesn't need this, I know. Should I apologize? I frown. Does he blame me?

Lopez clears his throat. "So Izzy...you've told Phil," he gives Phil an inclusive glance, "as much as you know about what's going on?"

I nod. "Up until today."

Phil's face is a mask, the single indication of inner turbulence a slight tapping of his fingers on the arm of his chair.

"Alright, then. Phil, here we go." Lopez smiles at Phil, a smile that Phil doesn't return. He sits rigidly in the chair, holding the paper coffee cup.

"Let's lay the groundwork first, if that's okay with you, Phil. My first question to you is this: did your HR department run a routine background check on Birdie before hiring him?"

Phil frowns. "We'd been friends and business associates for ten years or more; we felt it unnecessary."

Lopez holds Phil's gaze for a second. "Birdie has a history of sexual harassment. None of the charges stuck, but it's my understanding that the victims changed their stories at the last minute. It would have been a slam dunk." He takes a brief call, jots something in his notebook, then lays the pen aside. "As in so many cases, the perpetrator pays off the victims to shut them up. That would be my suspicion." He rises, pulls open a drawer on the metal filing cabinet, and pulls out a file. Lays it on his desk. I look at the file's label. Costanza, Elias, (Birdie). I shudder. "Also, embezzlement. Didn't you wonder why his last business tanked?"

Phil crosses his arms. "Yes, I did. I was outranked."

"One of the investigators just got back to me. Seems that what Tyler Samuelson said on the recording is factual. His mother died of a heart attack one week after she learned of the demise of the parent company. That much is corroborated. Of course, that wasn't directly Birdie's fault, but it's not a leap to imagine Tyler Samuelson grieving and triggered by running across him."

Phil runs his hand across the top of his balding head. "I didn't know any of this."

Detective Lopez lifts his palm toward me, as if serving me up for dinner. My turn.

"I'll start at the beginning. Tyler wandered onto the floor, and I approached, not knowing what I was going to do but with the intention of diffusing the situation. I thought he was trying to find me for some weird pushback on my reluctance to go out with him again. It freaked me out to see him on the sales floor, and all I wanted to do was get him out of there without making a scene. When he started telling me all this stuff, I panicked. One, I knew he had history with Birdie, and two, we needed to go somewhere private to listen to what he had to say. Winston and I took him to the conference room, and I recorded the conversation. Detective Lopez has the recording."

Phil looked like he'd been punched in the stomach. "What did he tell you?"

"Tyler and I must've talked about where I worked on our first and only date. He found the website, and...saw Birdie. He feels Birdie is responsible for his mother's death."

Phil looked at Lopez and me in desperate appeal. "I'm hoping this doesn't end up a huge lawsuit, Izzy. I can't see a way out right now, so forgive me if I'm at a loss."

"I was trying to keep Tyler off the floor," I huff. "Also, Tyler isn't responsible for everything. Birdie's trying to make it look like that, but Tyler thinks there's someone else."

Phil closes his eyes and tilts his head back.

"Birdie is an instigator, Phil." Lopez steeples his fingertips.

Phil tries to put the pieces together. "An instigator in what way?"

Detective Lopez leans back in his chair, crosses his legs. "If it goes the way I think it will, all of it. How much do you know?"

Phil makes an angry gesture toward me. "What she told me. That Birdie was rude to customers and had it out for her. And about..." He looks at me. "What's your ex's name? The one you told me showed up at Raphael's under pretense?"

"Ethan."

Detective Lopez blinks. "Ethan? The one I met at Raphael's?"

I bite my lower lip.

"What does he mean by 'under pretense'?"

"You already had so much going on with me...I didn't want to add to it."

His brow furrows. "Ethan could be part of this situation, too. Ever think about that?"

Had I?

"I never considered he could be involved with Birdie, but I told Phil that my ex had called Birdie. Ethan knew that the one thing that would rattle me is the threat of losing my job. So under the guise of 'concern,' he calls my boss, pretending to be all worried about how my online dating is becoming a problem. I don't know if he had any communication other than that, but...who knows? The night we ran into you at Raphael's, he told me he faked a profile to lure me out to prove a point. That's why I was so jittery when I saw you. I thought I was meeting someone new that I'd met online. He shows up instead." I stare at the wall behind Lopez's chair. "He also said he'd report me to Georgia Family Services and file for custody if I didn't drop dating online." My voice is whispery with shame.

Detective Lopez puts his palms on his desk, stands, and leans over it until his face is twelve inches from mine. "What he's doing is called *extortion*. Georgia law doesn't allow an ex-husband to threaten an ex-wife with custody issues. Much less the online impersonation, which is *harassment*." He glares at me, then drops back into his chair, pinching the bridge of his nose. "Is that it?"

Phil cracks a smile. "Isn't that enough?"

"More than enough," Lopez acknowledges. He shuffles pages into a file, shaking his head. "Izzy, please text me Ethan's contact information. Meanwhile, in light of Tyler's recording, we need to discuss what happened. Tyler will lawyer up, I'm sure, but an investigator is chatting with him right now. He's going to wait for his lawyer in a cell. Phil, put Birdie on leave or whatever it is that you do, but we'll need him on the bench until this is resolved, understand?"

Phil nods. His face is ashen. "Is he being arrested?"

"We have nothing concrete, since he's camping out on denial. We can't hold him for long, but we'll try to get enough for a warrant and a hearing. I've got Lonnie in an interrogation room right now. He's just a kid. He'll spill all he knows, and I imagine he'll get probation and a fine and be back in no time. If you want him back."

Phil focuses on the detective's face. "If you'll advise me whether he's being charged? I'll need to funnel this through my HR department. In the meantime, Izzy, do you need him?"

The crushing feeling in my chest subsides. Is he saying I get to keep my job? "I can't trust him, Phil. Not after this."

He nods. "We'll find you someone else."

"Thank you." I want to leap into his lap and wrap my arms around him in gratitude. I settle for imagining it.

Detective Lopez grins. "Ok. Stay close, kids. We'll be in touch."

I give the jacket back to Lopez.

Phil and I walk outside and pause on the sidewalk.

He sticks his hands in his pockets. "What a huge mess."

I say nothing. I'm stressed and weirded out and feel guilty. I have no idea what to say.

"Need a ride?"

"Can you drop me at the parking lot?"

"Sure."

"I appreciate your patience, Phil."

He gives me a somber look. "Isn't over yet."

We walk in silence to his car.

Chapter Thirty-One

The black Lincoln Navigator idles in the parking lot of Messner, Scott & Ellis.

Birdie strolls down the steps after a two-hour meeting with his attorney, who told him, among other things, that he better keep his nose clean. The infractions from Missouri could sway a jury, and if he wanted to take this to court, it could get expensive. His attorney asked point blank if Tyler Samuelson's allegations were true.

"No!" Birdie proclaims to the interior of his SUV. He rams the car into drive and speeds from the parking lot toward the *Sentinel*. "Deny, deny, deny...that's the ticket." He chuckles. "What proof do they have?" he mutters. His word against that creep Tyler's. Who are they going to believe?

His lawyer planned to send an email to Phil advising him that he had no grounds for termination and, if enforced, the newspaper would receive a wrongful termination lawsuit. His attorney also disclosed that since Birdie is over sixty, age discrimination may come into play.

He rubs his hands together and smiles. He will walk into the office head held high, the long-suffering, wrongly accused victim. He can't wait.

Tyler is no match for these attorneys. He'd be brought to his knees with a slander suit and assault charges. However, his attorney is right. He needs to think about what a jury will believe before proceeding.

His eyes narrow. He knows better than to use his work computer for private emails, but he didn't have time to clear out his office before he was spirited away by the ambulance yesterday. His hand rises to his throat. A flush creeps up his neck onto his face. The feel of Tyler's hands around his neck is still fresh. He could've bought it right on the damn sales floor. What a way to go.

He curses, jerks the SUV into the parking lot, and strides to the entrance like he owns the place. Rides the elevator to the second floor. Juts his chin and clenches his jaw. When the doors part, the first person he sees is Izzy. The next is Winston. A one-two punch.

Jon Hoyt from Classified walks up to Izzy's desk and stands there as if daring him to say anything.

"Good morning," Birdie says and walks into his office. His laptop is gone. Further, he notes that his office door, which he always locks...is unlocked.

He falls into his chair. The veins in his neck bulge. He feels his blood pressure shooting through the roof. With a growl, he grabs a duck-hunting paperweight off his desk and throws it into the wall. It hits one of the framed prints that his wife had picked out for him. The artwork crashes to the floor. The glass explodes and blasts across the carpet.

The receptionist knocks and walks in. "Are you okay?" She takes in the shattered glass, the broken frame. "I'll get janitorial up here in a jiffy, Birdie." She leaves.

Birdie smiles. He's untouchable. If the *Sentinel* wants a war, bring it on.

Chapter Thirty-Two

The sun streams through my window.

The day after. That's how I think of it…the aftermath of my wake-up call. The day I admit that I'm an addict—that I have no control over my nightly romps into fantasy. The day after Tyler goes ballistic on Birdie, and the day after, Tyler reveals his true self. The huge and horrifying reality of what I've done sinks deep into my soul.

What's the axis upon which all these events hang?

My freaking online habit, that's what.

I groan.

None of it seems real. Why would Phil keep me? According to the employee handbook, he has every reason to fire me.

I just want to go back to sleep. I toss the comforter over my head.

A knock sounds on my door. "Mom?"

I throw back the comforter, jet out of bed. "Come in. I overslept."

Peter cocks his head. "You were here last night, right?"

I frown as we walk downstairs together. Peter has his backpack slung over one shoulder. "You, Chad, Mimi, and I talked until eleven o'clock. Did you think I was going to run out that late?"

He grins slightly and gives me a look.

I wave my hands like flags of surrender. "Okay. You have a point. No. I didn't go out, and yes, I was here."

I delete the part about staying up until three a.m. answering texts and cruising new matches and, in general, acting out in my addiction when a crisis hits, as Brillo Pad had informed the group was something to guard against. I wish for a meeting more often. I can't imagine how I'm going to get past this. When tension strikes, the sites are my go-to.

I wander into the kitchen, lean against the doorframe. "You guys have your homework? Eat breakfast?"

Mimi puts her bowl in the sink. "Yep," she says, then trots over and crushes me in a hug. Tears come to my eyes. Had our talk last night meant that much?

Chad shrugs into his backpack and saunters over. "I, uh…am proud of you for going to those meetings, Mom."

Peter smiles. "Come on, guys. Time to go."

I wave them down the street. Run upstairs to get ready to go into the office, but first, I check the sites to see what trouble I'd gotten myself into. I'd been so desperate for an escape after the bizarre events of yesterday that I'd logged on as soon as I could. Like a junkie needing a fix, I was unable to tear my hands from the keyboard. Every stroke, every message, every flirtatious icon…felt like heaven. However, in the calm light of day, I can't remember what damage I'd done. Had I been drinking, too? Judging from my headache, yes.

I log on to one site…all good. Another…no glaring red flags there. The third one…oh, no. No. No! Four profile photos of smiling matches mocked me from the screen, each messaging that they looked forward to meeting me. Tonight. I'd arranged four meet-ups on one night? This is crazy, even by my standards.

I must've hit the jackpot. I also must've been toilet-hugging drunk. My heart is as heavy as a stone. I'd indulged in this behavior *after* repenting to my darling children for all the hurt I'd caused them and promising to give up online dating because they are my priority, always and forever.

I slap the laptop shut. Stalk into my bedroom. Find Brillo Pad's card and locate my phone. Someone needs to talk me off the ledge before I destroy my life.

I scream into parking lot at nine-thirty a.m. and hope that Phil understands why I'm late again.

Detective Lopez calls as I'm driving to work and tells me they'd interrogated Birdie and let him go and that he didn't think a suspension would stick, either. Birdie had been adamant about his rights as an employee.

What am I walking into this morning?

Alighting from the elevator like some sort of paranoid deer, I look right and left, then leap to my desk. My security blanket, Winston, isn't in the cube, and neither is Lonnie. I am alone with my fresh newspaper.

The queen of the pod.

I drum my fingers on my desk, then unfold my newspaper.

One of the other coordinators slips into Lonnie's chair. "Can I do anything for you, Izzy?"

She smiles, but it's a 'wow, you really stepped into it this time, didn't you' smile. I stare at her round, cherubic face. She can't be over twenty-one. She tells me she has Lonnie's log-ins, that she is overseeing production of my ads, things are on track. I thank her, and she leaves.

I drop my purse into its drawer. Slump in my chair, and under half-masted eyelids, notice whispering and pointed fingers aimed in my direction.

How do I get anything done today? What client would want to talk to me in my godforsaken current mood? I jam my arms across my chest and pout.

Winston walks in, smiles, twirls his driving beret on his index finger, and zings it like a Frisbee to the coat rack. It lands on a hook. I laugh. Once again, Winston restores me.

He sits at his desk. "What are you doing here? Don't you need to take a couple of days?"

I rub the back of my neck. "I guess I need to feel productive."

"Well, take it easy today. Give yourself a break."

I turn the pages of my newspaper to the comics. On purpose.

"What's going around?" I suck on my bottom lip and pretend I'm wildly interested in 'Garfield'.

"People think Tyler is some psycho you met online. They're talking about his motivation to attack Birdie. I don't think it's registered with anyone yet that Lonnie is involved. What happened with everything? Are you okay?"

I fill him in on the meeting with Phil and Detective Lopez. His eyes brighten that Phil had come down on my side, even agreed to give me a new coordinator.

"What about Tyler? Do they believe him?"

"It doesn't matter. Tyler assaulted Birdie, and that charge will stick. Birdie's denying ever meeting the guy."

"Figures." Winston rises to get coffee. "I'll be back."

I open my desktop computer, log in, and calculate my functionality. Chirpy and persuasive is off the table, so client meetings are out. Maybe I should have stayed home. No, that would be worse. And besides, what would I be doing? Yeah, scouring the sites for men isn't going to help anyone. The comforting feel of Brillo Pad's card rustles in my pocket. I drag it out and put it on my desk where I can see it.

I scan the sales floor for Phil. Where is he?

A chuckle bubbles up.

A few weeks ago, Phil was someone to avoid or make excuses to about being late. Now, I miss my ally and supporter. What a difference a stalker makes. And a creepy manager.

Jon Hoyt walks over from the classified department, his hands in his pockets. "Hear I missed all the excitement yesterday. How you doing?"

Before I respond, Birdie exits the elevator.

The hair rises on the back of my neck.

I stare at him. He scowls at me. A showdown.

I don't know what to do or what to say. I look away. Jon folds his arms and holds Birdie's gaze.

"Good morning." Birdie's voice is flat. He walks into his office.

I look at Jon. "He...he's supposed to..." I clear my throat. "I didn't think he'd be here."

Phil exits the elevator. His face is drawn. He sees me and motions for me to follow.

"I'm available for lunch if you want to talk later." Jon smiles, walks back to his desk.

I hear the sound of a crash. The receptionist hops up, runs into Birdie's office.

I walk to Phil's corner office, which is only a wall away from Birdie's.

"Close the door." Phil drops into his chair, his lips thinned out in that way they do when he's got a problem.

Phil sighs. "Just got back from Legal. Izzy, I'm afraid we're going to have to tolerate Birdie until we have evidence that what Tyler told us is true. Right now, it's straight-up assault. Maybe attempted homicide. Birdie's in the clear." Phil grimaces. "He's the *victim*. And it happened in our office building. The ramifications of that are huge." Phil grimaces. "The GM and I are putting our heads together on next steps, but I need you to play nice."

My eyebrows pull together. "What happened?"

"He got a lawyer. As anyone would. I didn't think it would be an issue for him to lay low for a few weeks, but Birdie isn't going for it. His attorney threatened us with a civil suit, a liable suit, wrongful termination, and everything but the kitchen sink. The newspaper won't want to air this publicly. The, uh…publisher is involved now. He's talking to our attorneys."

I sit in my chair, quiet.

Phil runs a hand over his head. "This isn't you, Izzy. This is Tyler. Nobody could've predicted that Birdie and Tyler's lives were connected." Phil groans. "If it's anybody's fault, it's the GM's. I asked him to do a background check, drug test, the whole deal. He refused. He and Birdie are real tight." Phil chuckles. "Used to be, anyway." Phil gives me a look. Points his index finger back and forth between us. "This little get-together right now? This stays between us."

I nod. "No worries, Phil."

We share a beat of silence.

He drums the desk with his fingertips, thinking. "You going to be okay with him here? Do I need to let you…take vacation or something?"

I shake my head. "Thanks. I gotta grow up sometime."

He smiles. "We'll figure this out."

I tap my chin, stare out Phil's window to the busy street beyond, deep in thought.

Proof. Phil is talking about proof. *Evidence.* "Did I tell you how Tyler got in?"

Phil frowns. "Why?"

"He came in through production. There's a separate door back there. He came in with Birdie's code. Birdie gave it to him."

Phil's countenance clears. "And we keep a list of who enters their codes and when." After I give him a window of time when Tyler could've entered, he walks to the door. "I'm running down to Operations to check it out. That's a good thought, Izzy." He leaves.

I walk back to my desk, glancing at Birdie's closed door. How does he expect to manage a sales team after yesterday?

Chapter Thirty-Three

I walk outside and breathe in the night air. My second meeting had gone better than the first, and Brillo Pad had asked if I'd get up and share with the group. It had been hard to get started, but once I did, I couldn't quit. With the sharing, a forty-pound backpack of shame lifted from my shoulders. Also, we'd celebrated seven days of my sobriety. Seven whole days of avoiding the dating sites. Each day is a victory, and I'm getting stronger. My phone, a work phone, had always been a non-starter since, at any point, Phil could jerk my phone. Not that he would, but the thought is always in the back of my mind. I'd have to turn the phone in eventually, and what then? I may not have time to scrub it. So. The laptop has the stronger pull.

Brillo Pad and I talk every night. She's become my lifeline. The moment I feel a flicker of desire, I call her. She passes me on the way to her car. I wave. "Good job tonight," she calls.

Jon strolls out of the building. "Hi, there. Didn't know if you'd come back."

"How could you doubt me?" I tease.

"Habit." He grins. "How are things between you and Birdie? He's been sneaking around the office like a dog with its tail between its legs."

"I avoid him. It can't be easy for him after he threatened the newspaper with legal action. How do you go back to work after that?"

"I wouldn't," Jon says. "Some things aren't worth fighting for. If there's a toxic work environment, I'd be gone."

"But he's the toxic environment."

Jon shrugs. "You look great, Izzy."

"Seven days clean, as they say." I laugh. "Even my kids are commenting that I look better."

"Good job. Keep comin' back." He smiles and heads to his car.

I walk over to a bench and sit. People walk out to the parking lot or chat in small groups. The peace I feel is life-giving. Renewing. I watch all the brave people confronting their issues file outside, and feel a curious synergy. "So this is what progress feels like," I whisper.

My gaze falls on a lone, tall, young guy ambling along, his eyes on the sidewalk. I squint. Lonnie? If he's going to a group, that's a good sign. After all, I don't want to totally give up on him. Once, we were friends...or so I thought.

I rise from the bench and start toward him. "Lonnie?"

He startles at the sound of my voice. I watch the shift in his posture as he makes a decision. He turns. Watches me and waits.

"How'd it go?" I ask as I approach.

We both know I mean the fallout from his chat with Detective Lopez. His "brave face" crumples. I am reminded he's just twenty-two years old.

"Not good." Lonnie swipes at one eye. "I told them the truth, Izzy. The whole truth."

"Okay. Now tell me. What happened, Lonnie?"

He digs the tip of one of his Nikes into the concrete. "First, I want to tell you how sorry I am...not that you'd believe me, but..."

"Try me. Let's go sit."

We walk to one of the benches that bracket the concrete walkway. The night is chilly and clear. A full moon smiles upon us. Lonnie sits at one end, and I take the other.

"I was trying so hard," he blurts, after a long pause. "All I wanted was to be like you, a major accounts salesperson, and I thought Birdie could help with that. He was friendly and supportive." His expression hardens. "He's a snake."

I agree.

"Look," he turns sideways toward me, puts one arm on the back of the bench. "I fight a drug problem, okay? I've been going to meetings for a

193

while. Somehow he must've found out about it." Lonnie frowns, looks away. "Birdie got me all warmed up, y'know…like we were friends…like he was my uncle or something, and wanted to give me a hand up." He shakes his head in disgust. "And then he asked if I 'knew someone' that sold benzos. After that, he was off to the races, and I didn't have enough self-control to turn down what he was offering." He goes silent a few seconds. "All I had to do was dig into your life and report back."

My mouth drops open. I can see it. If Birdie finds a weakness, he exploits it. Lonnie is responsible for his choices, but what kid wouldn't want to impress the new boss? And when Lonnie weakens, boom. Birdie is right there to leverage it. "I understand, Lonnie."

"But still, I shouldn't have done it, Izzy! I've ruined everything. My parents are…they've been so patient and put me in rehabs, and now…" he folds his arms around himself and rocks back and forth. "They want me to find my own place to live."

He turns his anguish on me, full blast. "I don't even have a job now. How can I pay for my own place? What should I do, Izzy?"

My heart goes out to him. However, I still don't trust him. "You rebuild, Lonnie. Accept the consequences. If it's a first offense, they will be lenient. If not, then you may need the experience to get you to pay attention before something worse happens." I stare at him a minute, his head hanging down, his fingers entwined and dangling between his legs.

"Lonnie, did you climb into my garage and put a note on my kids' car?"

His cheeks redden. He nods.

"Did you walk around my fence one night, checking the gate?"

He rubs his hands together. "Yeah."

"You tell the police that?"

He nods. "Like I said, I told them everything. Lot of good it did me."

The silence that floats between us is awkward.

"Lonnie, it's always better if you tell the truth. No matter what the consequences are, at least you won't carry the guilt." The words boomerang right back at me. How long had I lived a lie? My own consequences were coming down hard, right here. Right now.

Another pregnant pause looms, one I didn't know how to fill. I feel pressure from him, the kind that makes me uncomfortable.

"If you expect me to put in a good word for your job, I'm sorry, I can't."

The anguish dries up like the turn of a water faucet. His eyes grow dark; his jaw clamps down. "As if *you*, in all your puffed-up importance and leaving your kids to fend for themselves to go out and meet some dude every night, didn't get all the second chances in the world! When someone else needs a chance, you suck at it. Why did I know you wouldn't help me?"

He jumps up and leaves.

I feel sad for him, but assured that I'd made the right choice. Before becoming involved in my support group, I'd have given in to the emotional blackmail.

Not anymore.

Chapter Thirty-Four

I t is nine-thirty by the time I get home. Peter and Chad are watching TV in the den, and Mimi is upstairs in her room, reading. I had to smile at that. She'd been staying off her tablet in a nod to me staying off my laptop.

Maybe we're winning.

Yawning, I go into my bedroom and put on PJs. Grab my phone to pay bills on my bank app, and see an alert for a low balance.

My forehead wrinkles. What?

I do a quick scan of my checking and savings. Sure enough, my balance is beneath the minimum, and I need to make a deposit before I can make any more payments. Scrolling through my account, I notice that Ethan's child support hadn't credited this month.

Peter pops in. "Going to bed. Good night, Mom." I smile, tell him good night, not taking my eyes off the screen. "Something wrong?"

I put down the phone. "Oh, you know. Sometimes money is tight."

Peter frowns. "I can get a job."

"We've talked about that, honey. I don't want you to miss out on sports and Key Club." I rip my thoughts from the puzzle of the low balance. "I've got this. You don't have to work. You have all that ahead of you after college."

"Okay, but I will if you need me to." He gives me a hug, then walks upstairs.

A warm feeling blossoms in my chest. I can count on one hand the number of hugs I've received from him lately. I return to the banking site, wishing I didn't depend on Ethan's child support. We'd agreed not to quibble over alimony—that he'd hike the child support instead. But if that hefty payment didn't plop into my account, I had to scramble to make ends meet. Add to that, he's still catching up from the last few payments that didn't make it into my account. With a sigh, I walk into the den where Chad has fallen asleep, wiggle him, and tell him to go to bed. He gives me a sleepy smile, rubs his eyes. "'K. G'night, Mom."

I tell him I love him as he walks up the stairs.

Another kid down. On cue, Mimi sticks her head out of her bedroom. "Night, Mom."

Three down.

I continue to be amazed at the positive changes in my kids and acknowledge that sacrifice is the better part of valor. For me, sacrificing the tasty elixir of male attention takes a huge amount of valor.

I text Ethan about the oversight. Plug my phone into the charger. Stare at the laptop sitting there, closed.

No. *I won't.*

I pull away from the laptop.

Check my phone.

No text back from Ethan.

I press his number. Listen to the rings. Voicemail kicks in. "Ethan. I know it's late, but I'm missing this month's child support. Did you lose your debit card or something? Let me know."

I never leave a voicemail. He'll know I'm pissed.

The fridge starts humming loud, which startles me. I traipse through the house, turning off all the lights my kids have left on. Picking up plates, cups. A floral headband. Chad's glasses. I trip over the shoes scattered in the den, gather them in my arms and drop them in the shoe bin by the door.

I stare at my cell.

Still no text.

I call again. It rings and rings.

I don't leave another voicemail.

The drive to work the next morning is frustrating, in part because Ethan yet to make contact, but also because the sales force had been called in for a half-day Saturday seminar.

I'd had to move money from my small savings account. I stare longingly at Starbucks as I pass by without stopping. Single parents experiencing late child support shouldn't pay six bucks for a cup of coffee. My lips tighten. This is ridiculous. Ethan makes plenty of money. What's wrong with him? I try his cell again. No answer.

I park and start walking toward the office building, feeling a sense of relief. Work brings order to my messy life... it's something I can control. Something with structure. I frown. Or was, before Birdie. A split second before I put my foot on the first of four wide concrete steps that lead to the entrance, a smoking hot guy approaches.

"Hey there, gorgeous."

I blush. "Thanks." A small sizzle attacks my neck. So irritating. I need to manage attention from hot men in a more subdued manner.

Before I can get out another word, he shoves a 9x12 envelope into my hands.

"You've been served." He says, somewhat apologetic. "For the record, you do look gorgeous. Have a good day."

I stand there, numb and open-mouthed, watching him slip through a crush of chattering, happy people. People who don't get served with God-knows-what. People who don't feel the weight of the world on their shoulders every freaking day. People who have dependable child support.

The envelope in my hand feels heavy. I storm into the building and flop into my chair. Drop the envelope on my desk.

Winston's eyebrows rise. "Good morning to you, too."

I grunt at him. "I got served."

His pale, blue eyes grow serious. "With what?"

I point.

"You going to open it?"

In a full-on pout now, I shake my head and let the dark mood smother me.

Winston extends a hand across the pod-divide and wiggles his fingers. "Give it here. I'll do it."

I fling it on his desk. He rips off the top, pulls out a half-inch-thick sheaf of documents. Gives me a look I don't understand.

"Child custody." Winston hands the envelope and docs back to me. "Not the best way to start your day, I'm sure."

I jerk the packet out of Winston's hands. "That Ethan! He hasn't been returning my texts, and this is why." Glancing over the body of the Petition, I deduce that he wants full custody. With a groan that I feel in the marrow of my bones, I stick it in my purse drawer and slam it shut. Stalk away from my desk and outside in order to call Ethan and give him several pieces of my mind. As usual, he is sitting on his butt watching TV like he does all day every Saturday and ends the call before I even have a chance to wind up my diatribe. "You're such a jerk," I mutter and walk back into the office.

"I'm sorry, Iz," Winston says, lips pursing. His fingers sprint up and down the lanyard. "He's been such a thorn in your side, hasn't he?"

"I'd use stronger language, but yeah, he hasn't made my life any easier." A headache begins at my temples. "He must've been thinking about this for a while. Remember when I told you he popped up as one of the guys I'd been chatting with online? He was getting ammunition. For court." Angry tears start. "Dammit!" I swipe them away.

Winston's jaw clenches. He leans in on his elbows.

"Do your kids see him often? I mean, do they have any kind of relationship with him?"

I make a rude noise with my lips. "Whatever. The guy makes no effort to enjoy an actual relationship with them; he just wants to stick it to me. He must be tired of paying child support. They never hear from him unless I need him to watch them, and now I can't even use him anymore."

"Why not?"

I wonder why Winston is so interested in single-parent woes, but I'm glad I have his support. "He's been pumping the kids for information. I guess he's been thinking about this for a while, and I don't trust him with my kids. He's not a dad; he's a mercenary asshole who wants *me* to pay child support. And now..." I exhale and swipe more tears off my cheeks. Winston hands me a tissue. "Now, he's got the online dating thing on his side. He'll probably get full custody. I know how he works...he's a master of persuasion, and a good liar. He'll have the judge eating out of his hand, and I'll just sit there like a sobbing wreck of a mother—guilty as charged."

"It's not like that, Iz," Winston reassures his voice soft. "Let's not go there yet. You're getting help. That's all anyone can do."

"Winston, I can't afford an attorney. I haven't said anything, but Ethan is like…four months late on child support. It's hard right now. And I sure can't pay someone hundreds of dollars an hour."

Winston leans back in his chair, folds his hands, thinking. "Has mediation been suggested?"

I shake my head. "Already tried that. He said no."

Winston stretches his arms high, then threads his fingers together behind his head. "You have joint custody now?"

"I refused that option early on. I won full custody, and he got generous visitation. He wasn't happy about it, but that was years ago. He's become this weird, raging, monster lately." I shrug. "Or maybe his real self is presenting. Who knows?"

For once, Winston has nothing encouraging to say, and we sit there, silent.

We drink our coffee, read our papers, and dutifully march into the conference room when they call us in for the Saturday seminar.

Much to my surprise, the seminar adequately re-routes my mind for a little while. Plus, Birdie is keeping a low profile. Phil hadn't given me any indication that I should start reporting to Birdie again, so maybe things will work out.

My cell rings with Detective Lopez' number. I snatch it up. "Hey."

"Hi, Iz."

We exchange pleasantries before he gets down to business.

"Tyler is cooling his heels in a holding cell. Wanted you to know. So…no more notes?"

I smile. "Lonnie admitted to me that Birdie put him up to that. What's going to happen to Lonnie?"

"He's just a kid. I think the Court will take that into account. It'll have to play out. A hearing is scheduled."

"Phil told him to resign."

"That has to feel good."

"It doesn't, but it's life. Consequences. I can't trust him."

"Had to happen. He'll find his way, Izzy."

We fall into an easy silence.

"What about Birdie?" I whisper, glancing at his office door. Curtains cloak the glass wall.

"His lawyer has him all clammed up, and the DA isn't too excited about taking the case. It's Lonnie's word against his."

"But Tyler..."

"Tyler destroyed all credibility when he tried to strangle Birdie. He's poison. His accusations won't stand. It's not against the law to be a scumbag."

"And the police reports, and the restraining order don't help when I thought he was he was a threat." I tap my fingers on my desk. Will Birdie walk? Forever steamrolling people's dreams? Will the *Sentinel* stand fast against his accusations? Or will Birdie's lawsuit gain momentum and cloud their pristine reputation?

"Tyler *was* a threat. Maybe he had good intentions, but the way he went about it was all wrong. Discussions are taking place about the recording you made. There's some issue about it being admissible, but it's still in play."

"Did Phil get back to you with what he found out? About the code?"

"We talked about it. There's no way to verify. Tons of people use that door. For all we know, he could've walked in behind someone, and they held the door for him. We can't use it."

"What did Birdie say?"

Detective Lopez grunted. "Said he gave his code to a couple of other people, who conveniently don't work there anymore."

My shoulders slump.

"I'm sorry it isn't better news, Izzy. However, this is a good thing...Tyler's getting Court-ordered mental health rehabilitation while he's waiting on trial."

I think about that. The grief he'd been dealing with over his mother's death. The shock of seeing Birdie again. His rage. His desire to warn me about him. "I think that's great. Tyler's had a hard time."

"We'll see what the DA has to say. Anyway, that's the update. You doing okay?"

Should I tell him about the latest garbage dump in my life? Ethan's custody suit?

No. Why should I ruin his day with Ethan's vendetta against me? It isn't a crime to sue someone for custody, and Detective Lopez doesn't need my personal issues on his plate, along with everything else.

"Doing fine," I say.

Chapter Thirty-Five

Birdie blows a smoke ring in the air and smiles into the darkened room. He pauses, tilts his head at the screen. How should he describe himself? By now, he's learned most of the tricks that seduce Isabelle Lewis.

Pushing the cigar to the other side of his mouth, he resumes typing, speaking aloud what he concocts: "Art shows, Broadway, books (the classics), fine wine..." he smacks his lips. "That should finish up the 'interests' section. What woman can resist any of that?" He laughs.

A shaft of light spills into the room. His wife enters. Birdie looks up.

"Did you call me?" she says, her expression hopeful.

Birdie frowns. "Working."

She backs out of the office without a word.

"Damn woman." He hates that she tiptoes around him like he's some kind of dangerous criminal.

Birdie finishes his fake profile with a flourish. When that idiot, Ethan, had contacted him in an effort to keep Izzy offline—as wrong-headed as that had been—he'd grabbed the opportunity to develop what had become a valuable relationship.

He pushes himself off his chair, walks to the portable bar beside his desk in his home office. Pours himself a generous amount of bourbon, neat. Savors the last few draws of the cigar, then snuffs it out. Sits in a leather armchair, crosses his legs, and sips the bourbon. He'd learned that Ethan had been developing quite the evidence for a custody lawsuit with Izzy. Birdie had been thrilled after learning about Ethan's scheme to lure Izzy to Raphael's as proof of irresponsible parenting. What a great idea to draw her out with a fake profile to prove the habitual poor choices that result in leaving her kids all alone—poor darlings—to sneak off into the night to meet a stranger. Wouldn't that classify as a danger to herself and others?

Birdie smiles, sips.

Yes, Ethan is a valuable asset, indeed.

His attorney tells him that Birdie should warm to the idea of a liability suit. After all, they should have protected their employees from Tyler, an unbalanced person. Birdie could've been killed, after all. His attorney insists they can win the case if proof exists that management was aware of the issue beforehand.

Birdie swirls the bourbon in the glass with a slight movement of his hand.

Management had played it safe. They hadn't suspended, terminated, or asked him to resign. Wrongful termination is off the table. He can't be effective as an employee under the current circumstances, but he can lay low and see what develops. Nobody there can touch him in a legal way, but the work environment for someone that's a liability threat? Not good.

If Isabelle Lewis had been removed as he'd planned from the beginning, none of this would've happened. He'd be well on his way to a promotion, bonuses, and a top position at a well-respected, daily newspaper.

Except…Izzy.

"Bitch." He drinks the rest of his bourbon, slams the glass on the side table.

Footsteps scurry to the door. A tentative knock. "You okay?"

He tells her he's fine. The light steps recede.

He turns his attention back to the task at hand.

Is it true that a strong liability case is his for the taking? Should he risk the fraud charges at his former business becoming public? How can that result in anything good? Well, except he might very well win a nice settlement. But still…the work environment is untenable. Is it worth it to hang around?

He crushes the dead cigar in the ashtray with a paperweight. "Need to *make* it worth it."

He smiles at the fake profile he's creating. Ethan had paid the bartender to give him video footage of fake meet-up with Izzy and plans to use it in court. Admissible or not, it'll sway the judge. Ethan will win custody, unless his attorney warns against the risk of using the video.

Can he use Ethan's trick to his advantage?

Of course. A hundred bucks work wonders with a bartender. Maybe two hundred, if the person is greedy. He shrugs.

The dust will settle if he is patient, doesn't sue, and performs his job as best he can under the circumstances. In the meantime, Izzy will fall apart after the custody battle, and his door of opportunity will be wide open. A serial online dating habit, a disastrous custody suit, and the deranged people she collects from her activities should form an excellent foundation from which to suggest that Izzy resign. On the heels of this, he'll waltz into the GM's office to ask if bygones can be bygones since he's told his attorney to drop their liability suit. They'll owe him. He'll be a hero and there's a strong possibility the *Sentinel* will move him into the vacated ad director spot. Worth a try, anyway.

The removal of Isabelle Lewis is still possible.

The longer he looks at the dating profile he'd just created, the more he feels the urge to celebrate. His plan is brilliant. This can work. It really can.

"Margaret?" Steps approach. She opens the door. "Yes, dear?"

"I feel like going out tonight."

She smiles. "I'll go get ready."

"Make it quick," he says.

Chapter Thirty-Six

Two long days pass, and I try my best to get back to normal. When Darlene asks to meet after work, I'm all in. I have a night off from Peter's football, Mimi is spending the night with a friend, and Chad is doing his homework in the den. All is quiet on the Ethan lawsuit front as well, so I've avoided paying a huge, freaking retainer to an attorney. That being said, a night including Darlene and a glass of wine sounds excellent.

I'm smiling as I stride into the noisy bar.

I lean across the table to hear Darlene as the server returns with our drink orders. "Sorry, it's so loud in here," I half-yell.

"Let's move," she mouths.

We take our drinks and find a quieter spot at a high top table.

It takes effort for her to settle her five-foot frame into the tall chair.

"Glad we get an opportunity to catch up. You've been busy, haven't you?" she asks.

I groan. "Understatement of the year."

I tell her about Detective Lopez's update and that Birdie gets to keep his job for the time being.

She frowns. "How are you dealing with that?"

"I don't have a choice."

"Are you considering a different job?"

The possibility crossed my mind, but how would I replace the flexibility? The bonuses? The relationships I'd built with my clients? "I'm going to wait it out. Birdie can't stay there forever. Nobody wants him there."

I spend a little time explaining liability issues. Darlene is livid. "These cat-

and-mouse games the law plays. Whatever happened to 'at-will' contracts?

"I think we do have those kind of contracts. But in this case, a lot of issues enter in. The guy could've died. I mean…seriously."

We drink in silence.

I am just about to launch into a long-winded diatribe against Ethan and tell her about the custody suit when my cell rings. It's Lopez, or I wouldn't have picked up. With an apologetic look at Darlene, I tell her I have to take it.

I slip off my chair and find a quieter space to chat. "Hey. Something new come up?"

"Where are you?"

I blink at his bluntness. "In a restaurant with a friend from work. I'm heading home in thirty minutes or so."

"Where were you two nights ago?"

My mind spins. What is he getting at? "Uh. Let me think. At home with the kids. I didn't go anywhere. We've had a quiet couple of days."

"What time? Will your children corroborate that?"

"Well, yeah, sure." I pause. "What's going on? You're scaring me."

"Anything else? Are you sure you didn't go anywhere at all?"

"I took them for ice cream last night. We went to Daisy Dip around eight. Peter's girlfriend dropped by, and I treated them. Two nights ago, I stayed in. I was exhausted. What does this have to do with anything?"

A pause. "Why didn't you tell me about the custody issue with your ex?"

My eyebrows shoot up. "Why would I need to? I thought you had enough going on."

He sighs. "Izzy, your ex is Ethan Gerard Lewis, correct?"

My hand rises to my throat.

"The ME puts his death at forty-eight hours, approximately eight p.m. A concerned neighbor checked in on him and called nine-one-one. Homicide asked me to get you down to the station. Give me your location. I'll pick you up."

Chapter Thirty-Seven

Once again, my kids have to grant Mom another late night, but this time, I have no choice in the matter. I sit stiffly in the sedan as Detective Lopez pulls into the station and parks. Spotlights aimed at the flagpoles in front of the building burn a hole in my retinas. The flapping of flags in the night breeze provides a gloomy soundtrack that underscores my mood. Lopez stares at his hands on the steering wheel.

"I don't know what to think, Izzy."

"You and me both." I fold my arms across my chest and sigh.

He twists in his seat to look at me. "It doesn't matter what I think. Homicide has already uncovered the Petition for Full Custody, the restraining order against Tyler, and the police reports. On paper, you seem..." The glow of the spotlights and flapping flags cast darting shadows across his face as he searches for the right word.

"Seem what? Unbalanced? Unfit? Congratulations, you sound just like Ethan."

"I wasn't going to say any of those things, Izzy. I'm trying to be diplomatic, but it's not working. You seem a probable suspect. We have to rule you out."

The anger seeps out of me. I can't fathom the full scope of what is happening. How is this even possible? I feel as if I'm in an alternate reality. My lower lip quivers. *Ethan is dead.* "What...how did..." I clear my throat. "What happened to Ethan?"

"Forensics isn't completed yet, but we think it may have been someone with medical experience. A simple cut to the carotid artery underneath the jaw. Death was instantaneous." He closes his eyes, takes in a breath. "I have to ask before I turn you over, Izzy. For my own personal assurance. Have you ever worked for a medical professional or had training?"

I feel my body melting. Like candlewax, the passenger seat in the sedan holds an amorphous blob, nothing more. My thoughts run rampant. Detective Lopez? How could he even ask that question? *Self-control, Izzy. It's just a question, not an accusation.*

"No, Detective Lopez. I'm a sales rep. I've never had a medical job or training."

"Parents?"

I give him a steely-eyed silence.

He studies me. "I'll take that as a no."

I pull myself together, jerk open the passenger door, and start walking toward the station.

The interrogation takes twenty-five minutes. The homicide detective is kind. Detective Lopez had waited, and on the ride back to my car, we don't say much. I speed home and race inside. I am desperate for peace. Hugs from my kids. A sitcom. Something. Anything.

Once I make sure the kids had finished homework, eaten dinner, and accomplished a skirmish-free evening without me, I relax. The cops will check my story, which will put their cop-minds to rest. All will be well.

I open a bottle of red. Walk outside to stare at the stars, the waning moon. I need to re-route my thoughts, not dwell on the unthinkable. I finish the glass of wine. My fingers twitch. No. *No.*

I scramble into the house, search for my phone. Where is it? When I cannot find my phone, I search for Brillo Pad's card. I tear my desk apart. Nothing. I sit at my desk, my heart thrumming in my chest. The pull is shattering. Astounding.

I open my laptop.

And I'm gone.

I am roused from sleep the next morning by knocks on my bedroom door and worried kids. Dragging myself from my bed, I join them in the hall. I hug them in a daze, realizing I'd not yet told them about the death of their father.

How I dread that conversation.

Then I remember the horror of yesterday. All of it. I curse softly, pad into my bathroom for a shower.

As the water slides over me, I scrub myself with vicious, punishing strength. What had I done? Had all my restraint and support group meetings been for nothing? What is wrong with me?

I step out of the shower, my body red from the scourging. My eyebrows draw together as I get dressed. When had I come home, anyway? How late had I been out? Had the kids known?

I hope not.

This is the last time. I lift my eyes to the ceiling. *I promise, God.*

I arrive at the office mismatched and unprepared for the sales meeting. Reluctant to meet Winston's questioning gaze, I tuck my purse in the drawer and trudge to the back to get coffee. Birdie is alone, lingering at the coffeemaker. He chuckles when I approach. "Another late night?"

I refuse to talk to him. Anything I say he uses as a weapon against me, so why try?

He studies me, a smirk on his lips. "How long did you wait, *Belle?*"

My dating app name. "How long did I wait for what, Birdie?"

His face splits with a smile. "At the bar last night. Isn't it interesting that the minute your ex is no longer a threat, the custody case goes away, and you can get back to what you do best...feed the beast." He shrugs. "I think Phil should know how late you were out last night, so I was nice enough to purchase a recording of the security footage for him. And we should include that nice detective friend of yours. We can't have any more Tyler's around here, now, can we?"

I shudder. I'd waited a *long* time, drinking more than usual. And the bartender had been evasive and edgy.

In a thunderclap of understanding, I realize it had happened again. Birdie set me up! Just like Ethan. I try to pour the coffee, but my hand is shaking so hard it's difficult. I keep my eyes low. I don't dare risking looking at Birdie. He would see the murderous intent simmering there.

How could he possibly know about Ethan's death? Had it made the obits already? Impossible. I stare at the sludgy coffee and resist an urge to throw it in Birdie's face. Phil walks up, senses tension, and throws me a questioning look. After he fills his mug, he jerks his head toward his office. "Izzy. Can I see you a sec before the meeting?"

I am unable to unleash my feet from the floor. Phil takes my elbow and whispers in my ear. "Walk, Izzy. I've got you."

"You need me in the sales meeting, Phil?" Birdie calls after us.

"That won't be necessary, Birdie," Phil throws over his shoulder.

He pours me into one of the chairs in his office, then closes the door. His steps are light and quick as he rounds the desk and sits. "What's going on?"

"I'm a horrible human being."

"Okayyy…"

I peg my red-rimmed eyes on his intense, blue ones. "Did you hear about my ex?"

He shakes his head. "Should I have?"

"Ethan. My kids' dad. He…he was murdered."

Phil's eyebrows launch. "Oh no. I'm so sorry, Izzy."

"I was interrogated yesterday. Homicide. Somebody slashed his carotid." Tears slide from my eyes.

"Take all the time you need, Izzy. Take a week."

I shake my head. "That's not why I'm telling you this. Since Ethan was suing me for custody of our kids, the cops consider me a suspect. And the online dating stuff has become a bigger issue than I ever thought possible. It's his primary catalyst for the suit." I choke out a sob. "So I'd murder him? Because I want his lawsuit to go away?" I whisper. "Phil. I don't know what to do."

Phil picks up the fidget spinner on his desk for something to do with his hands. "They're just following protocol. You're in a group. It's not an issue anymore. Not to me. They're fact-finding, Izzy."

"I'm being set up, Phil."

Phil's eyes bounce over to Birdie walking through the cubicles on the way to his office. "By who?"

"Okay, I had a lapse last night. It was all too much. I...I lost it after I finally got home. After Detective Lopez told me about Ethan, he picked me up for interrogation. I was a complete basket case, Phil. I didn't get home until late."

Phil is silent.

"Birdie and Ethan must've developed a relationship? That's all I can come up with." I choke back a sob. "I was hysterical last night. I needed to re-route my brain, y'know?"

He nods. "And that caused the lapse. A crisis is a huge trigger. It happens. We just get up and start over."

"Not so easy when it's *Birdie* who set up the profile I responded to. That's what was happening over the coffee a few minutes ago, Phil. He'd just bragged about having freaking video of me at a bar waiting to meet someone. No one showed, because he set the whole thing up to get video. He made a fake profile, just like Ethan did early on. I'm sure that's where he got the idea."

Phil's jaw tightens. "Why in God's name would he do something like that?"

"He has an agenda, and the first step is getting me fired, which means destroying my credibility with my employer." I stare out his window at the sky, the tops of office buildings. "It's more than that, though. After Chad's accident, Family Services got involved. They're watching me like a hawk to verify that I make...certain lifestyle changes. All of these incriminating events make me look like a terrible parent. Ethan was leveraging his little impersonation gimmick to further his custody case, but with his death, the case goes away." I spread my arms. "See? It doesn't look good." I swipe away nervous tears. "And now...even Detective Lopez has doubts. They think I went ballistic after I was served with the custody action and flew over to Ethan's house and killed him." A shiver runs up my spine. I am so cold. "I have an alibi. And...and no medical experience. I don't know if that's enough."

Phil runs a hand over his head. "Izzy," he says. "You're not capable of murdering anyone." He pauses, squints at me. "What does medical experience have to do with anything?"

I stammer through an explanation.

Phil grunts. "Don't even go there." He stares at a photo of himself and the publisher of the *Sentinel* on his desk. "Birdie's trapped us, you know. I'm getting the sense that he's a professional con. Plus, the lawyer he hired is all about the show. The media follow him around like slobbering dogs. Birdie's not shy about spouting off allegations, and the media don't exactly love the newspaper, so the coverage is spun to their advantage, not ours." He looks out the window, rubs his jaw. "The Tyler situation put us in the spotlight. Local news went nuts over it. 'Struggle for Survival on Second Floor of Sentinel,' he quotes, chuckling, pointing to an article on his laptop. "You'd think the person responsible for that headline would know that alliteration is a thing of the past."

"*I* caused all this. I'm so sorry. Please forgive me, Phil."

He wags a hand in dismissal. "You couldn't have known Tyler would attack Birdie. Even Tyler didn't know what he was doing. I lay it at the feet of grief. He's been grieving for two years, and if grief isn't dealt with, it becomes rancid. He was out of control."

We sit silent.

Birdie struts by Phil's office, talking on his cell and laughing. Phil strokes his chin as he watches. "Listen, Izzy. I have an idea."

"Don't we need to get to the sales meeting?

"It'll wait three minutes. Here's what I have in mind."

I pulled my chair close.

Chapter Thirty-Eight

In spite of Birdie's intentions to crucify me...hope is reborn.

Phil and I have a plan.

I savor a secret smile, and walk into the conference room with a slight bounce in my step.

Right behind me, Phil walks in and stands at the front of the conference room in full-on general mode. He gives us updates on ad budgets and trends, the state of marketing and advertising throughout the country and our region. After twenty minutes of discussion and questions, he puts his hands behind his back, widens his stance, and presses his lips together.

All thirty of us lapse into silence.

Phil clears his throat.

Then he proceeds to dump the whole story on my colleagues about the issues I'm facing. My cheeks burn with shame.

He could've warned me.

However, thanks to my recovery group, I'm learning that transparency is good for the soul, with the side benefit of humility. Humility is a virtue, right?

I sigh.

After Phil is done, questions abound. The sly looks floating my way evolve into grudging respect and empathy. It feels good to come out into the open with my struggles. Phil assures us that the *Sentinel* family has locked arms behind me and that we must put on a good game face where Birdie is concerned due to legal ramifications. His finale is a whopper of a warning to keep opinions and ruminations to ourselves, give one another the benefit of the doubt, and except for the grace of God, we could all be in the same shoes as Birdie or Izzy. I wince a little at being lumped together with Birdie, but be that as it may...most of this mess is my fault. I have to own it. Live with it. And forgive myself in time.

Winston walks with me afterward, elbows me in the side, and smiles. "That's a big win, eh, Iz?"

My secret smile returns. I think about the plan Phil and I had concocted. "Can you hang out a bit before you go on your calls?"

His brow furrows, but he says he will.

I sit in my cube, glancing at the corner office every few seconds. Phil stands in front of his desk, looking out through the thick glass, watching the team get back to work at their desks and the sales assistants churning back and forth between their assigned sales executives and the production department. Business as usual.

My eyes are glued to Phil. He walks behind his desk, picks up his landline and makes a call. When the call ends, he rubs his face with both hands. After a few seconds, and with a jut of his chin, he looks at me and jerks his head toward the back.

My heart in my throat, I leap from my chair and trot to the coffee nook where—as Phil and I had discussed— Birdie cannot resist gathering scraps of information about the sales meeting to which he was uninvited.

I slow my pace as I approach. The other managers conveniently slip away, leaving only Jon Hoyt, Milton, the classified ad manager; and me.

Birdie tosses a smirk in my direction.

I smile. "What's so funny, Birdie?"

"It's no secret, Izzy."

I glance at the others. "Tell us." I spread my arms. The transparency of the sales meeting has made me strong. "Tell all of us, Birdie, what's so hilarious."

He steps closer. Mutters in my ear. "You are gonna to be begging for mercy."

"Can you repeat that, please?" I asked.

Jon sips his coffee and eyes Birdie. Milton folds his arms.

Birdie frowns. "Why are you all treating me like a leper? Izzy is the one who opened the door to that psycho that tried to kill me. Did y'all forget about that?"

"So you retaliate by creating a fake dating profile to trap me, Birdie? By using Lonnie as your errand boy to spy on me? What's the end game here, Birdie? We all want to know," I taunt, with a glance at Phil.

Milton's eyes grow round. Jon's scowl deepens. He inches closer to me. *Just a little more. A little more. C'mon, Izzy. You can do this.*

Birdie's face reddens. "I don't have an end game, little girl." He jerks his index finger at me. "You're the one who's creating problems. Running to Phil with complaints about me. How did you think I was going to react?"

Jon, Milton, and I remain dead silent.

Birdie bares his teeth and growls, "What? I'm the damn victim! Izzy caused the whole thing. What the hell is wrong with you guys, protecting her?"

"Tell them how you knew Ethan, Birdie." I am the picture of innocence. The queen of the pod. Lighter than air, in the midst of my witnesses. "He's my ex," I explain to Jon and Milton.

He attempts to calm himself. Blows out a breath, jabs his hands on his hips. "With pleasure. Ethan came to me hoping I'd provide some…uh…assistance in pulling you out of your make-believe world that affected your work and your children. He was concerned." Birdie glances at Jon and Milton. "As anyone would be."

Milton's eyes bulge. His forehead creases. "And you allowed that conversation to happen? Birdie, that was…well, *inappropriate* doesn't even begin to cover it. At the very least, you should've told Izzy about it, and maybe HR. Did you?"

Jon puts his mug aside.

"Izzy had become a problem," Birdie mutters.

My eyebrows fly up in pleasant surprise and stay there. He's *admitting* what he thinks about me, and it's obvious he's unclear about the line between right and wrong. The plan is working. Where's Phil? He's supposed to be part of this.

Birdie grows more agitated. He pokes his thick forefinger at me. I am *so* sick of looking at the end of his finger. "You weren't keepin' up with your accounts. I even offered to help. Then you went off-grid and took..." He points at Jon. "Classified accounts!"

This is turning out way better than I thought it would.

"Tell us about how you and Lonnie got all cuddly, Birdie," I suggest.

Birdie starts to realize which way the wind is blowing, and snaps his mouth shut.

"How are all those fraud charges in Missouri coming along, Birdie? You still on probation?" I prod, keeping my voice even.

He is quiet. His eyes are icy.

Jon and Milton look at each other. This is new information to them.

"I heard you faked a dating profile to get Izzy out of the house," Jon deadpans, adding fuel to the fire. "What the hell, dude?"

I didn't know Phil had had time to clue him in, but whatever...I almost laugh at Jon's willingness to help. Almost.

"I never showed up," he protests. "Anyway, it doesn't matter. They'll have a hell of a time proving that I was involved and..." His large, juicy lips part in a cry of frustration.

I allow a small grin. We're getting to him.

"What did you give the bartender in return for the security camera footage, Birdie? The Homicide Division needs to schedule a sit-down and talk about it," I continue.

He blinks at Jon and Milton. In a shaky voice, he asks, "What are you doing?"

"Did you write those notes, Birdie? The ones that I thought Tyler left, but didn't? The ones Lonnie admitted *he* left? For you? What was that about? You have something against Tyler? The man who lost his mother because you *bankrupted* her?" I swallowed, hard. Birdie was about to explode. "Seems to me it should be the other way around."

He curses, his voice soft and dangerous. "She had a heart condition...that wasn't my fault."

I lock eyes with him. "You keep telling yourself that, Birdie."

Detective Lopez and Phil round the corner.

Birdie pales, takes a couple of steps backward.

"Tyler has a lot more on the ball than you give him credit for, and now, he has nothing to lose. I believe his story. And this?" Detective Lopez circles his index finger at us. "This little pow-wow can't be classified as hearsay, bud. We got a warrant for your phone records, by the way. Wow. Lots of calls between you and Ethan Lewis. Did you think latching onto Izzy's ex would be a *good* thing?" Lopez shakes his head. "Congratulations. You're now on top of the suspect list in Ethan's homicide."

"This is entrapment." Birdie's eyes dart right and left. His hands clench.

"Your word against mine, bud. Who do you think they'll believe?" Lopez' smile bathes me in relief. I'm off the hook. And the Bird has a lot of questions in his future.

Lopez grips Birdie's arm. Birdie, furious, lashes out with a left jab and misses Lopez by inches. His gaze lands on me. He lunges. His coffee mug goes flying. The hot liquid spackles the air before anointing us. I jerk away. Jon rushes in behind, throws his arms around Birdie's shoulders, and holds on. Birdie realizes he's not doing himself any favors and shakes Jon off, trying hard to get a handle on himself.

Jon, Phil, Milton, and I form a loose circle around him. He has nowhere to go unless he runs over one of us.

Breathing hard, shooting all of us looks that could kill, he offers the detective his wrists. Detective Lopez spins him around and cuffs him.

"If you're thinkin' I had anything to do with Ethan's death," Birdie mutters. "I don't. I have an alibi." He juts his chin toward me. "*She* needed him gone, not me."

"And *you* needed *her* gone. So you see my dilemma. You can tell us all about it down at the station." Lopez propels Birdie to the elevator.

On his way out, Detective Lopez tells me he'll call later on.

I stand there watching, wondering if they can hold Birdie. I smile at the thought of Birdie's lawyer freaking out on him for letting this happen. When Phil and I had put our heads together before the sales meeting, we'd agreed that Birdie's feathers would be easy to ruffle. And sure enough, they were.

The rest of my workday includes catching up on reports, making sales calls, and clueing in Darlene during my frequent trips to production. I'm numb, but no longer walking on eggshells since Birdie is neutralized.

As for Phil, he'd stuck his hands in his pockets, walked into his office, and resumed his workday like nothing happened.

Me, not so much. Winston held my hand all afternoon, metaphorically speaking, and as I leave for the day, I no longer feel like I'm drowning.

I arrive home at two-thirty p.m. and sink into my recliner.

Interesting how looming and ongoing catastrophe can change perspective.

I lean my head back and think about the conversation that must take place. I hadn't even had time to grieve poor Ethan, much less prepare myself to give the sad news to our children. Who could have done that to him? Should I tell the kids how he died? How does a mom tackle telling her children their father was murdered?

Not that they had much of one in the first place, but still. He was their father, and they sustained a certain loyalty.

I do not feel that loyalty, but I want to honor theirs.

I stare at my closed laptop on the coffee table as if it's the enemy. I jerk it into my lap and delete every last dating site, go to my settings, and block them as well. Then I delete the corresponding apps from my phone. At least when the urge strikes, it'll be too much trouble to install them again. Maybe I'll forget how to do it. On purpose.

My cell buzzes. I pull my cell out of my purse and look. Jon Hoyt.

"Hey."

"How you doing?"

"How do you think?" I smile.

"Thought you might need a distraction. Want to get coffee?"

"Thanks, Jon, but I need to connect with the kids tonight. I'll take you up on it another time, though."

"Sounds good. In the meantime...do you want to talk?"

I think about that.

"Yeah. I do."

Jon and I talk until I hear the kids' car in the driveway. When the call ends,

I feel lighter. Jon had some great things to say. Encouraging things. My next support group meeting is tomorrow night, and I can't wait. I smile. Maybe knowing Jon will be there has something to do with that.

I walk out onto the porch to greet my kids.

Chapter Thirty-Nine

Birdie's wife opens the door to his home office and walks in. "You called me?"

"I need to tell you some things," he says to her. "Please sit."

Her face lights up. "You got the promotion!"

Birdie's smile is fleeting. "Not quite, dear." He selects a cigar, snips it, lights it. Starts puffing. Stares at the wall.

His wife seats herself, purses her lips and folds her arms.

"A few complications threw a monkey wrench in my plans. I'll not be working here much longer."

Her manicured brows draw together. She places her palm on her cheek and leans into it. "I thought you were doing so well there."

"I am, I am…" he assures her. "I've been accused of harassment." His sigh holds the essence of a victim wronged. "It's not true, but people believe what they want to."

He doesn't notice the slight tightening of his wife's posture. Or her warm, brown eyes growing cold.

He puffs the cigar. "I think it's time I look for something else."

She is quiet and still.

"I'm thinking California. A friend of mine reached out, and it sounds like a good opportunity."

"An opportunity to do it again, Birdie?" She slides forward in her chair and straightens, a pert smile on her lips.

He frowns. "What do you mean?"

"Do you think I'm a complete fool, dear?"

How does she know?

"How dare you accuse me of such a thing?"

"If I call Human Resources, what will I find in your file, Birdie?"

He pounds his desk with a fist. "There are privacy laws, dammit!"

"So you see, there are things you don't tell me, all locked away under privacy laws, just like last time." She smiles. "I want to believe you. Every time, I want to believe in you." Rising from her chair, she leans across the top of his desk and tap-tap-taps a 9x12 envelope with a pink, freshly manicured fingernail. "Have you looked at this?"

"What is it?"

She hands it to him.

Birdie rips off the top, pulls out paperwork. Reads the first page. A flush creeps up his neck. "You're divorcing...*me*?"

"I think it's about time I look for something else, too."

The door closes with a soft click behind her.

Chills race down his arms. He pounds the top of his desk in frustration. She may be less savvy than he'd like, but at least she'd believed in him. Supported him. Stayed, when others walked away.

Now, in addition to suspected homicide, attempted assault, and entrapment charges, he's looking at a battle over the division of assets and alimony. Swiping drops of perspiration from his forehead, he finds his attorney's most recent call, and clicks on the number.

Chapter Forty

The discussion lasts long into the night. I try to deal with each child according to personality—listening to the sobbing of Mimi, observing the stoic patience of Peter, and watching Chad turn into an angry piece of stone. Even an undependable, problematic dad is better than none. Peter, ever the caretaker, does his best to reassure his younger siblings. We finally get to bed around two in the morning. I tell them all I know, and in the end, they seem sad, but satisfied.

I don't sleep a wink.

The school agrees that a long weekend is a good idea, and the kids and I take the day to drive to Savannah. We walk the riverfront, admire the waving woman statue, do lunch on Bay Street, and have ice cream cones afterward. I don't feel the huge, emotional wallop of a husband passing on, but I do feel my children's loss. Ethan's parents had driven in from Atlanta to take care of the funeral arrangements and asked if the kids could participate in planning. My kids have always had a good relationship with their grandparents, and I am glad for their presence. The funeral will be hard. Especially since Emerald Spring PD have yet to pin down a suspect.

My cell rings. Detective Lopez. I brush my hair out of my eyes and blink up into the Savannah sunshine. "Hey."

"Hi, Izzy."

My gut fizzes. What now?

"This is an update, Izzy, that's all. Don't worry. Birdie's lawyer had another fit, climbed the walls, and I don't blame him. There isn't one bit of evidence that he had anything to do with Ethan's homicide. However, we now have cause to pursue entrapment, extortion, possessing an illegal substance, and attempted assault. I'm inclined to believe Tyler and Lonnie, and I think a judge will believe them, also. That's where we are. Birdie made bail but is on a monitor. Figured you'd feel better knowing."

I smile. "Thank you, Detective." The Savannah River laps gently along the boardwalk. "Guess what I'm doing right now?"

"Taking a breather, I hope."

"My kids and I are in Savannah enjoying the day. Last night I had to tell them their father was murdered, and tomorrow, they join their grandparents at the funeral home to plan the funeral. So I thought just for today...I'd treat them to anything they want. Let them be kids." Tears straggle down my cheeks.

"I'm sorry, Izzy."

"Yeah," I whisper. "Me too."

"In other news, you've been given the all-clear. Everything lines up with what you told us. There wasn't even enough for a warrant to search your house. And besides, they have no hairs, fibers, no prints, no shoeprints at the scene. Whoever did it was meticulous, I'll say that. Neighbors saw nothing, heard nothing. At this point, we have zero leads."

"Could Birdie..." I let the thought hang.

Detective Lopez chuckles. "Whoever did this to Ethan was a master of finesse, maybe due to medical training. After hanging around Birdie—who, by the way, has no medical background that we could find— I don't think he's capable of subtlety. Have you seen those hands? I doubt he'd be able to make an exact, clean kill cut. Someone knew their anatomy." He pauses. "Sorry. This can't be easy for you to hear."

"It isn't."

"I'll let you get back to it. No more notes?"

I smile. This had become a joke between us. "No more notes, Detective." We end the call.

I stare off into space until the kids' voices pull me back. We hike to the car and drive to the trolley station for a tour of Savannah. In three days, the kids and I will put their father in the ground. It doesn't seem possible.

The funeral is long, sad, and traumatic. For me, for the kids and their grandparents, and for the gaggle of Ethan's friends that had shown up. The children and I are invited to sit beside Ethan's parents, and his mother sobs through the whole service. I think about Chad's accident on The Bluffs and how quickly life can change. My son could just as easily have been the one in the casket at the front of the church. My heart aches for this grieving mother, the grandmother of my children.

Afterward, we stand in a line, listen to well wishes and farewells and how much Ethan will be missed. My back aches, and my stomach growls with hunger. When had I eaten last? I can't remember. Maybe yesterday.

I shuffle the kids over to Ethan's parents after the last guest leaves.

"Y'all have a nice couple of days." I smile. Ethan's mother hugs me. "Thanks for letting us have them for a few days."

"You bet." I wave them off. Winston and Jon approach.

"It was a nice send-off," Winston remarks. He is dressed in a dark suit, minus the bow tie.

Jon scrutinizes me. "You surviving?"

"Do I have a choice?" The joke falls flat. "Birdie's out on bail. They haven't ruled him out as the killer, though."

"The plot thickens," Winston murmurs.

"How about Starbucks? I'm paying." Jon suggests.

Because the kids are with their grandparents, I take the next couple of days off. Phil is understanding about the request, and I detect a hint of relief in his voice. I can't ignore the fact that I'd become a problem for the newspaper, and wonder if I'll be the next one out the door. Through Darlene, I learn that Birdie cleared out his office with security guards watching his every move. I feel vindicated. Free to enjoy my job again…if I still have one.

Winston checks in a couple of times a day, which warms my heart. Since my own dad died years ago, perhaps God gave me Winston as a replacement. He cheers me up with office scuttlebutt, of which I am no longer the primary subject. Now, people talk about Birdie and Lonnie. Lonnie has vanished, Winston tells me, and I wonder if this is true. I guess I'll find out at the meeting tonight.

Walking down the entryway toward the meeting feels like coming home. The women from my group wave me over, and we sit together in the big auditorium and chat about innocuous stuff. This is a balm to my battered soul. By the time we file into the Love and Relationship group's meeting room, I'm prepared for another dose of how to fight the beast. I'd had no idea so many women struggle through withdrawals when a man isn't around. Like me, we are all sad junkies needing a fix. I look forward to the day the desire to log onto the apps is dead. It will happen. I am determined.

Brillo Pad beams at me as I enter the room. "I'm proud of you, Isabelle. Some women can't accept the truth. If you've made it three times, you'll be coming back for more. I believe you can do this."

I give her a hug. "Me, too," I whisper and find a seat.

I push off the stress of Tyler. Lonnie. Ethan's funeral. I push away my sorrow over my kids losing their father, their grandparents losing a son. I pull together all my focus and shove it into one funnel: learn how to be a hundred percent woman without needing a guy to fill an insatiable void. Before I can attract the right kind of man—a good and healthy desire—I'm learning how to become the right kind of woman. The women's stories are epiphanies to me. Their journeys to climb out of impossible situations often mirror my own. It feels like I've arrived at the end of a long power outage and plugged into a live socket. How had I not known these things?

Their stories break my heart, as mine breaks theirs. But we are learning and joined by a common thread...*hope*.

After our meetings, Jon finds me. We meander outside and sit on a bench. I appreciate his quiet support. I scan the space for Lonnie, not expecting to see him, but hoping. "Have you seen Lonnie tonight?"

Jon shakes his head. "He's in a bad place right now."

"I hadn't heard that."

"He talks to me once in a while. Y'know...drugs, alcohol...the pull is the same. Different, but the same. I'm his safe place, I think."

"What's going on with him?"

"He's bottoming out. No money, no job…it's the kind of pressure that makes addicts run back to drugs. Being high helps them forget their problems. It's denial of the most savage kind. I hope he has family."

I groan. "He said his parents kicked him out."

"God help him," Jon says.

"Another gift from Birdie," I say through gritted teeth. "I told you that, right? That Birdie had him stalk me, leave notes, delve into my personal situation…in exchange for drugs?"

"He told me. I hope I don't ever see that guy again—selling is one thing but to exploit someone who's been clean for a while? He deserves everything he gets, Izzy."

"Maybe the charges will put Birdie in a cell."

Jon frowns. "He needs to be taken down, that's for sure. Any news about Ethan?"

"Nothing. They're talking about someone from his past, maybe. He had a lot of girlfriends."

"Any medical professionals?" Jon smiles.

"Not funny."

"Sorry."

I sigh. "It was nice to discover that he'd made a will. I didn't even know about it. He set up a trust for the kids. I found out from his parents."

"That's great, Izzy."

"After all the bad things I said about him, he turned out to have some good qualities. Maybe I can afford college for them now. It would be nice not to have to take out loans."

"I'm happy for you."

I stare into Jon's kind face. Had I noticed that his brown eyes were warm and reassuring? That I didn't have to check my makeup every ten minutes with him because I had no need to look perfect? We lock in on one another.

I tear my eyes away before I say something I can't take back.

I get up from the bench, stick my hands in my jacket pockets. "Time to go. Need to check in on the kids."

He stands. "I'm proud of you, Izzy."

Warmth blooms in my chest. Tears pond and spill. "Thank you, Jon."

He places gentle hands on each side of my face and thumbs away my tears. We gaze at each other. He leans in for a kiss, and I melt into it. The kiss lasts a long time. I pull away and stare into those warm, brown eyes for a full three seconds before I tear myself away.

Chapter Forty-One

Birdie stomps around his house, cursing the electronic ankle monitor and his damn attorney who hadn't even tried to get him out of it. The monitor option had presented itself, and his attorney had jumped on it, assuring him it was a better option than a cell. And that was that. "How am I supposed to limp around in this thing for six weeks?" He groans. His feckless attorney hadn't been able to arrange a decent court date, either.

He scowls. Why did they think him such a flight risk? His cell lights up with a call. Lonnie. "What?"

"How's it going? I heard...I heard you got tapped."

"Thanks to you, dumbass. Don't you know how to keep your mouth closed? Thought we had a deal."

A beat of silence. "Is this a secure line?"

"How the hell should I know?"

Above his head on the second floor, he hears his wife move around in their bedroom. She'd arranged her affairs packed, and gotten ready to leave him in record time. He wonders how long she'd been planning it.

"What do you want? I've got stuff goin' on here." Birdie narrows his eyes. "How are you out, anyway?"

"Got a good public defender, and I'm capable of a believable performance when necessary. They bought it. I got probation and a fine. Have to find a place to live and a job, though." After a pause, he continues. "I didn't tell them everything, Birdie. Just enough to get them off my back."

Birdie thinks about that. "What don't they know?"

229

Lonnie chuckles. "I didn't tell them I was *in* her house. I played the part of a young, stupid victim, all about the drugs."

Birdie's forehead wrinkles. He'd never thought any different. Maybe he'd been wrong.

"That note you wanted me to plant in the garage? I thought it was crap. So I waited, and the next night I watched her. Izzy leaves her blinds open, and I could see clear as day right through the window. She stayed up late, talking on the phone, real happy and stuff. So I wrote a note that was more...intimidating, might be the word, and referred to how late she stayed up. She was freaked about finding the note the next day and told me all about it. It was hard to act concerned without laughing my head off."

Birdie's mouth drops. "How did you get into the garage? She has a security system."

"I'm on friendly terms with her daughter."

"What do you mean?"

"I found her on Instagram. She's very uh...mature for her age." Lonnie laughs. "Her profile says she's fourteen, but from Izzy, I know she's twelve. Anyway, she told me how she tricks the system. It's easy."

"And here I thought I was *corrupting* you. As it turns out, you're already there."

Birdie, much encouraged, reaches for a cigar and lights it. His wife thumps down the stairs with her suitcase. Thump. Thump. Thump. Bang.

"Ow! Dadgumit!" she erupts.

"Hold a sec," Birdie says. He dashes to the stairs. "Need help?"

His wife glares. "I do not." Holding her head high, she strides down the hallway with two large pieces of luggage. Birdie hustles to open the door, thinking he might as well be pleasant about this. It'll play well in front of the judge. He plays out the scene in his mind—'Judge, I even opened the door for her and offered to help with her bags when she walked out. She was furious, but I was kind. After all, I didn't want her to leave.' With a tight smile, he opens the door for her. She walks through.

"Bye, honey." Birdie puffs the cigar in his mouth.

Her face a neutral mask, she loads the car and leaves. Not once does she look back.

He returns inside. Picks up the cell. "Okay, I'm good now."

"I wrote a better note that made her think she had this creepy stalker, right? So after everything blew up, I started thinking…she's had a hard time with her ex. She talked about it at the office, and I overheard a gnarly conversation about a custody battle. If anyone had motive to kill a guy, it would be her. And…the cops still have no suspects. Anyway…I thought I could…make it right?" Lonnie ventured hesitantly. "Since now you know I can get into her house, is there any way to use it to make this easier on you?"

Birdie's face lights up. He waves his cigar around in the air. "Lonnie, I think you need to come over. I'll make it worth your while."

"On my way."

Chapter Forty-Two

"It's hard without the kids here. At least I had a distraction with homework and cooking dinner for them and all that. Three solid distractions. Right now, I'm alone, drinking wine, and feeling…"

"…Locked, loaded, and ready for love?" Brillo Pad's voice on my cell is teasing. "You shared that with us at the meeting, remember? We laughed about it."

I smile. "Not so funny right at this moment."

"I understand. Good for you that you reached out. It's progress, Izzy."

Holding the cell to my ear, I walk to the vintage serving cart I'd bought at a flea market and refinished it to make into a bar. Hand-painted dahlias adorn my favorite wine glass. I love dahlias because of Darlene. My laptop sits on the kitchen table. I stare at it. Maybe I shouldn't even have a laptop. I pour the wine and remove myself from its orbit.

I look around the empty house, which feels too big, too dark, and overwhelming. At least when I'm online chatting up various guys or the kids are in the house, I don't feel so alone. Tonight… a few days out from the funeral, work, traitorous assistants, and a boss bent on destroying me…the need to connect is strong. I am weak with desire. Brillo Pad has outdone herself with availability. I'm on my third call to her in the past two days.

"Izzy, have you made friends with the other women yet?"

She gives me three numbers of women that have been attending for a long time. Veterans.

I laugh. "We are a pathetic army."

"We're the lucky ones. Most women think this type of behavior is normal."

"*I* did. It took an incredible amount of torture for me to rip the blinders off. There were signs, but the pull was too strong. I just buried them. I knew, though. In my heart, I knew it was becoming an issue."

"Making the non-existent perfect man your life's goal is on the way out, dear."

"Yes. Agree."

"Good to talk to you again. Have a nice evening. Use those phone numbers. All of us have been where you are."

My fingers are a little shaky as I push the 'end' button. I shove the cell into my back pocket and walk outside. The evening is cool, and clouds float across a sliver of moon. I find the North Star and toast it with my glass. The kids arrive home in the morning, and my plan is to hit up my life again, full speed ahead. Or something.

An hour later, I'd cleaned the kitchen, avoided my laptop, and put on my PJs. I sit in bed with a new book on my Kindle. Suspense instead of Rom-Com. Romance is out until I get a handle on doing life like a civilized human being. By the end of the second chapter, my fingers tingle, and I clearly see them on my keyboard, resurrecting the websites I'd blocked.

I'd left my laptop downstairs on purpose, so I wouldn't grab it in a moment of weakness. Like now. Every beat of my heart says, 'Walk. Down. Stairs. Walk. Down. Stairs'...I rub my face, throw off the comforter. "This is ridiculous," I seethe in the privacy of my bedroom. I close my eyes and press my temples with my fingertips. In my mind's eye, Brillo Pad's lips form the oft-repeated mantra of the group— 're-route.' *Re-route, Izzy.*

Instead of going downstairs, in desperation I throw off my PJs, turn the shower on full blast and step into the steam.

It works.

After the shower, I am fast asleep in minutes.

"Hi, Mom," Mimi runs into my arms as she exits her grandparents' vehicle in the buttery sunshine of early morning. Chad and Peter follow with the bags.

Ethan's mother walks to the front porch, gives me a hug. "Please keep us informed about the…" Her eyes water, she looks away, takes a breath. "Ethan's case. Will you?"

I assure her that I will and give her Detective Lopez's cell number. "He'll be glad to talk to you also, Lenore. Keep in touch."

They power down the windows and wave as they drive away.

Lenore's sorrow is catching. Rubbing my arms as if I were cold, I walk into the kitchen to join the kids. "Have you had breakfast?"

"Grandma and Grandpa took us to Cracker Barrel. I'm good," Peter says, stuffing his backpack. "Need to leave in thirty minutes if we're going to make it to school on time. Mimi! Chad!"

"We're ready!" Mimi sings, jumping up and down. "I don't need breakfast either, Mom."

Chad walks into the kitchen. "We can go early if you want," he tells Peter. In the blink of an eye, they're out the door and down the street.

I have to take a second. No fights? No bad temper? No eye-rolling?

I think about the years of struggle to get them ready for school on time. Perhaps the somberness of Ethan's funeral made an impact? I will sit down and chat with them about it tonight. Or maybe I should take the win and not try to dissect it to death.

I let out a long sigh and straighten my shoulders. "Izzy. Go get dressed. Think about stuff later. Focus on having a peaceful day."

My phone buzzes as I trot downstairs to grab my purse. I glance at the number. Detective Lopez.

"Morning." I'm smiling, because things seem to be sorted out, and I'm hopeful that the avalanche of misery will fall on someone else for a change. I've had my share. *Peace* is the rule of the day, and I want it to stay that way. Please.

"Not supposed to do this, but I wanted to give you a heads-up."

My heart stops.

"Homicide has a warrant to search your house. They should be there in five. Can you let them in? Wouldn't want them to break your door."

I am speechless. My jaw drops. "I…I…"

"They got a tip. It's procedure. After you let them in, look at the scope of the warrant and make sure you understand what they're doing, where they're supposed to look. Don't say anything. Don't talk to them. At least one cop will be assigned to watch you as they search."

"What, so they make sure I don't make a run for it?" My hopes plummet to my feet. I throw my purse on the floor. "Haven't I been through enough? What's going on, Detective?"

"You'll have to look at the warrant. I'm so sorry. If they don't find what they're looking for, you're good. If they do, you'll need an attorney."

"An attorney?" I squeak. "I can't afford a freaking attorney, Detective."

"You'll have one assigned, then. It'll work out. But I doubt they'll find anything."

A hard knock sounds at my door. "POLICE. WE HAVE A SEARCH WARRANT. OPEN THE DOOR."

"That's them." I end the call. Thank God Detective Lopez prepared me. Before I open the door, I take a moment to compose myself.

When I open the door, my eyes widen at the small army of cops on my front porch and down the sidewalk. "Good morning," I tell the group of uniforms headed up by a somber-looking man with a document.

He waves it in my face. "Isabelle Lewis? We have a search warrant. If you'll step aside."

"May I look at the warrant, please?"

He shoves it into my hands, gives his team a signal to wait.

Trembling, I scan the page. It's a full sweep—the entire house and anything attached. For the assault implement utilized to murder the victim, Ethan Gerard Lewis. With a gasp, I hand the document back to the detective. He gives me a curt nod, gives his guys the 'go' signal. Dazed, I call the office and tell them I'm running late. I drop onto the couch in the den, fold my hands in my lap, and watch them tear through my house like a horde of locusts.

Two hours later, the sounds are less worrisome, more focused. They coalesce in my laundry room on the first floor. My hand drifts to my chest. My eyes close. Who called this in? They'd already cleared me; why is this necessary?

They won't find anything. I'm well past 'upset' and zeroing in on 'mad as hell.' A hot flash crawls up my back and out of my mouth. "They're *not* going to find anything," I declare to the petite female detective sitting across from me. I jerk an arm toward the laundry room. "This is crazy. I've already been cleared."

Her calm cop-face says nothing as she babysits the potential perp. I imagine she's following search protocol: 'Don't talk. Just let her vent and see what comes out.' I can almost hear the conversation, and it makes me furious. "I didn't murder my ex-husband!"

She winces, but keeps her mouth shut.

Measured steps walk down the hall. Into the den where we are sitting.

The lead investigator pulls off blue, nitrile gloves and stuffs them in his back pocket. A uniform hands him a plastic baggie. Holding the baggie inches from my face, his next words shock me to my core.

"Recognize this?"

I blink at the baggie. My lips part. Something like an X-acto knife is in the bag. My eyebrows shoot up.

It's a scalpel.

"Is that it? Is that the murder weapon?" I am shaking so hard it is difficult to stand. I reach for the back of the couch to lean on.

"There are traces of blood on this item, ma'am. We will need to verify the DNA on this item, but we have secured a warrant for your arrest." He jerks his head at one of the uniforms.

I'm twirled around, cuffed, and stuffed into the back of a patrol vehicle.

My neighbor is in her yard watching, her eyes as big and round as dinner plates.

Chapter Forty-Three

B irdie walks into his kitchen, grimacing at the overflow of dishes in the sink and the pots and pans that hold congealing bits of food on the counters. "One thing that woman was good at...cleanin' up the place."

With a long, gravelly sigh, he starts rinsing dishes and putting them in the dishwasher. A half hour later, order is restored. Should he grovel at Margaret's feet? Hope that she'll set the divorce petition aside? No. Not worth it just for someone to keep house. A lot cheaper to hire a maid. Margaret had never been on her own. She'd be swimming in problems up to her neck and begging him for another chance soon enough.

A knock sounds. He walks out of the kitchen to the front door. A young man stands on the stoop. Hands him an envelope. "You've been served, sir."

He pulls out the wad of paperwork. Petition for Discovery. Scanning the bullet points, he becomes furious. He presses the number to the bank, then hesitates. What good would it do to close the accounts and open new ones? A judge will look at this action as childish and selfish. Better to let her hang herself. If she spends too much or withdraws large sums of money, it'll play right into his hands. "A detail," he mutters to himself as he walks through the home. He grimaces at the smell emanating from the bathroom. How long since that toilet had been cleaned? The kitchen is one thing, but a toilet is another. He curses.

Five weeks until his trial date.

He glares at the ankle monitor, plops into his recliner, and falls into a fitful sleep.

His ringtone blasts through the room. Then again. And again. Birdie rubs his eyes and stalks over to grab his phone. Lonnie.

"Yeah?"

"I did it."

Birdie wonders if the cops are listening. He's not sure how all that works, but since their monitoring systems track him through his ankle bracelet, the room is more than likely bugged, too. "Don't say anything else. I'm allowed thirty feet from my house. Meet me in the backyard. There's a gate at the back of the fence. Park a couple blocks over, okay? Be discreet."

Lonnie and Birdie sit in patio chairs overlooking Birdie's sumptuous backyard.

"It's nice that you're not in a cell," Lonnie remarks.

Birdie snorts in disgust. "Tell me what happened."

"You'll love it." Lonnie chuckles. "Night before last, I ran by her house. All quiet, y'know? Like the kids were gone. Sure enough, they were. So I did the trick with the refrigerator magnet over the magnetic square thing security companies put on windows and slid open a downstairs window. No alarm and I was in. Guess where I was?"

Birdie puts his hand over his eyes. "Just keep going, kid."

"Laundry room! It was lit— perfect spot to hide the scalpel." Lonnie laughs. "And you are gonna get such a kick."

"Out of what?"

"On the way to her house, I nicked some stray cat on the street with it. See? So it'd have blood on it."

"Brilliant," Birdie mutters.

"I know, right?"

"Did it not occur to you that they'll run that blood? They'll analyze it, and it'll return as animal. I hope you wore gloves." He scowls. "Did you?"

Lonnie frowns. "A'course I did. The transparent, plastic ones. Just like doctors wear."

Birdie stares out into the yard, thinking about how meticulous he'd been with his landscaping. He wonders if, after the divorce, he'll be able to afford lawn care. He runs his hands across the stubble on his cheeks with a sigh. Returns his attention to Lonnie. "This time, are you going to keep your mouth shut?"

He frowns. "Last time, I was forced. 'Coerced' as my attorney put it. They turned me inside out with threats of jail time and a record."

Birdie presses his lips together and stares at Lonnie until he gets nervous. "Look, man, I'm sorry you're in this mess."

"Are you?" Birdie gives him a ghost of a smile.

"I didn't know it'd turn out this way."

"I trusted you, and at the first sign of pressure, you squeal like a pig."

"Hey, bro—"

"The answer is no."

Lonnie's eyebrows draw together. "Didn't ask a question."

"But you're going to...your hands are shaking, you're sweating. You need oxy."

Lonnie shrugs. "Well, yeah, but...you said you'd make it worth my while, so I thought—"

Birdie smiles. He'd let the fool *think* he had drugs on hand. "I don't care what I said. The answer is no. Get out."

Lonnie stands. He is pale. "We had a deal."

"Deal's dead, bud. Now get out of here."

Birdie rises and walks into the house. Closes the door and shoves the deadbolt home.

Lonnie's head hangs. He shoves his hands in his pockets as he walks through the backyard. Birdie watches him slap open the gate angrily. After a bit, an engine starts. The vehicle roars away.

Birdie's shoulders relax. Lonnie is gone.

Clearing his throat, he looks up the number for Emerald Spring PD.

He asks for Detective Adrian Lopez and is put on hold. The hold music is lyrical and uplifting.

"Lopez."

"Detective Lopez, this is Birdie Costanza. I have some information you'll be interested in."

239

A beat of silence. "Shouldn't you be talking to Homicide?"

"I want to talk to you."

Birdie hears the rustle of paper. The click of a pen. "Give me your address."

Chapter Forty-Four

"We're all innocent in here, honey." The young woman pushes her oily, rancid hair over her shoulder. "You'll learn that. Not one of us is guilty." Her laughter sounds like a rusty hinge.

I look around the holding cell. Three attractive women in short skirts, heels, and lots of make-up trade war stories. I long to bolt. How did I end up in a cell with real, live hookers? My tears dried up hours ago. My pulse is off the chain. I need a shower and a good dose of Darlene, or I might go mad in here.

Including me, there are seven women in this holding cell. It has a single toilet in the corner, wide-open so everyone can watch a person do her business, and slim benches attached to two of the walls, upon which one of the women is snoring so loud that the others are making jokes. In the adjoining cell, someone pounds on the wall non-stop and shouts their allegiance to Allah. My mobile phone, shoes, money, and jewelry were seized. One of the guards called a public defender for me, and he gave me about ten minutes of his time and let me use his phone to call my neighbor and text my kids. Six hours later, I am taken out of the cell and fingerprinted. A DNA swab is roughly inserted into my mouth and nose. Two hours after that, I am interviewed and recorded, but my state-issued attorney is not in attendance, so I wonder if that is a problem. When the security guards ask what I want to eat, I choose lasagna. It is microwaved and rubbery. I take a couple of bites, then shove the plate away.

If there is a hell, this is it.

I take off my jacket, fold it, place it on the floor. Settle my butt and claim my space against the wall. It's impossible to sleep. Every light in the place is blazing, and half of the holding cell population is shouting, screaming, or sobbing. The other half is vomiting or seated on communal toilets.

There are no clocks. I have no idea what time it is or whether it's night or day. I figure it has to be night because four of the women stretch out on the floor. No blankets, no extra mattresses, nothing. I sit on the cold floor with my back against the wall and try to sleep sitting up, but my back is killing me. Guarding my little plot of cell space, I rise and arc my back in a cat-stretch.

"Izzy."

I blink. Locate the voice outside the bars.

Seeing Detective Lopez brings tears to my eyes.

"Sorry, I couldn't get here sooner. Hey. I have some great news. Birdie ratted out Lonnie. The scalpel was a plant. It didn't take but thirty minutes to get him to confess. We have to sort out their stories, but looks like Lonnie's on the hook, and you're out. They're doing paperwork now."

I drop to the floor, my hands over my face.

Detective Lopez squats down and whispers. "I know this is hard. It'll be over soon. I'll hang out here until the paperwork arrives, okay?"

I raise my unwashed, sweaty, tear-stained face. "Thank you, Detective."

"You're welcome, Izzy." He pulls a chair over to the cell and sits. "I'm right here."

One of the women on the floor rises up to one elbow. "And we're so freakin' happy about that, lover-boy. Can we get some sleep now?"

I laugh.

Later, my hair and body squeaky clean from a long shower, I pull on my PJs in jubilant gratitude. I take a few minutes to express my thanks to God, because I'm quickly becoming a believer. I'd never prayed so much in my life as in that hellhole.

I'd not gotten home until the wee hours, so I left my kids at Annie's. She'd see my text first thing in the morning and send them over.

I shake my head. I'm probably the talk of the neighborhood.

I look at the clock on my dresser. Three-thirty a.m. I'm wide awake and thinking about Lonnie and Birdie. I'm not all that surprised about Birdie, but Lonnie? Had he hated me that much? To plant the supposed murder weapon in my house? My eyebrows knit together. How had he bypassed my security system? Detective Lopez and I had talked as he took me home, and he said he'd get someone to check entry points. I'd put in that system to keep us safe. So what now? My chin quivers. My arms snake around my shoulders. Someone had set me up to take the fall for Ethan's murder. Why? Who?

I sweep away my sloppy-cry tears. Push my hair off my face. Why can't I sleep? I'm exhausted.

My eyelids fall to half-mast.

Five short minutes is all it'll take to unblock the dating apps on my phone.

Brillo Pad's sweet face floats before my eyes. NO, she says.

But I'm terrified!

NO.

Images of smiling, available men kaleidoscope through my mind. The familiar behavior within the warm cocoon of texting new men feels secure. Comfortable.

I'd be less alone. Safe.

My laughter borders on hysterics.

I think about the cold, airless, depressing, holding cell. The sounds, smells, and sights of criminals shuffled from one holding cell to another. The terror of sitting there, helpless, for something I didn't do.

Safe? That 'warm cocoon' is what got this whole mess started.

My laptop is downstairs. It'll take only a few minutes to unblock the sites.

Go get it. You'll feel better.

"That's such a lie!" I yell into the quiet of my bedroom. Pounding my pillow into submission, I drop my head onto it and sleep.

On this, the first morning of liberation from the fetid holding cell…even the thumping bass of the kids' music has no power to bother me. The breakfast teasing between brothers doesn't irritate me, either. Mimi's squeals of protest when one of her brothers pokes her in the back doesn't phase me. The scant two hours of sleep doesn't bother me, either.

With an extreme sense of contentment, I lean against the doorjamb and fold my arms across my chest, watching Peter back the car out and pull into the street with my precious cargo on board. They all wave. Mimi blows a kiss.

I am curiously devoid of irritation. I don't know how long this feeling will last, but I hope it lasts long enough for me to remember how torturous things can get and choose less onerous activities to slake my soul thirst. Smiling, I close the door and head upstairs to get ready for work.

A parking space presents itself when I pull in. "The benefits of being five minutes early," I murmur as I walk to the entrance. I'm never early, but maybe I should start trying. I smile as I power open the ponderous doors. My mind is no longer clouded by Birdie-dread. Another benefit to being on time is not having to dash up the stairs to make up for the slow elevator. I am patient and peaceful as I wait, grateful there is an elevator option in this building instead of resentful that it's so slow. This benevolence thing going on inside me is nice. Foreign, but nice.

Winston walks inside and joins me. Phil enters. Then Darlene. We get on the elevator together and joke around on the way to the second floor. No one knows about my nightmare holding cell experience, and I am happy to keep it that way. Dare I hope that life will return to normal? I think about my resistance to the dating apps on my phone and the dating sites on my laptop. The wonderful reassurance and support from Brillo Pad and the group she rules like a drill sergeant.

Better than normal.

We exit on the second floor, and the three of them hang out around my desk, all chatty and bubbly. A circle of friendship. This is so comforting and kind that I want to cry. No pressing for updates, no 'I told you so's', just solid support.

Jon Hoyt walks over. "I heard there's a party over here..." He smiles at me. My face flushes. Jon. The KISS. Happily for me, he doesn't act weird.

He is low-key and pleasant. He, too, is one of my solid supporters. I lapse into listening mode, enjoying the easy laughter, quips about football or the weather. My gaze wanders around the sales floor. Assistants fly around, salespeople stroll in from the elevator, ditch their stuff on their desks, walk to the breakroom to grab coffee and return to their cubes. I breathe deeply of the smells, sights, and sounds of life returning to normal.

Phil notices my silence. "Izzy? You okay?"

I straighten in my chair. Smile. "I'm more than okay, Phil. I'm grateful."

He laughs and pats my shoulder. "Good to hear. Grateful account executives sell more advertising."

Soon, Winston and I are all alone in the pod. He leans forward on his elbows, eyes bright. "You're good, then?"

I give him the highlights of the last few days, deleting the holding cell experience or Lonnie's insidious plan, which is too raw. Too fresh. I might never share it. Maybe I can pretend it didn't happen.

"They ever get a suspect in Ethan's homicide?"

My mind zips to Lonnie. Is that why he planted the scalpel in my laundry room— to take the spotlight off himself? But what motive would he have to kill Ethan? He's twenty-two and, as I've recently discovered, stupid as a rock.

I shake my head. "All they know is that it had to be someone with medical experience, since the scalpel cut was accurate and well-placed." I shrug. "At least 'scalpel' is their best-educated guess. They told Ethan's mother that it is impossible for someone who didn't know anatomy to be that precise. The consolation is that it was quick. He bled out fast." I suppress a shudder.

Winston threads his fingers together, looks down at his desktop, thinking. "Did I ever tell you I did a military stint in the Persian Gulf War?"

I shake my head as I smooth my fresh newspaper pages and, as always, sniff the bloom of ink on newsprint. "Nope." I flip to the 'Living' section.

"I was a medical corpsman for the Marines. I was on the ground, in the field, as a first responder."

I glance at him. My classic hoverer. My staunch protector, my support. The man who'd acted as my backup dad for years. I study his bow tie. The calm gaze. My eyes linger on his steady hands.

My hand rises to my throat. My lips part. "I didn't know that."

Winston's smile is thin. "Combat changes a person."

My heart is beating a mile a minute. "I'm sure it would, Winston."

"Time to get out there." He grabs his driving beret and slaps it on. Pulls sunglasses from his shirt pocket.

I watch him get into the elevator.

I sit at my desk a long time, staring at nothing. And everything.

Chapter Forty-Five

Winston trots down the front stairs of *The Emerald Spring Sentinel*. He stretches his arms high overhead, enjoying the bright and sunshiny morning. He walks to the parking lot, unlocks his car, and sits inside. Digs out his cell, texts, then lays the phone aside and waits.

A smiling, energetic woman with wiry, short, gray hair approaches and taps on the window. Winston motions her to the passenger side, and she enters the vehicle. The woman asks for a cigarette. Winston scrolls the windows down a few inches, reaches in his pocket, pulls out a lighter, and offers her a pack. She takes one. Winston lights it, then lights one for himself.

"It was a damn miracle you found me," she remarks, blowing out a plume of smoke.

Winston smiles. "I believe in miracles."

She laughs. "No doubt. On the battlefield surrounded by bloody, dying Marines that took a bullet or triggered a land mine...the miracle was that we survived."

"That's a fact." Winston grins and glances at her. "We helped a lot of Marines survive out there too, Sarge." His eyes rove the area for prying eyes as he talks. "We did a lot of things we never thought we'd have to do, too. Unthinkable things. It's amazing what a person is capable of in the trenches." After a pause, he says, "It's good to see you again, Sarge."

"It's Claire, buddy. Just plain, ole' Claire trying to help a few damaged women find safe passage through an ocean of bad guys." She blows smoke out the crack at the top of the passenger side window.

Winston shakes his head. "I don't know how you do it."

"You mean the support groups? It's not just Isabelle, you know. You should listen to these women. It's the same sad, sick story over and over. What possesses these girls to marry men like that? And the worst thing is that unless they get help, the behavior's repeated. And Isabelle? She was letting this guy *watch the children*. After some digging, I found him on a sex offender registry." She snorts. "The way things were going, he woulda probably gotten custody. The court system is a joke. She should thank you."

Winston exhales. Pinches the bridge of his nose. "That makes me feel a little better."

They fall into an easy silence. Winston and Claire finish their cigarettes and toss them out the window. He shoves his hand in his pocket and pulls out a wad of cash. "Here's the other half of what I owe you." Claire takes the money without counting it and tucks it into her purse. "Thanks."

"The more Izzy talked about how much she liked the leader of her group, the more familiar it sounded. When I called on the pretext of needing help for a friend, and they gave me your name, I couldn't believe it. Then you called." Winston chuckles. "Your voice is hard-wired into my head for all eternity, Sarge."

Claire laughs. "Long time ago."

Winston clips on his seatbelt. "If he'd gotten those kids, I don't know what would've happened to Izzy."

"Huh," Claire remarks. "She never told me she goes by Izzy."

They watch fluffy, white clouds chase each other across a brilliant sky.

"If you ever need anything, send up a flare," Winston says. "And I mean it. I've slept better ever since..." Winston clears his throat. "Ever since I've been sure that Izzy and the kids are safe."

Claire reaches into her purse and pulls out a thick, folded batch of paper. "This'll make you feel even better. Found this when I had to sneak into a closet at his house."

Winston unfolds the papers. Frowns. "He was convicted, for God's sake. How could she not have known?"

"Records were sealed. I checked." She lifts a shoulder. "Isabelle wouldn't know how to get info that his attorney hid. This type of predator fools a lot of women. Yeah, Ethan was a perv. Big-time. Don't beat yourself up. I'm not."

He gives the documents back to her.

Claire shakes her head and pushes his hands away. "Keep it. When you start feeling bad about what we did, read it."

Winston taps his fingers on the steering wheel and stares outside. He hears the faint sounds of traffic as he watches the Spanish Moss adorning the trees sway in the breeze.

"I'm sorry we can't be friends, Sarge," he tells Claire.

"Me, too." She smiles and puts her hand on his shoulder. "Okay. I was never here, and we've never met," she says as she exits the vehicle. She turns around and raps a couple of times on the window as a final goodbye.

Winston watches her until she disappears around the corner.

He runs his palms the circumference of the steering two times before he grips it tightly and exhales a long breath.

The worker bees begin streaming out onto the sidewalks, bound for an early lunch. He tilts his driving beret just so, places his sunglasses on his nose. Then he starts the car, shoves it into gear, and pulls away.

Into the wild.

A Note from the Author

My best friend and I were talking the other day, and I told her about this story. She asked me, in whispered horror, if I had ever done this sort of thing. Was any of the story true? I said no, of course not, that I take events from my life and stretch and pull them in a thousand ways, exaggerate them so that they are more creepy and entertaining. Then I smile, because I say that same thing about *everything* I write. It's up to the reader to sort fact from fiction. The truth is, we're all capable of damning and disgusting things, and we often take these secrets with us to our graves. For me, I dust them off, bring them out into the light of day, and fold them into my manuscripts. It is both redemptive and cathartic.

Acknowledgements

I'd like to first acknowledge my publisher, Level Best Books, for their belief in this book, and my editor, Harriette Sackler, for giving me valuable feedback on how to make it better. This book is based on the first story I ever wrote when I was a young, stumbling, wannabe writer that knew very little about what makes a good book tick. Twelve long years later, I've rewritten and polished the story and shaped it into a very different book. As always, my thanks go out to my husband, Jim, who patiently supports me through the process of writing. I also want to send out big hugs and kisses to my four grown children, who lived through many edge-of-cliff episodes and scary times when I was a single mom. We made it, didn't we, kiddos?

About the Author

Kerry Peresta is the author of the popular Olivia Callahan Suspense series and Back Before Dawn, standalone suspense. Additional writing credits include a popular newspaper and e-zine humor column, "The Lighter Side," the short story "The Day the Migraine Died," published in *Rock, Roll, and Ruin: A Triangle Sisters in Crime Anthology,* articles published in *Local Life Magazine, The Bluffton Breeze, Lady Lowcountry,* and *Island Events Magazine.* She is past chapter president of the Maryland Writers' Association and a current member and presenter of the Pat Conroy Literary Center; a member of Hilton Head Island Writers' Network, South Carolina Writers Association, Sisters in Crime, and International Thriller Writers. Kerry is the mother of four adult children, and spent thirty years in advertising as an account manager, creative director, copywriter, and editor. When she's not writing, you'll find her working out, riding her bike, or enjoying the beach and Lowcountry marshes of Hilton Head. Kerry and her husband moved to Hilton Head Island, SC, in 2015.

SOCIAL MEDIA HANDLES:
https://www.twitter.com/kerryperesta
https://www.instagram.com/kerry.peresta
https://www.facebook.com/klperesta
https://www.facebook.com/kerryperesta

AUTHOR WEBSITE:
https://www.kerryperesta.net

Also by Kerry Peresta

The Olivia Callahan Suspense Series:
The Deadening
The Rising
The Torching

Other Works:
The Hunting

CPSIA information can be obtained
at www.ICGtesting.com
Printed in the USA
BVHW041718120723
667142BV00001B/11